NESSA'S SEDUCTION

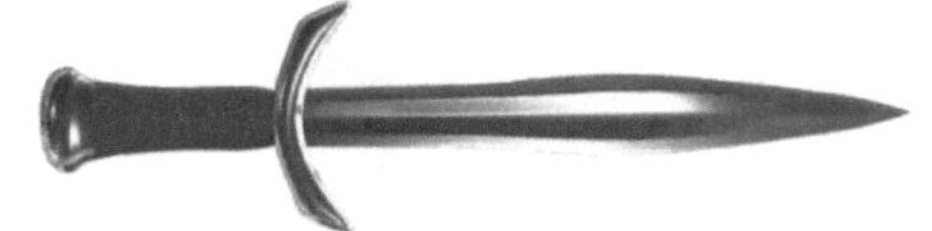

GUARDIANS OF ALBA
BOOK ONE

JAYNE CASTEL

WINTER MIST PRESS

Nessa's Seduction, by Jayne Castel

Published by Winter Mist Press

ISBN: 978-0-473-57735-3 (paperback)

Edited by Tim Burton
Cover design by Winter Mist Press
Cover photography courtesy of www.shutterstock.com
Dagger vector image courtesy of www.pixabay.com

Visit Jayne's website: www.jaynecastel.com

***

For Timbo.

***

Historical Romances by Jayne Castel

DARK AGES BRITAIN

The Kingdom of the East Angles series
Dark Under the Cover of Night (Book One)
Nightfall till Daybreak (Book Two)
The Deepening Night (Book Three)
The Kingdom of the East Angles: The Complete Series

The Kingdom of Mercia series
The Breaking Dawn (Book One)
Darkest before Dawn (Book Two)
Dawn of Wolves (Book Three)
The Kingdom of Mercia: The Complete Series

The Kingdom of Northumbria series
The Whispering Wind (Book One)
Wind Song (Book Two)
Lord of the North Wind (Book Three)
The Kingdom of Northumbria: The Complete Series

DARK AGES SCOTLAND

The Warrior Brothers of Skye series
Blood Feud (Book One)
Barbarian Slave (Book Two)
Battle Eagle (Book Three)
The Warrior Brothers of Skye: The Complete Series

The Pict Wars series
Warrior's Heart (Book One)
Warrior's Secret (Book Two)
Warrior's Wrath (Book Three)
The Pict Wars: The Complete Series

Novellas
Winter's Promise

MEDIEVAL SCOTLAND

The Brides of Skye series
The Beast's Bride (Book One)
The Outlaw's Bride (Book Two)
The Rogue's Bride (Book Three)
The Brides of Skye: The Complete Series

The Sisters of Kilbride series
Unforgotten (Book One)
Awoken (Book Two)
Fallen (Book Three)
Claimed (Epilogue novella)

The Immortal Highland Centurions series
Maximus (Book One)
Cassian (Book Two)
Draco (Book Three)
The Laird's Return (Epilogue festive novella)

Stolen Highland Hearts series
Highlander Deceived (Book One)
Highlander Entangled (Book Two)
Highlander Forbidden (Book Three)

Guardians of Alba series
Nessa's Seduction (Book One)

Epic Fantasy Romances by Jayne Castel

Light and Darkness series
Ruled by Shadows (Book One)
The Lost Swallow (Book Two)
Path of the Dark (Book Three)
Light and Darkness: The Complete Series

"Wherever you go, go with all your heart."
—Confucius

1

AT THE GATES

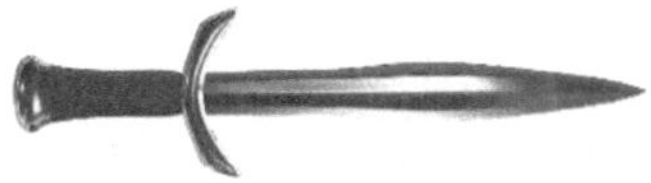

Dunfermline, Scotland

Late winter, 1304

SHE STRAYED CLOSE to the gates of the enemy camp—close enough to draw the attention of the guards.

Pretending not to notice their lewd stares and coarse comments, Nessa plastered a smile onto her face and tightened her grip upon her basket, even as nervousness constricted her belly. She resisted the impulse to pull her heavy woolen cloak tight, swivel on her heel, and march home. Instead, she glanced wistfully back in the direction she'd come. Perched high above the jumble of slate roofs of Dunfermline town, the abbey loomed dark against the fading sky.

No matter where one traveled in Dunfermline, the abbey was a constant landmark—one that was as yet untainted by the English. The sight of it galvanized Nessa's resolve, causing her anxiety to settle. Tearing her gaze from the abbey, she focused upon the mail-clad guards flanking the gates.

She'd braved this spot for a reason. She couldn't flee now.

The men were still staring at her with wolfish grins. She stood just yards from the entrance to a temporary settlement—a township that comprised a sea of white and red pavilion tents and fluttering pennants. Somehow she needed to get in there—but an outer perimeter of 'war wagons', carts equipped with high wooden shields with openings for archers to fire through, blocked her path.

Ignoring the guards' leers, Nessa peered into the camp. Somewhere in there was *The Hammer*, Edward Longshanks himself. That bastard needed to die—but she hadn't been charged with assassinating the English king.

Nessa's purpose here was a very different one.

Still observing the camp, she wrinkled her nose. The reek of the army—peat-smoke, manure, and stale sweat—hung heavily in the dank, chill air. It was so cold this afternoon that the skin of her exposed cheeks prickled. More snow was on its way; she was sure of it.

But snow wasn't the only thing she was certain about.

Ye shall meet him today … the Englishman ye must seduce.

That morning, just after dawn, she'd cast the bones, and they'd given her the sign she'd been waiting for. If she wanted to make contact with one of the king's knights, she needed to get inside the English camp—today.

"Ho, wench!" One of the guards called out. "What have you got in your basket?"

"That Scot slut won't understand you," another guard chortled before making a crude gesture. "She doesn't speak our tongue."

Heat ignited in Nessa's belly. This dull-wit was mistaken. She'd grasped every word. Forcing herself to keep smiling, she patted her basket. "I have trinkets … to bring you luck."

Her words brought looks of surprise. Nessa had taken care over the last years to learn their tongue. Her English was a little halting and strongly accented—and not half as good as her French—yet she wagered few Scots used it.

Recovering from their surprise, the men exchanged smirks.

"Come here then," one of them drawled, beckoning to her. "Show us your wares."

The suggestive note to his voice galled, yet she couldn't show her distaste. She'd been in Dunfermline since Samhuinn, watching and waiting. She wouldn't let her hatred of the English make her lose focus.

Colina would be wondering why it was taking Nessa so long to discover Edward of England's battle plans—when and where he would strike next. The High bandruì—druidess—had instructed Nessa to find work at a tavern frequented by the English and use a blend of wiles and witching to seduce one of the knights within Edward's inner circle. Her first step was to cross paths with a king's man and then take him to her bed. After that, she was to use the craft on him to loosen his tongue.

Yet with so much at stake, Nessa wanted to ensure she seduced an Englishman who could actually help her, and in truth, she didn't want to work as a tavern wench. She'd decided to do it her own way. So she set herself up in a cottage on the edge of the town and established herself as a healer: a wise woman who knew some hedge-craft, a woman who employed more than salves and tinctures to mend what ailed her patients.

She'd busied herself in her new life, and now the time had come to find a suitable target.

Moving close to the smirking guards, Nessa readied the working she'd prepared. In her free hand, she carried a 'cairn stone'—a lump of smoky quartz—which she'd imbued with her witch-will during the full moon of the night before.

"What luck are you in need of?" she asked, meeting one of the guard's gazes boldly. The cairn stone pulsed cold against her palm in response to the question. Witching surged through Nessa's blood, and the wind picked up, whistling across the shallow valley.

The guard stared at her, blinking. As the stare drew out, his expression grew slack.

Nessa fought the urge to grin. Soon she'd have these two fools eating out of her hand.

"What's all this?"

A powerful male voice intruded, jerking the guard out of the enchantment she'd started to weave upon him.

Shaking his head, as if to clear it, the guard's attention shifted away from Nessa, his stance going rigid.

Silently cursing at being thwarted—for she'd been about to suggest the guard let her pass into the camp—Nessa glanced over her shoulder to see three men approaching. They strode over the humpbacked bridge that crossed the burn between the town and the camp, their spurs clinking on stone.

Nessa went still, her gaze settling upon the newcomers.

Dressed in heavy hauberks, with their coifs pulled down, they wore crimson surcoats covering the mail. The three knights were all big men; they were also clean-shaven, something that wasn't common among the Scots. One was balding, another was dark-haired. The third knight, the one who strode out front, had light-brown hair cut short—and a surly expression.

Nessa stepped back from the guards, her pulse racing.

Her attention remained upon the knight leading the others, certainty and relief settling in the pit of her belly. She'd thought she'd have to gain access to the camp in order to cross paths with one of the king's knights—yet The Three had blessed her this day.

I've found him.

The lead knight halted before her, his expression inscrutable. "State your business here, woman."

Nessa flashed him a smile. "Trinkets to bring you luck, brave knight." She gestured to her basket. "Or would you prefer I read your fortune?"

All three knights had now stopped before Nessa. Her words brought looks of surprise to the balding and dark-haired men, although their surly friend frowned. He'd called out in English, yet, like the guards, the knights hadn't expected her to speak their tongue.

Of course, these men would likely speak French as well. However, she'd wanted their full attention—and now she had it.

"Best I don't know what the future holds," the bald knight replied, favoring her with a flirtatious smile. "A soldier's life usually has a violent end."

His dark-haired friend snorted. "Aye, better let the Lord decide." Nessa saw that the knight wore a small silver crucifix around his neck; it glittered dully in the fading light.

The ill-tempered one continued to observe Nessa, his gaze hooding. "How is it you speak our tongue?" he asked, clearly suspicious. His voice was a low rumble, a deep timbre that was pleasant on the ear.

Nessa inclined her head, meeting his eye. She wasn't about to be cowed by this man—instead, she took his unfriendliness as a challenge. "I lived on the borderlands for a while," she replied, "and healed a number of English soldiers."

His gaze narrowed. "So you're a healer, not some peddler of witch ways?"

Nessa inclined her head. He was a sharp one. "Perhaps I'm both?"

He held her stare. "And what is it you're selling?"

Needing no further encouragement, she dug into her basket and withdrew a length of rope. "Can I interest you in a Druid's Ladder?" she asked. "It'll cost you just one penny. To draw good fortune to you ... tie a knot toward you upon a waxing moon and picture the thing you want."

The knight's handsome face—for she'd noted he was handsome, with a strong jaw, proud features, and a finely molded mouth—stiffened.

Ignoring his reaction, Nessa dug into her basket once more and produced a smooth, dark river stone with a white line running through it. "Or two pennies will buy you a Wishing Rock. Keep it with you at all times when you wish for things, and your desires will come true."

The knight's brows crashed together. "Is that right?" he growled, while next to him the dark-haired, crucifix-wearing knight muttered something under his breath and crossed himself. "Sounds like nonsense to me. Take your baubles and peddle them elsewhere, *witch*."

His reaction wasn't unexpected. However, Nessa wasn't put off. She held the knight's stare. "Or, if you prefer, I can cast the bones and tell you if providence shines upon you?"

The knight's bald companion smirked at this. "Hugh de Burgh makes his own luck." He then cast a pointed look at his friend. "Isn't that right, Sir Hugh?"

Hugh de Burgh.

Nessa once more fought the urge to grin. Indeed, fortune was shining upon *her* this day. She'd heard of this man—few in Dunfermline hadn't—for he was the English king's commander, a man who would certainly know Edward's intentions.

The bones hadn't failed her. Now, she just had to find a way to make the dour knight warm to her.

"Shut up, Nicholas." Sir Hugh cast his companion a baleful look.

It was then that Nessa saw the knight's right hand was bound. A linen bandage swathed it, and a dark stain seeped through the material.

Nessa's pulse quickened, excitement constricting her chest. This was her chance. "Shall I take a look at that for you?" she asked, careful to keep her tone calm and solicitous.

"No," Sir Hugh replied gruffly. "Just move on, woman. This isn't market square. Go and sell your trinkets elsewhere. None of us are interested in your witchery."

Nessa stilled. He'd spoken those last words in fluent Gaelic, something that unbalanced her. Of course, some of these men had been campaigning in Scotland for years now. This Hugh de Burgh had the weather-beaten look of a man in his mid-thirties, a man who'd lived through many battles. It shouldn't have surprised her that he spoke her tongue.

"This isn't *witchery*," she replied softly in Gaelic, spearing him with her gaze once more. "I'm a healer ... and that hand will fester if someone doesn't tend to it."

Nessa placed her Druid's Ladder and Wishing Rock back in her basket and took a step away. The man's rudeness didn't bother her. She'd made contact—trust would come later. It didn't matter that de Burgh's attitude toward her bordered on hostile, for she'd noted the way he held her eye far longer than was necessary.

The knight hid it well, but she sensed his interest.

"My cottage sits on the edge of the woods north of town," she told Hugh, continuing in Gaelic. It was obvious from his friends' confused and irritated expressions that neither of them understood their exchange. "I suggest ye pay me a visit … if ye wish to keep that hand."

2

THE KING'S MAN

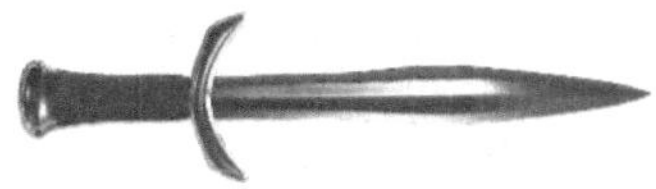

HUGH DE BURGH watched the woman walk away, his gaze tracking her.

"She's a comely one ... for a witch," Robert le Breton spoke up next to him. Hugh tore his gaze from the blue-cloaked figure, to see that his friend was fingering the crucifix around his neck, as if hoping it would protect him from lustful thoughts about such a woman.

Next to Robert, Nicholas Harrington cast his friend a withering look. "Dolt ... did you really think they are all gap-toothed hags?"

Ignoring his friends' conversation, Hugh's attention drifted once more to the departing woman.

"Still," Nicholas continued "I'd happily give that one a swiving." A pause followed. "She seemed to take a liking to you, Hugh?"

"Did she?" Hugh replied, affecting an uninterested tone. He glanced back at his friends to see that Nicholas was favoring him with a sly look.

"Aye ... and you spoke to her in Gaelic." Robert's brow furrowed. "What did you say?"

"That I didn't need her assistance, and that she should leave."

Nicholas snorted. "Miserable bastard ... some of us were enjoying her company."

Hugh's mouth thinned. Of course Nicholas had been—the knight had a weakness for women. And despite that he was bald and had a face like an old hound, lasses actually liked him.

Hugh wasn't so easily distracted. Even so, the woman, who had now been swallowed up by the gathering dusk, was the loveliest thing he'd set eyes on in a long while.

He'd marked her as he'd approached the bridge. It had been impossible not to. Tall and well-formed, with thick red-gold hair that fell unbound over her shoulders, she carried herself like a queen. She wore a sky-blue kirtle, with a darker blue cloak over the top, and carried a basket as if she were a wife off to market. As Hugh had drawn near, he'd seen that she had milky skin, a pretty face, expressive green eyes, and full lips.

His gaze had lingered on that mouth a moment too long, and he'd felt his groin tighten in response. Lush and red: those lips were made for sin.

His swift physical reaction had irritated him, but it was far too long since he'd had a woman. Even when she'd produced her ridiculous witchy trinkets, he'd found himself captivated by her.

Her sensual smile and knowing eyes had drawn him in. She was no innocent blushing maiden; although her face was unlined, he guessed she'd seen five and twenty winters at least. She'd met his eye boldly and hadn't even flinched when he'd been rude.

"Even so." Robert's voice roused Hugh from his reverie. He then cast a pointed look at Hugh's hand. "She's right. You should take care with that."

"I am." Hugh glanced down at his bandaged extremity before shrugging. He'd already been to see the camp's physician twice. The man had cleansed the wound, rubbed salve upon it, and put on clean bandages. However, the cut—one he'd taken in a skirmish outside Dunfermline just before Yule—throbbed constantly these days and now felt hot to touch. "You fuss like an old woman."

Robert shrugged, taking the point. He then glanced up at the heavens. Snow was starting to fall: white flakes fluttered down from the darkening sky. The gloaming always came on them so early this far north. It was still difficult to get used to, even after all this time. "Come on then ... let's get ourselves some supper." Robert met Hugh's gaze. "Do you want to join me and Nicholas in my pavilion ... we can both beat you at knucklebones afterward."

Hugh snorted before shaking his head. "It'll have to wait till tomorrow. The king expects me for supper this eve." In truth, he'd have rather dined with his friends. Edward had been on edge of late and had been pushing for an early departure from Dunfermline—something Hugh was against. Such discussions weren't good for one's digestion.

The three of them moved toward the gates.

"Mind yourselves with that woman," Hugh murmured to the guards. "If she comes near the gates again, you're to chase her off."

The guards all nodded vigorously. However, Hugh's attention settled upon the one who'd been standing the closest to the Scotswoman. The man now wore a sheepish expression. "You're not posted out here to flirt with local lasses, is that clear?"

The man's throat bobbed. "Aye, Sir Hugh."

Hugh cast the guard a narrow-eyed look, hauled his cloak about him, and entered the camp with Nicholas and Robert. His boots crunched on snow, his chainmail jangled, and despite the warning he'd just issued the guard, his thoughts returned to the comely figure clad in flowing blue.

My cottage sits on the edge of the woods north of town ... I suggest ye pay me a visit ... if ye wish to keep that hand.

A scowl marred Hugh's brow. Aye, she was a bold one. Such women were trouble.

Hugh quickened his step, moving ahead of his friends. The cold was raw, and his breath steamed in a cloud before him. They made their way down a thoroughfare toward the heart of the camp. On the way, they passed clusters of smaller tents, where most of his men slept, as well as make-shift stores, fowl coops, and byres.

The three friends had just returned from visiting an alehouse in town—and as always when Hugh re-entered the camp, the noise, dirt, and stench of so many men living at close quarters struck him. Passing the privy tents, which had been erected over sink holes, Hugh took shallow breaths through his mouth.

Nicholas mumbled an oath under his breath as they walked past before stifling a gag.

Hugh's mouth thinned. Indeed, after nearly four months of use, the reek of the privies was almost unbearable. He'd have to see about having them shifted.

The three knights walked on, and the stench faded, replaced by the odor of overcooked cabbage. The sulfurous smell drifted from cook fires throughout the camp, a reminder that supper was approaching— cabbage and turnip pottage from the smell of it. Hugh was grateful his position afforded him more palatable fare.

Ahead, he spied the circle of the inner perimeter—a space shielded by supply wagons rather than armored ones. To reach the gate, the three men walked through the training arena, which was empty at this hour. Hugh, Nicholas, and Robert spent the best part of their mornings here, taking men through drills. Despite the long wintering at Dunfermline, they had to keep their soldiers fighting fit.

At the sight of the arena, which was little more than a sea of frozen mud at present, Hugh's brow furrowed. The king wasn't the only restless individual in this camp. The winter hadn't yet ended, but his men were impatient to move on.

A few men-at-arms had grumbled about the long wait that morning. Hugh had told them that only a fool went to war in the midst of winter this far north, which had shut them up. However, restlessness still simmered.

Entering the inner perimeter, Hugh moved through the grand pavilions—one of which belonged to him—to the largest tent of them all, in the heart of the camp.

Vast, with four peaks and a cartwheel and spoke design, the king's pavilion was impossible to miss.

Banners hung down its sides: the red and white flag of Saint George and the Plantagenet banner of Edward's family—three golden rampant lions against a crimson background.

Bidding his friends 'good eve', Hugh strode toward it, jaw clenched. He was in a bullish mood this evening. If the king wanted an argument, he'd give him one. The snow fell heavily now, swirling around the tent in flurries. Two soldiers stood guard outside, flanking the entrance. Shoulders hunched against the cold, they greeted Hugh as he approached, and he nodded back.

Bending his head against the stinging wind, Hugh ducked inside.

"Hugh … glad to see you remembered to join us." The king's low, yet powerful, voice greeted him.

"Of course, sire … I would never forget." Hugh straightened up, brushing snow off his shoulders as his gaze swept across the plush interior of the king's tent. This might have been a temporary structure, yet it was far more comfortable than most keeps.

The tent's woven sides had been insulated with heavy woolen hangings and tapestries, and thick furs and mats covered the ground. Braziers burned in each corner, warmth suffusing the space. Banks of candles lined the walls, casting a golden light over the tent's interior and the poles and spokes that held up the vast roof. An array of large stuffed cushions, stools, and bench seats lined the living area of the pavilion.

A long oaken table sat in the center of the space, and King Edward of England lounged at the head of it, his tall frame folded into a carven chair. Edward was getting on in years, halfway through his sixth decade to be exact, and his once blond hair was almost entirely grey, as was his neatly trimmed beard. Yet when Hugh met the king's ice-blue gaze, he was reminded that England's 'warrior king' was just as formidable as he'd ever been. He dressed like the soldier he still was, in a heavy hauberk, and the body under it was strong.

The king reminded Hugh of a mighty oak. In many ways, the man seemed ageless, and yet when he fell—as one day he would—the ground would shake.

The pair of them had locked horns several times over the years, although the king respected Hugh's opinion. Edward didn't like toadies, but sometimes Hugh tired of having to stubbornly hold his ground on certain matters. He had a feeling this eve would be one such occasion, for Edward had a glint in his eye that Hugh knew well.

"Take a seat." Edward waved a ring-encrusted hand to the empty seat to his right before gesturing to a circling page boy. "Fill up his goblet."

The lad moved eagerly to do his king's bidding, filling the empty pewter goblet with French wine.

Hanging up his cloak by the entrance to the tent, Hugh moved to his place at the king's side, lowering himself down onto the bench seat. He then took in the ample spread of roasted fowl, fresh oaten bread, the ubiquitous pottage, and aged cheese before him. His belly growled, reminding him that the noon meal seemed hours away now.

Of course, Hugh wasn't taking supper alone with the king. The prince and the queen consort, Margaret, had joined them, as had Lamia, one of the queen consort's ladies-in-waiting.

Hugh nodded to his supper companions, and was just taking a sip of wine, when Prince Edward spoke up. "So, are the men ready to depart, Sir Hugh?"

One and twenty, and keen to prove himself, the prince bristled with the same ill-concealed impatience as his father. Edward the younger was also tall and muscular, although he wore his dark-blond hair shaved close to his scalp in a severe style.

"Aye, Your Highness," Hugh replied, keeping his own expression veiled. "They're always ready to march ... although that doesn't mean they should."

"And why's that, Hugh?" Margaret asked. The queen spoke English with a heavy French accent. However, it pleased her husband that she learn his native tongue, and so she made an effort to speak it.

Hugh's mouth lifted at the edges. "Because winter isn't done with us yet, Your Highness … and this one is particularly harsh."

Margaret's brow furrowed as she took his words in. Small, with a pert face and curly walnut-colored hair, she'd insisted on accompanying Edward on his campaigns, as his first wife, Eleanor, had done. Her belly was starting to swell with her third child, yet that hadn't stopped her from remaining at her husband's side.

The king snorted. "That's a dull answer to my dear wife's question." The king then cast his wife an indulgent look. Edward had been lucky in love—more fortunate than most folk, Hugh included. He'd adored both his wives and now had an enormous brood of offspring: sixteen by his first wife, and two by his second. Likewise, the queen consort smiled back at her husband. The look of devotion that passed between them made Hugh go still. *His* late wife had never gazed at him like that in all the years of their marriage.

"A little snow shouldn't bother us," Prince Edward piped up, scowling. "We're Englishmen, not warm-blooded Spaniards."

Hugh drew in a deep breath and counseled patience with the hot-headed prince. "The snow isn't done with, Your Highness," he murmured. "The last thing we need is to be caught in a blizzard with Scots closing in on us." He paused then, frowning. "They know this land better than we ever will."

"Well said, Sir Hugh." Lady Lamia spoke up then. "The Scots are a hardy breed … we'd best not under-estimate them."

Hugh shifted his attention from the prince to see that the court lady was observing him keenly. He'd caught her doing that rather a lot of late.

Clad in a form-fitting, dove-grey cotehardie, a snowy ermine stole about her shoulders, Lamia was slender and possessed a gamine beauty. She had white-blonde hair that she wore pinned high upon her crown, with a few artful oiled ringlets framing her face. Her eyes were unusual: they were so pale grey they were almost colorless, like a winter's sky.

Surprised that he'd found an ally at the table, Hugh nodded. "Aye, history has a list of unfortunates who did just that, Lady Lamia."

"But fortune favors the bold, does it not?" the prince pressed on.

Hugh suppressed the urge to snort. *It also favors those who use the space between their ears.* However, he wisely didn't voice the sentiment. He held a privileged position as the king's commander, yet there were some lines that he wouldn't overstep.

As such, when Hugh replied he was careful to keep his tone low and respectful. "If we move too early and more snow falls ... as is common in Scotland ... we risk our horses foundering and our men losing limbs to frostbite." He glanced then to the head of the table, meeting the king's eye. "As such, I'd prefer to wait till winter loosens its grip, sire."

Edward scowled back at him. The king helped himself to some fowl breast and speared the meat with his eating knife. "Even so ... a wintering army cannot grow complacent. I don't want my men fat and lazy come spring."

Hugh held his eye, meeting his liege's challenge. "They won't be."

3

A COLD NIGHT

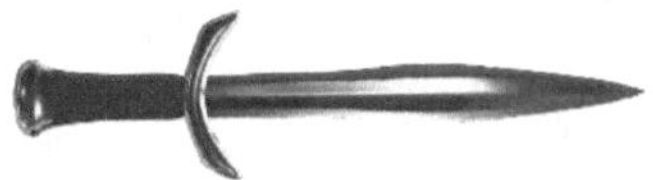

THE CROW WAS waiting for Nessa upon her return home.

Perched on the doorstep, feathers fluffed up with cold, and its head hunched into its neck, the bird watched her with gleaming coal-black eyes as she approached.

The sight of the crow made a smile stretch across Nessa's face. The snow was falling thick and fast, and the wind dug its claws through her clothing. She longed to get inside, yet her visitor was a welcome sight indeed.

It was almost as if Colina had known today was special—for she'd sent her familiar south in search of news.

"Poor weather for travel, Eclipse," Nessa greeted the bird. "Ye shall be staying the night, I take it?"

The crow merely shuffled to one side, allowing her to open the door.

The High Bandruì was the only one who could actually share thoughts with the crow. Nonetheless, the bird could understand the other members of the order.

Nessa threw open the door, and Eclipse flapped indoors. Following the bird in, she pushed the door shut behind her and barred it. She lived alone in a cottage that sat apart from other houses. Despite the foul weather that would keep most folk huddled by their hearths, she was always careful.

Nessa had ways of keeping men with ill-intentions away, yet none of her methods were infallible.

Blinking, as her eyes adjusted to the dimly lit interior of her cottage, Nessa swung her gaze to where Eclipse now perched upon the wooden window-sill.

The bird fixed her with a penetrating, demanding stare that she knew well: Colina wished for an update.

"Ye timed yer visit well," Nessa informed the familiar, crossing to the hearth and peering into the pot of bubbling stew she'd put on earlier in the day. The strong aroma of mutton filled the small space. "I have finally met someone who should be able to reveal The Hammer's secrets to us."

Eclipse sat silently, waiting for Nessa to elaborate.

"His name is Hugh de Burgh," she continued, shedding her damp cloak and hanging it up behind the door. "He's the king's right-hand. Now that I've established contact ... I can begin my seduction." She flashed Eclipse a grin. "Worry not, I'll have the details we need soon enough."

Nervousness fluttered in Nessa's belly then. Despite her confident manner, she was a little on edge after meeting the knight. Colina had chosen her for this mission, for she was comely and self-assured and had already proven herself extremely capable in the past. However, she'd never deliberately 'seduced' a man before to get him to spill his secrets. She'd need nerves of steel for what was to come.

"At least he's handsome," she murmured, voicing her thoughts aloud. "That should make it a little easier."

The crow merely cocked its head, inviting her to continue.

"Hugh de Burgh is gruff and a bit ill-mannered," she said, sorting through her impressions of the knight. "Not one to trust or to take others into his confidence easily."

She didn't add that de Burgh's attitude toward her had been frosty. It mattered not, for she'd noted the way he'd held her eye far longer than was necessary.

He hid it well, but she'd sensed his interest.

Slinging a woolen shawl across her shoulders, Nessa crossed to the low table near the window—which was piled high with a jumble of baskets of herbs, clay bottles, and leather pouches—and cut herself a slab of bread from the loaf she'd made that morning.

Feeling the crow's beady gaze upon her, she glanced over at it. "I will ensure our paths cross again," she assured the bird. "And soon."

Studying the bird's unnervingly bright eyes, she felt a tightening in her chest, a pang of envy. Only the most powerful of druidesses drew a familiar to them—and Colina was the only current member of their order who'd done so.

Life could get lonely sometimes, moving from place to place—always the outsider. She could have done with a familiar to keep her company. An owl perhaps, or a cat.

But Nessa's witching didn't burn as bright as the High Bandruì's. Hers was rooted in the earth, her skills in the healing arts. And as such, she'd gotten used to her own company—she'd had no choice.

Helping herself to a bowl of stew, Nessa perched on a stool before the glowing hearth and ate her supper. The stew was scalding, and she had to consume it slowly or risk burning her tongue. All the while, she felt Eclipse's stare upon her.

Of course, Colina wanted to know what else she'd learned of late.

"The English keep largely to themselves," she admitted after a pause. "Edward's army is well defended, and there have been no rumors of where he will move onto in the spring." She paused there, swallowing a spoonful of hot mutton stew. "I go daily to the market in town and make sure I listen to every rumor … every whisper." She shook her head then, frustration bubbling up within her. "But The Hammer has gone silent of late."

Nessa stirred the remnants of the stew with a spoon, her lips pursing. Impatience simmered within her. "The English king is getting old," she murmured. "Perhaps his ambition wanes."

The crow gave a soft, disbelieving caw in reply, and Nessa huffed a wry laugh. "Ye don't believe that either, do ye?" Her jaw tensed then. "War-mongering, pox-ridden cur … I can't wait for the day we send him and his lackeys back across the border with their tails between their legs!"

Eclipse gave another caw, although this one sounded like a resounding agreement.

For nearly a decade now, the English had launched campaigns north of Hadrian's Wall. Edward Longshanks, 'The Hammer of the Scots', was relentless.

He had to be stopped.

Finishing her stew and bread, Nessa then poured herself a cup of apple wine. She huddled close to the fire, poking the brick of peat that burned there, with a stick.

The cold drilled into one's bones tonight, as if the Crone herself walked abroad, leaving the world frozen and silent behind her.

Nessa shivered, pulling her shawl closer. She might not be as old as The Hammer, as her order named him, yet she felt every one of her thirty winters this evening. Even her dedication to the Guardians of Alba, which smoldered like a glowing coal in her belly, couldn't warm her.

I've lingered in Dunfermline long enough. It was time to complete her task and move on.

Hugh braced himself for the chill as he stooped to exit the king's tent. But even though he'd prepared himself for it, the icy wind cut straight to the marrow. He was bone-tired tonight, his shoulder and back muscles aching from the harsh training he'd gone through that morning, and from the cold that still managed to drill into him, despite his thick layers of clothing.

Muttering a curse, Hugh pulled his cloak tight about him before casting a look at the two shivering guards flanking the tent entrance. Guttering torches outlined their pale, taut faces.

"Go and get yourselves cups of mulled ale," he instructed brusquely. "Before you drop from cold."

"Aye, Sir Hugh," one of them mumbled through frozen lips. "Thank you."

Hugh nodded before striding away from the king's pavilion. His own tent sat just a few yards away, although the journey seemed endless on a night like this.

A blizzard swirled about them, blocking out the darkness. Hugh's mouth thinned. No one was likely to make an attempt on the king's life in weather like this. Even so, the men would need to return to their posts shortly.

Entering his tent, Hugh found his squire diligently polishing his master's armor. The lad sat upon a stool, Hugh's plate armor and greaves spread out around him. His face was screwed up in concentration as he worked a shine onto Hugh's helmet.

"Leave that, Thomas," Hugh instructed. "I don't need to see my face in my helm."

Thomas Charlton, a lanky lad of fifteen, and the eldest son of the Earl of Apley, glanced up. "I like to keep them looking nice, Sir Hugh."

"Aye," Hugh huffed, shrugging off his cloak. "But such tasks can wait till tomorrow."

Moving to the center of the tent, and passing the glowing brazier that warmed the space, Hugh took in the comfortable surroundings. Indeed, despite the fingers of icy air that still managed to force their way in through the gaps in the awning, this pavilion was as comfortable as his bed-chamber back at Grosmont Castle. Furs covered the ground, and guttering candles illuminated the billowing tent walls; the wind had picked up. A large bed dominated the center of the space, and a rectangular table sat a few feet to its right. Hugh usually took his meals in here, and generally preferred it.

Dining with the king put him in an ill-temper of late.

Thomas set about putting away the armor while Hugh undressed. He undid the sword belt about his waist and placed his longsword upon a low table. A leather scabbard encased it, decorated with the de Burgh crest and motto: a gauntlet with the words *Lux vitœ*—the light of life.

Removing his surcoat, Hugh then pulled the heavy hauberk under it up around his waist. He leaned forward and touched his toes, shrugging off the heavy chain mail shirt so it slid over his head and rattled onto the furs. He'd learned years ago that trying to remove it like one did a tunic merely resulted in a lot of struggling, sweating, and swearing.

An instant later, Thomas retrieved the surcoat and hauberk, hanging them up next to the knight's gleaming armor.

"Do you need anything else, Sir Hugh?"

Hugh shook his head. "No ... get to bed, lad."

Not needing further encouragement, the squire dug out the sheepskin he slept on and rolled it out a few feet back from the brazier—not too close to the fire lest it spat out embers during the night, yet far enough away from the door to avoid drafts. He then made a nest for himself under a pile of coarse blankets.

Hugh's mouth quirked as he watched the squire's ritual. Thomas had been with him for the past three years. The lad was quiet, hardworking, and he slumbered like a hibernating hedgehog. These days, Hugh's own sleep had grown restless. He went to bed tired, yet often found himself staring up at the darkness for hours before exhaustion finally dragged him down into its clutches.

A lukewarm bowl of water sat next to the bed. Thomas, the good lad that he was, had retrieved it for him.

Stripping off the gambeson—a heavy, quilted tunic— he wore under his hauberk, Hugh crossed to the wash bowl. Picking up a hard cake of lye, he quickly bathed. Robert, who boasted that he washed once a month, often delighted in making fun of his friend's evening rituals. Hugh rarely missed his nightly wash—a habit his father had instilled in him. However, he didn't linger over it this evening. Jaw clenched against the cold, he stripped off his chausses and hose, leaving on his loose linen braies, before he doused the candles upon the bedside table and climbed under the covers.

Lying there in the half-darkness, for only the glow of the brazier now lit the interior of the tent, Hugh listened to the howling wind, the creak of the tent, and the crackle of embers. Moments later, the rumble of Thomas's snoring joined the other noises.

Hugh sighed. The lad's snoring had grown wearisome over the past years, especially since sleep often eluded *him* these days.

He was aware then of the dull, throbbing ache in his right hand. The cold had distracted him, yet now he was warm under the covers, he noted it once more. Placing his other hand over the tightly wrapped bandage, Hugh winced. It was becoming increasingly tender, and he could feel the heat of the wound even through the thick layer of linen wadding.

You could pay that healer a visit?

The thought made his lips thin. Aye, he could. Or perhaps the harassed camp physician needed to take another look at the wound instead.

4

HE WILL COME

NESSA MADE HER way to market through a world blanketed in white.

Basket slung over one arm, her boots crunching into the pristine ermine crust, she breathed in the sharp air and enjoyed the sting on her face.

She didn't appreciate winter's numbing chill, but there was a beauty to this season all the same that she loved. Nessa was nature's child—and had always felt strongly connected to the passing seasons. It was a connection that aided her use of the craft.

Breathing in the scent of wood smoke, which mingled with the heavier, more pungent odor of burning peat, she navigated the narrow streets of Dunfermline and made her way to the small square at the heart of it.

Even on a snowy day such as this, the farmers, bakers, and merchants were hawking their goods, their cries reaching Nessa before she caught sight of the snow-encrusted awnings. A number of men and women moved through the square, their faces ruddy with cold.

Nessa greeted the vendors she passed with a smile. She never missed the daily market. It was a source of news, but also companionship. As much as she was used to her own company, she'd found herself succumbing to loneliness of late. It was likely the long, cold winter, she told herself—but these days she often lingered at the market, chatting to the woman who sold hot pies, while she sipped a hot cup of mulled wine.

But she wasn't here just to gossip with the local women today.

Gaze narrowing, she surveyed the milling crowd, in search of the glint of chainmail, the flash of a crimson cloak. Now that she'd made contact with Hugh de Burgh, she intended to press her advantage. However, there was no sign of the knight, as yet.

Eclipse had flown off with the dawn, taking word of her progress to the High Bandruì. Colina, usually so serene, had developed an urgency of late. The English were gaining a foothold in Scotland, and nothing seemed to be able to halt their progress. Nessa desperately needed to learn where and when the enemy would strike next—but gaining such information took time and patience.

Moving through the market, Nessa's brow furrowed. The English were a plague upon this land. She didn't want to lie with a man who had spent the last few years slaying her countrymen. Yet she would—for Scotland.

Of course, to seduce Hugh de Burgh, she had to meet up with him again.

Now that she had made contact, she had something to anchor her witching upon. She suspected he would come to her eventually, after their encounter at the gates, but decided there was no harm in giving him a little nudge. That morning, as the grey light of dawn filtered through the cracks in the shutters, she'd written a charm upon a scrap of parchment as she'd burned mugwort. She'd then whispered those same words to the rising sun. She carried the parchment with her at present, rolled tight and slipped into the bodice of her kirtle, against her heart.

He will come.

She knew it with a certainty that sat heavily in her bones, as it often did when she worked a charm. She just needed to exercise some patience.

Hugging her basket close, Nessa walked over to where a man was selling fruit and vegetables. There wasn't much to choose from this time of year, but Nessa bought some apples. They were the winter store, and as such, a little wizened. Yet they would taste sweet, and she could stew some with honey.

The vendor flashed her a smile. "Chilly enough for ye, lass?"

"Aye, let's hope it's frozen the English in their beds," she replied, grinning back.

The man snorted before leaning close. "I was at *The Drovers' Inn* yester eve and heard a rumor … that those whoresons are planning to push north once the snow melts … to take Inverness."

Nessa's gaze widened, her pulse quickening. "Aye, Darach … and who told ye such?"

"One of the serving lasses told me an English soldier bragged of it to her … said that Longshanks wants the Highlands next."

Hot and then cold swept over Nessa. The Hammer's warmongering knew no bounds. "Bastard," she muttered. Tucking the detail away, she promised herself she'd investigate this rumor further. She'd pay a visit to *The Drovers' Inn* later and speak to this serving lass herself.

Handing the fruit and vegetable vendor a penny, Nessa wished him a good day, turned—and ran straight into a wall of chain-mail.

Reeling back, she raised her chin and stared up into a sneering face.

Clad in a hauberk and stained surcoat, and reeking of onions, the English soldier had just deliberately collided with her. The man's blue eyes glinted before he murmured in English, "Watch where you're going."

"Aye." A second soldier stepped up next to him, grinning. "Clumsy bitch."

Nessa viewed them, her mouth pursing. They were both young and not as finely clad as the three Englishmen she'd met the day before—men-at-arms rather than knights. She'd worked a charm in order to cross paths with Hugh de Burgh this morning, not these two louts.

"Apologies," she replied in English, her tone cool. "It won't happen again." Then, dropping her gaze even as ire now boiled in her belly, she stepped aside.

"You speak our tongue?" The first soldier frowned. "How's that?"

"It's easy enough to learn," she replied. "Now, if you will excuse me."

"Going somewhere?" The man side-stepped, following her. "I think not ... we'll have some fun first."

Nessa glanced up, twisting her head to see that, still grinning, the second soldier now moved behind her. He caged her in, while his friend loomed over her, smirking. The smell of onions was so overpowering that her eyes started to water.

"How about a kiss?"

Nessa's mouth twisted, the reply slipping from her lips before she had the wisdom to check it. "I'd rather kiss a dog's arse."

The soldier's leer faltered. "Mouthy Scot bitch." He then shoved her, sending Nessa into the arms of his friend. "That can be arranged later."

"Aye." The second soldier grabbed Nessa, roughly squeezing her backside. "But right now, we'll take what we—ooff!—"

Nessa drove her elbow back, into the man's chest, cutting him off. Around her, she was aware of a rumble of angry voices. However, none of the vendors had yet come to her aid. Nessa's belly twisted, heat washing over her. These people all hated the English, but none were bold enough to intercede.

And yet part of her understood their reluctance. Both soldiers wore longswords at their hips and knives strapped to their thighs. They were also huge men with hard eyes—folk were wise to be wary of such individuals.

That wasn't of any help to Nessa though.

Snarling a curse, the first soldier grabbed her by the hair and hauled her against him. A large hand fastened over her breast, pinching hard. "I'll take that kiss now."

Meanwhile, his friend had recovered from the jab to the ribs. Growling curses, he crushed himself up against

Nessa once more, grinding his groin into her backside. She was now jammed between them.

Fury kindled hotter within Nessa, igniting in her veins. She'd not tolerate this—even if defending herself would draw unwelcome attention. It was too public a place for using the craft, yet she had other methods of protecting herself.

Nessa's hand strayed to the dirk hidden under her heavy winter cloak. These two would soon regret laying hands on her.

An instant later, the brute whose foul breath gusted across her face jerked away.

Staggering, Nessa realized someone had just yanked him backward. She then caught the flash of a fine crimson surcoat. A third figure, taller than either of the soldiers, stood between them now.

Hugh de Burgh grasped both men by the lowered coifs of their hauberks and smashed their skulls together. A satisfyingly hollow 'clunk' echoed through the marketplace.

He then sent the pair of them careening into the fruit stand. Apples went flying, scattering like large blood-red rubies onto the snow.

Drawing her cloak tightly about her, Nessa looked on while the king's commander surveyed both soldiers coldly.

"Your names?" he growled.

A beat of silence followed. The soldiers looked scared now, the whites of their eyes stark against their flushed faces.

"John Fullar," one of them rasped.

His friend, the one that reeked of onion, swallowed hard. "William de Clopton."

"Get back to camp ... and I'll deal with you both later." The knight's voice was flint-hard and as icy as the wind that cut through the market.

Neither soldier argued with him. Nessa knew by the look on their faces that they were aware exactly to whom they were speaking—and they feared him.

Scrambling to their feet, they hurried away, leaving the ruin of the fruit stand behind them.

Heart still pounding in her ears, Nessa watched them go.

"Look what ye've gone and done," the vendor spluttered. His round face purpled as he glared at the knight who remained behind. "My apples will be bruised! No one will buy them now!"

Nessa cast the man an irritated look. He rushed to the defense of his wares but not women in peril.

"They'll be fine," she muttered. Wondering why she was aiding someone who hadn't bothered to assist her, Nessa then sank to her knees and started to gather the fallen fruit. The snow had indeed broken their fall.

"Here." The deep rumble of a man's voice rolled over her, and Nessa's skin prickled with awareness. "Let me help you."

An instant later, a large hand plucked a red apple out of the snow, leaving a perfect spherical imprint in its wake, and passed it to her.

Bracing herself for the impact, Nessa took the apple, raised her chin—and looked into a pair of appraising hazel eyes. The knight crouched before her, his gaze level with hers.

"Tapadh leibh, Sir Hugh," she thanked him, viewing him under her lashes. She placed the apple he'd passed her back in her basket before reaching for another.

Hugh de Burgh caught her eye once more. "You remembered my name," he said gruffly in the same tongue.

Nessa favored him with a coy smile. There was no time to waste—she needed to start working her seduction upon this man now. "Aye ... it was only yesterday we met, after all."

His head inclined. "You know my name ... but I do not know yours."

"That's easily fixed." She continued to look at him, even if she was aware they were still drawing curious stares from vendors and market-goers alike. "My name is Nessa."

He gazed back at her, no trace of a smile upon his face. "Nessa," he said after a brief pause, pronouncing her name carefully as if committing it to memory. "I must apologize for the behavior of those men ... they will be dealt with."

Nessa stilled at the hard edge to his voice. She didn't doubt him.

The knight's expression softened then. "Did they hurt you?"

Nessa shook her head before gathering up the rest of the scattered apples. "No ... thanks to ye."

Together the pair of them rose to their feet.

Lifting her chin to meet his gaze once more, Nessa reflected that Hugh de Burgh was indeed ruggedly handsome. The fine lines around his eyes and the grooves bracketing his mouth confirmed that he was a mature man, in his mid-thirties at least. The knight was dressed as he had been the day before, in a glittering hauberk and blood-red surcoat that made him stand out in the crowd of men and women in checked plaid, fur, and wool.

Sir Hugh didn't seem to care that folk were staring at them. He wore a longsword at his hip and carried himself with breathtaking arrogance. It was almost as if he dared anyone to aggress him.

Nessa could feel the suspicious looks of the vendors and market-goers alike boring into her. They'd all be wondering why she was conversing with this Englishman.

"What are ye doing at market?" she asked then, deliberately injecting a breathless note into her voice. "Apart from rescuing women."

"Just making sure the folk of Dunfermline are behaving themselves," he replied.

Nessa arched an eyebrow. He'd said that too in Gaelic, heedless of the scowls surrounding him. "And are they?"

The corners of his mouth lifted just a fraction. She couldn't believe it: the dour knight was close to smiling.

"It appears so." His expression sobered once more. "It was my men who were not."

Nessa's attention drifted down to his right hand, which she noted was still bound, although it appeared to have a clean bandage. "Ye've had that wound tended to then?"

"Aye," he grunted. She glanced up to see he was frowning. "Although the camp physician tells me it just needs time."

"Has he treated it?"

The knight shrugged. "Not really."

Nessa's gaze held his. "Such wounds are dangerous. If ye come with me, I can take a look at it."

His mouth thinned. "So, ye can mend injuries better than a trained English physician?"

Nessa swallowed the sharp response that bubbled up within her. In her experience, such men were often butchers who killed as many patients as they cured. But since she was trying to charm this man into her bed, she choked the rebuke down.

"I am only trying to help ye, Sir Hugh," she said, careful to keep her voice soft and inviting. "But if ye do not wish it, I shall bid ye good day. However, if ye *do* wish to keep that hand, ye know where to find me." She paused then, favoring him with one last smile. "I thank ye again, for coming to my aid."

Nessa then turned and walked away. And as she went, she felt the weight of his stare upon her.

Nessa's smile widened as victory thrilled within her. The trap had been well and truly set—now all she had to do was wait.

5

THIS WILL NEED CARE

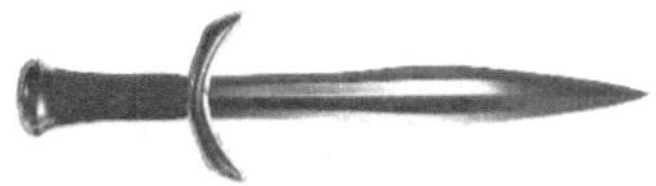

THE WOMAN CLAD in blue disappeared into the crowd. Hugh watched her go. He couldn't help himself. Everything about Nessa the healer was sensual—her walk and the gentle sway of her full hips included.

He became aware then of the quizzical and hostile looks he was attracting.

Hugh didn't often visit the market, and he wasn't sure what had possessed him to do so this morning. He'd awoken to find the blizzard spent and a deep crust of snow upon the world. And then, after a cup of hot broth and a slab of buttered bread to break his fast, he'd gone to visit the physician. Subsequently, he'd left the camp and walked into town.

He looked down at his bandaged hand. Curse the woman. Did she really think he risked losing it?

He'd seen the way the physician's gaze had shadowed earlier that morning, heard his muttered assurances of how it would heal given time. But when Hugh had seen the wound, a chill feathered down his nape—it was red and swollen. Hugh was a veteran, he'd seen similar wounds before, and such an injury didn't usually bode well.

Hugh's gaze narrowed, and he swiveled on his heel, cutting a swathe through the milling crowd in the direction of the camp.

Enough of this nonsense. It was an odd coincidence that he'd literally run into the comely healer he'd met the day before, especially after months of their paths never crossing—although it was just as well he had.

Hugh's frown deepened then. He had two men-at-arms to seek out.

John Fullar and William de Clopton would soon find themselves digging privies and emptying slop buckets for the next moon.

Stepping back inside her cottage, Nessa muttered a curse.

She wasn't the tidiest of individuals by nature, yet this morning she cast a critical eye over the cluttered interior of her dwelling.

Fyfa would have a fit at this. A wry smile curved Nessa's mouth then. Indeed, Fyfa, one of the sisters of her order, loathed untidiness. Growing up, she'd always despaired at the disorder of Nessa's sleeping alcove. Nessa hadn't seen Fyfa in years and wondered if she was still as neat and organized. It was likely—for Nessa's messy ways hadn't changed with the years either.

Focusing once more on her shambolic cottage, Nessa's smile faded.

If she was shortly to have company, she needed to make her home more inviting.

Throwing open the door and shutters, despite that chill air rushed in, she set about clearing up. Firstly, she tidied the wooden table that she used for everything, from preparing food to making salves and tinctures for healing. As such, there were baskets of dried herbs to stack, dusty bottles to put away, and the work surface to wipe down.

After that, she took out the furs she slept on and shook them in the crisp air.

Glancing up at the sky, she saw the faint halo of the sun attempting to shine through the clouds. There was no heat in it this time of year, yet it was a brave attempt nonetheless.

She brought the furs back inside and re-made her bed. Nessa then stepped back, her cheeks warming at her presumption.

Are ye really so certain he'll succumb to ye today?

Nessa's lips compressed. Timid women didn't lure men into their beds. She had to be confident in her ability to seduce Hugh de Burgh. So much depended on her gaining his trust. They had to know where the English would focus their attention next and when precisely they planned to move on. Earlier, after leaving the market square, she'd gone to *The Drovers' Inn* and found the serving lass who'd passed on the rumor about Inverness being the enemy's next target. Yet Nessa had left the inn frustrated; the lass was goose-witted and couldn't recall most of the conversation.

No, if Nessa wanted to know the enemy's plans, she had to beguile a man who had the king's ear.

Moving across to the window, she deftly drizzled a line of honey across the window-sill, murmuring a charm as she did so. It was a simple working: one scattered salt to ward a place, yet drizzled honey to beckon something—or *someone*—in. She wasn't going to leave anything to chance today.

Grabbing a broom, Nessa then started to vigorously sweep the dirt-packed floor of her cottage. A frown marred her brow as she worked. She really needed to clean her home more often. However, such tasks always seemed of little importance compared to those of gathering herbs and preparing healing salves. Today, she welcomed the industry—it took her mind off the nerves that danced in her belly.

It was well after noon by the time she'd finished tidying. Closing the window and door, Nessa put another brick of peat on the fire and heated a cauldron of water. The morning's work had left her sweaty and dirty.

Nessa wrinkled her nose. If she wanted to welcome a male visitor, she needed to be clean.

Stripping off in front of the hearth, she washed deftly before using a tincture of rosemary and lavender to cleanse her hair. Drying herself off afterward, she dressed in a fresh lèine and blue woolen kirtle. Blue was the color of her order—she rarely dressed in any other color. Nessa then prepared herself some bread, cheese, and apples for supper.

She'd hoped to put on a stew—for appetizing smells often made a man feel welcome—yet the day was waning, and after her morning's industry, she was worn out.

Perched by the fire, her hands wrapped around a cup of warmed apple wine, she wondered if she should work another charm, a stronger one than drizzling honey across the threshold. There was witching that could make a man calf-eyed and lustful.

But she was reluctant to use such a working. Indeed, this was perhaps the real reason she hadn't followed the original plan.

Aye, she'd used the craft that morning, to draw Hugh de Burgh to the market so that she could speak to him. But that had been a gentle beckoning charm, one that only gave the man a nudge in her direction. To induce someone into falling into her arms was something else.

Nessa scowled then, irritated at her pricking conscience. *He's an Englishman ... he doesn't deserve to be treated well.*

Many of the sisters of her order would have told her to save her scruples for someone more worthy—and yet she resisted using the craft on him in that way. In her opinion, there was something abhorrent about coercing someone against their will to lie with her; it was a flagrant misuse of her witch-will.

It was the only aspect of being a bandruì that sometimes made her uneasy—it was a responsibility to wield such influence over others. Perhaps, if she became desperate in future, she would use such witching. But for now, she preferred to use his attraction for her as bait.

Rising from her stool, Nessa went to the door, opened it, and peered out. The shadows grew long, and snow had silently started to fall once more.

For the first time that day, doubt niggled at her. *Maybe he won't come after all?*

Nessa muttered an oath under her breath. It served her right for being overconfident. Maybe she overestimated Hugh de Burgh's attraction to her.

"The cottage needed a clean anyway," she growled, shutting the door. "The day hasn't been wasted."

Brooding, Nessa went to the work table and sorted through the herbs she'd been drying. Placing a handful in a stone mortar, she picked up a wooden pestle and started to pound the herbs into a powder. It was satisfying work, one that helped ease the tension coiled within her. Mixing some boiled water with the ground herbs, she transferred the ointment to a small clay jar. This salve, made of dried woundwort flowers, was useful in cleansing soured wounds. Fresh woundwort was better, yet there wasn't any to be found in the depths of winter.

Nessa was just poking the smoking lump of peat on the hearth with a stick when a heavy knock at the door made her start.

Gripping the stick, she straightened up, her pulse quickening.

He's here.

Nessa drew in a deep breath, brushed off her kirtle, and went to the door. "Aye," she called, naturally cautious. She was a woman living alone after all and was wary of visitors even if she was expecting someone.

"Nessa?" A low yet powerful male voice reached her. "It's Hugh de Burgh."

Schooling her features into an expression of gentle concern, she stepped forward, lifted the bar that locked her inside, and opened the door.

The knight stood on her doorstep.

The snow fluttered down gently, settling on the ruby-colored, fur-trimmed mantle he wore about his broad shoulders. He wore an unreadable expression, and his gaze was veiled. He'd paid her a visit, yet she sensed he wasn't sure about the wisdom of doing so.

She felt his distrust.

Nessa favored him with a warm smile. "Come in, Sir Hugh." She stepped back and gestured for him to enter. "Get out of the cold."

He obeyed, although he stamped his boots on the step and shook out his cloak before he did so.

A considerate man, Nessa noted. She hadn't met many of those over the years.

She took his cloak from him, noting the fineness of the weave, and hung it up behind the door. Suddenly, the interior of her cottage seemed overly cramped. He was a big man, tall enough that his head almost brushed the heavy beams that stretched overhead. Bunches of drying herbs and hangings of bones and feathers swung from many of them, so he would need to be careful.

"You said you'd take a look at my hand?" he said gruffly. Once again, he spoke Gaelic rather than English. It was something Nessa appreciated, a mark of respect he didn't have to give her—and yet did.

Nessa nodded. "And I will ... come, take a seat by the fire."

He obeyed, yet the tension in his broad shoulders was impossible to miss.

His heavy hauberk jingled as he sat down. Pulling up a stool of her own, Nessa met his eye, taking care to hold it a fraction longer than was necessary. "Let's take a look at that injury," she murmured.

Wordlessly, Hugh held out his bandaged hand, and she unwrapped the bandage. And the moment she exposed the wound, she fought the urge to frown.

His camp physician was a fool to let this go on untreated.

The wound, which was long and thin—and looked to have been caused by a blade—was indeed festering. It was red, swollen, and had a sickly-sweet stench that worried her. But even more worryingly, thin red lines had started to spread out from it.

"This will need care," she murmured.

Hugh frowned. "So, it has soured?"

"Aye."

Nessa knew she was supposed to be drawing this man into her net, yet it wasn't in her nature to soften her words about such matters. She had to let him know it was serious, or this injured hand could be the end of him.

It wasn't the best time of year to heal such an injury. A Storm Moon rode the night sky during the month of February: it was a time of cold, snow, hunger, and storms. Yet they had just begun the waxing crescent phase of the moon, a time of intention, which *was* favorable.

Nessa rose to her feet, crossed to her work table, and collected some items in a basket before carrying it to the fireside. "This will hurt some," she warned the knight.

Hugh grunted, making it clear he cared not.

Nessa resisted the urge to smile; most men were like that—until she made them whimper like bairns.

Unsheathing a small, thin-bladed knife from her belt, Nessa held it over the flames, waiting until the blade glowed red.

She then deftly lanced the wound. Blood and pus ran over his outstretched hand. Yet, to his credit, Hugh didn't flinch or make a sound. Only his face gave him away: white and pinched.

Wiping his hand clean with a cloth, she then poured vinegar upon the wound.

The hiss through Hugh's clenched teeth made Nessa's mouth curve in sympathy. She knew it would burn like the devil.

Don't have sympathy for him. She chastised herself as she wiped away the vinegar with another cloth, careful not to touch the wound. *He has spent years burning Scottish towns and cutting Scottish throats. Ye should be using yer blade on his throat.*

Aye, perhaps, but Nessa was a healer first and foremost, a protector of life. She couldn't stand by and not help the sick and injured. Even one of the enemy. Plus, if she healed him, it would be easier to gain his trust.

As if reading her thoughts, Hugh cleared his throat. "Why are you helping me?"

Nessa glanced up. "Ye are hurt."

Their gazes fused. "Aye ... but I am English."

6

CLOSE YER EYES

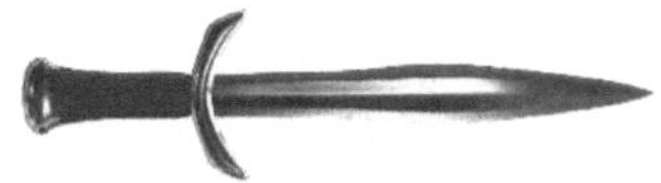

NESSA HUFFED A soft laugh, feigning embarrassment. Even so, the man had a penetrating stare, one that demanded truth. He was no fool. She considered her next words carefully. "Aye," she murmured, deliberately softening her tone. Hugh de Burgh wore a guarded expression, and he wasn't likely to bed her in such a state. "But ye are in need of my help."

She deliberately trailed her fingertips along his wrist before reaching for the pot of salve she'd made up earlier. "It seems yer camp physician doesn't know what he's about."

Hugh snorted. "He's busy tending injuries more serious than mine."

Nessa resisted the urge to scowl. *Then he's clearly a fool.* She didn't voice the observation; she was trying to get this man to lower his defenses after all. "Close yer eyes," she instructed.

Hugh's lantern jaw tensed, his gaze narrowing. "Why?"

"I'm going to put this salve on yer hand and work a healing charm."

The knight's frown deepened. "A *charm?*"

Nessa smiled. "It's merely something many wise women in this land use as part of their healing. Humor me, please."

Hugh gave her a wary look before he complied.

Nessa got to work. She covered the wound in salve before cupping it with her hand; the heat of the soured cut burned against her palm.

Closing her own eyes, she murmured the words Colina had taught her as a bairn, words that were as old as her people.

"Wrap ye in wool,
Bind ye with care,
Protection from pain,
Send harm back to its lair."

A breeze whispered through the smoky interior of the cottage then, and she heard the hearth gutter. A witch-wind, bringing with it the rich aroma of damp earth and the resinous scent of pine and crushed herbs, wrapped around them.

Hugh's hand grew rigid under hers, but Nessa squeezed it in silent warning. She then repeated the words once more, and the wind gusted through the cottage, causing her to shiver. She stopped speaking, and the witch-wind died away.

Nessa opened her eyes and glanced down at where her hand still covered Hugh's. The heat against her palm had lessened just a little. The spell was done.

"That's it," she murmured. Tiredness settled over her, as it often did after witching. "Ye can open yer eyes now."

Hugh did as bid, his hazel gaze fixing her. His expression looked even warier than earlier, and Nessa's chest constricted, panic darting through her. This wasn't going as she'd hoped. The man was more guarded than a fortress.

"What was that strange draft?" he asked, his voice rough.

Nessa shrugged, even as the tightness in her chest increased. She hadn't wanted to work a healing charm, yet the wound on his hand had required it. "Just a gust of wind hitting the cottage," she replied, hoping to put him at ease. "It happens sometimes ... I should really get a stonemason to take a look at the walls. It's far too drafty in here sometimes."

His gaze didn't waver from hers. "That tongue you whispered … what was it?"

"An old language." She broke eye contact, reaching for a fresh bandage to wrap his hand. "One that healers have used for centuries in this land."

"So, it wasn't witchcraft?"

Her mouth quirked at the suspicion in his voice. "And if it were, Sir Hugh? Many things in this world cannot be explained. I use some of the old ways in my healing." She lowered her voice, hoping to affect a beguiling tone. Time was running out, she had to penetrate this man's shields. "What harm is there in that?"

She started to wrap his hand. Holding his wrist firm, she deliberately made sure that she touched his skin rather than the sleeve of the quilted, long-sleeved tunic he wore. His skin was warm, and she felt his pulse quicken slightly under her touch.

Noting his reaction, victory flared within Nessa. He was doing a fine job of appearing surly and distrustful, yet her closeness was affecting him.

It hit her then that it wasn't one-sided. Seated before him, so close that their knees were almost touching, she was keenly aware of the man's presence. She inhaled the smell of leather and the warm, masculine spice of his skin.

Heat flowered across her breast as she worked, her breathing becoming shallow. She could feel his gaze upon her, burning into her. Perhaps he would reach for her once she finished wrapping the bandage?

Her belly fluttered at the thought.

She tied the bandage firm and raised her gaze once more. However, she didn't release his hand. Instead, she traced her fingers along the bandage and up to the exposed skin of his wrist. It was a bold move, yet she needed to get him to linger in her cottage. "Ye should be right now, Sir Hugh," she murmured, her voice lowering. "But ye came to me just in time."

"Thank you, Nessa." His voice was low, with a husky edge to it that made her feel a little light-headed. She was supposed to be seducing him, yet there was something about this man's presence that drew her in, made her want to reach out and trace her fingertips along the strong line of his jaw. Would his features soften if she kissed him? English or not, it had been a long while since she'd found a man this attractive.

The moments drew out, and then Hugh drew back his arm. He abruptly rose to his feet, severing the connection between them. "I should go."

Fighting disappointment, Nessa stood up and plastered a smile upon her lips.

Curse her, she couldn't fail—and yet Hugh walked to the door and retrieved his mantle. He appeared to be avoiding her eye now.

Nessa cleared her throat. "I suggest ye come back in a day or two," she said, careful to keep her tone light. "I'll check how it's healing and change yer bandages."

Hugh de Burgh gave a brusque nod. Then, still not looking her way, he lifted the bar from the door and let himself out. A gust of wind swirled in, bringing with it fat flakes of snow. An instant later, the door thudded shut, leaving Nessa alone.

Hugh strode away from the cottage as if the very hounds of hell were yapping at his heels.

He had to get away from this place and the winsome woman who inhabited it—before he forgot himself.

From the moment he'd stepped inside Nessa the healer's home, he'd felt something within him shift. The cottage had been warm and welcoming: it smelled of dried herbs and peat smoke. It was far less luxurious than his pavilion back at camp, yet he'd wanted to linger.

It had a woman's touch—something he'd not even realized he'd been missing over the years.

But even more than the homely surroundings, he'd wanted to linger in the Scotswoman's presence.

She was strange—the strangest woman he'd ever met. It was as if she existed outside the bounds of society. She appeared to have no family here and hadn't even given him her clan name. Nessa lived alone, apart from the rest of Dunfermline, a healer who employed strange arts.

Even now, the memory of that unusual draft, one that had smelled like he stood deep in a murky pinewood, made his skin prickle.

She'd assured him it was nothing, yet instinct told him differently.

She was at once nurturing and caring—an experienced healer who knew what she was about—and yet disarmingly sensual. Every time she touched him, he imagined her fingertips lingered upon his skin.

He hadn't been able to stop staring at that lush mouth of hers.

And that was why he'd had to leave. He wasn't in the habit of bedding witches.

Clenching the hand she'd tended, he pulled his mantle close. He wasn't sure what she'd done exactly, but the bone-deep throb across the back of his hand, which had been steadily worsening of late, had eased.

Aye, he should stay away from the woman. On his way back from the Holy Land a few years earlier, as he'd crossed the continent, he'd heard stories of folk hunting and burning witches. Fear of women who were different to others hadn't yet reached this far north, but all the same, Nessa should be more cautious about whom she revealed her abilities to.

Hugh muttered an oath under his breath and strode on, bending his head against the snow. Fortunately, he knew the paths around Dunfermline well, for it was getting dark and the swirling snow almost entirely obscured his surroundings. He'd visited her later than he'd intended—and almost hadn't come at all.

Despite that his hand now felt markedly better, he almost wished he hadn't.

Nessa stared at the closed door for a while after the knight left her cottage.

"Thrice-cursed fool," she murmured. "Ye've scared him off."

She hadn't wanted to use witching on his hand, yet the tell-tale signs of festering that was on the verge of taking hold had spurred her into doing so.

Once more, Nessa cursed. She wasn't supposed to be helping the man; she was supposed to be seducing him. Who cared if his damn hand rotted, poisoned his blood, and sent him to an early grave?

He was the enemy. It shouldn't bother her if his injured hand ended up being his doom.

Nessa scrubbed a hand over her face and moved to her work table, reaching for a clay bottle of apple wine. If she'd been canny, she'd have offered the knight some warmed wine before she'd taken a look at his hand. It might have made him relax a little, made him respond to her.

She didn't care what the bastard thought of her—and yet his rejection held a sting. Maybe she'd misread him. Maybe he didn't find her attractive as she'd thought.

Jaw clenched, Nessa poured herself a cup of wine and returned to the fireside. She took a sip, her mouth puckering as she swallowed it. This bottle tasted a bit sour; she'd have to replenish her stocks the following day, just in case she hadn't chased Hugh de Burgh off for good.

I wish my sisters were here, she thought then, wistfulness seeping over her. *They'd have sage advice.* Indeed, Fyfa and Breanna would have taken delight in working a charm to bring Hugh de Burgh to his knees—if only Nessa wasn't so stubborn about using her own wiles to seduce him.

The three of them—Nessa, Fyfa, and Breanna—had grown up together in the order. Although they weren't actually related by blood, they were closer than sisters, all foundlings who looked to the High Bandruì as their mother. Colina had repeated often over the years that anything important always came in a trio—three wishes,

three coins in a fountain, and three strokes of ill luck—
even the goddesses themselves: the Maiden, the Mother,
and the Crone.

Indeed, Nessa had always thought she, Fyfa, and
Breanna were stronger together than apart, yet their
missions had sent them in different directions. Fyfa was
now wed to Hume Comyn, the steward of Stirling Castle.
She'd been sent there a few years earlier, to find herself a
position in the castle where she'd be privy to the political
decisions of Scotland's rulers. Breanna, the wildest of the
three and a true warrior of the cause, spent most of the
year in the Highlands, ensuring the lines of
communication between the north and south remained
open.

Nessa sighed then, weariness descending upon her.
No, her sisters weren't here; she'd have to regain Hugh
de Burgh's trust herself.

7

CAREFUL DOES IT

THREE DAYS PASSED after Hugh's visit to her cottage.

In the meantime, Nessa got to work.

Clearly, Hugh de Burgh wasn't going to darken her door again unless pushed. Berating herself for using too light a hand with the knight, Nessa worked drawing charms at dawn and dusk and took care to drizzle fresh honey across the threshold each day.

But still, he stayed away.

The third day was drawing to a close when Nessa went to feed her pony. Honey—so named for the golden dun color of her coat—was impatient for her warmed mash. The cold had turned the garron ravenous, for the snow lay in a thick crust, preventing her from grazing. As such, Nessa made sure the pony had plenty of hay and a daily bucket of mash.

Picking up a hog-bristle brush, she applied a few strokes to the Highland pony's thick coat. The repetitive activity eased a little of the tension within Nessa. She'd spent most of the afternoon whispering drawing charms over a pot of burning sage; tending to the pony was a welcome distraction. It was surprisingly cozy inside the lean-to at the back of her cottage, and she was sweating by the time she finished.

I'll try another working tonight, she promised herself, brushing horsehair and hay off her skirts. She would sacrifice one of her fowls at dusk—Clover had recently stopped laying eggs and was ready for the pot anyway—and use its blood for a more potent charm. It was time to leave her scruples behind.

Jaw set, she left Honey to her meal and trudged around to the front of her cottage through thick snow. They'd had a fresh dusting every morning for the past few days; the spring melt still seemed a long way off.

Rounding the corner of her cottage, Nessa drew to a halt.

It was a windy, grey afternoon, the sky brooding with the promise of more snow—yet Hugh de Burgh's chain-mail glittered all the same.

He was standing before her door and had raised a mailed fist as if about to knock.

Sensing movement to his right, the knight swiveled, his gaze sweeping to her.

Nessa stilled, relief gusting through her. Clover would have a brief reprieve—for here he was. At her door, by his own volition.

"Sir Hugh," Nessa greeted him, favoring him with a half-smile. She was beginning to realize that seduction was a delicate art. It wouldn't do to appear too eager, as if she'd been awaiting his return.

He inclined his head, his mouth pursing, even if his hazel eyes gleamed in the wintry light. "Nessa ... have I visited at a bad time?"

"Not at all ... I was just feeding my pony." She gestured then to his right hand, presently covered by a chainmail glove. "Would ye like me to take a look at that?"

He pulled a face, revealing slight embarrassment. "Aye, if you wouldn't mind."

Nessa resumed her path to the door. "Come in then ... it looks like it's going to snow again. This winter seems endless, does it not?"

He gave a grunt of agreement. "My men grow restless," he admitted. "We've been wintering here since November."

Nessa cast him a glance over her shoulder as she threw open the door to the cottage. "Will ye move on as soon as the thaw arrives then?" she asked casually.

Hugh shrugged, his gaze veiling. In an instant, his manner became wary once more. "Our departure isn't yet planned."

Marking his response, Nessa turned away, leading him into her cottage. Her belly tightened. The man was suspicious by nature. She wasn't going to find him easy to extract secrets from.

"A cup of warm wine?" she asked, shrugging off her own cloak and hanging it up behind the door before taking his.

He paused a moment, as if debating the wisdom of such things, before giving a brusque nod. "Aye, thank you."

Encouraged, Nessa flashed him a proper smile and then gestured to the fireside. "Please … warm yerself."

Retrieving two cups, she filled them with wine she'd been mulling over the fire. The evenings these days seemed colder than ever. A cup of hot wine as the sun went down seemed to keep the chill at bay.

Hugh had removed his mail gloves and was indeed warming his hands over the glowing hearth. Nessa noted that he appeared to be avoiding looking her way. Was he nervous?

"I'm looking forward to feeling the sun upon my skin again." She passed him a cup of wine. "Are the winters this harsh where ye are from?"

Hugh took a sip of wine, and the tense set of his shoulders appeared to relax slightly. "A little less so … perhaps."

"Where is home then, Sir Hugh?"

He did look at her then. Their gazes met and held for a moment before his mouth lifted at the edges. "Grosmont Castle … it sits on the Welsh borders."

Nessa continued to hold his gaze. She noted the way his features softened when he spoke of his home.

"So, ye are a Marcher Lord?" she asked. "Appointed by the English king to keep control of the border."

"Aye, when I'm at home. These days, my younger brother rules Grosmont in my stead."

"When was the last time ye went home?"

He huffed a weary sigh. "Too long."

Nessa viewed him over the rim of her cup. This man was one of the enemy, but he intrigued her all the same. She heard the weariness in his voice. Hugh de Burgh was tired. She wagered that if The Hammer called a truce in spring, he'd happily return to his castle on the Welsh borders.

"Tell me of Grosmont," she asked, taking a sip of her wine. "Is the castle grand?"

He smiled, and Nessa's breathing stilled. It was the first proper smile he'd given her, and it was devastating. His left cheek dimpled, and the expression revealed just what an attractive man he was.

Heat spread through Nessa's belly, a warmth that had nothing to do with the wine.

Careful does it, Nessa, she counseled herself. She needed to keep her wits about her.

"It is a great stone keep, built nearly three centuries ago now, surrounded by a deep moat." Hugh's smile widened to a grin, revealing surprisingly white and even teeth. "To keep angry Welshmen out."

Nessa huffed. "Of course, Edward now has control of Wales, does he not?"

Hugh nodded, his grin fading. "Aye, his son, Edward of Caernarfon, rules those lands at present."

Nessa cocked an eyebrow. "At present? Ye don't believe he'll hold onto Wales?"

Hugh shrugged. "Power shifts in the blink of an eye, Nessa," he murmured. "Who knows who the ruler of Wales will be a decade from now."

Nessa took another sip of wine, eyeing him under her eyelashes. She didn't want to like Hugh de Burgh, and yet she found herself warming to him. There was something irreverent about him, something she hadn't expected to find in The Hammer's commander.

Setting his wine aside, Hugh held out his right hand to her. It wore a fresh bandage. "Did you want to take a look at your handiwork?"

Nessa put down her cup, and taking hold of his wrist with one hand, unwound the bandage with the other.

Those angry red lines had faded. The wound had now scabbed and was no longer swollen and pus-filled. "It's healing well," she observed.

"Thanks to you," he murmured.

Nessa raised her chin, meeting his eye once more. The way he was looking at her now made the heat in her belly spread up to her chest and throat. There was an intensity to his gaze that caused awareness to prickle through her.

Her attraction to this man was a boon indeed—it would certainly make this task easier.

"I thought I'd frightened ye away the other day," she replied softly. She was taking a risk, being so candid, yet she sensed this man preferred directness. "Ye looked at me as if I were about to sprout devil horns."

Hugh snorted, although awkwardness flitted across his features. "Your methods are … unusual … I'll admit," he replied. "But they clearly work. I appreciate what you did, Nessa."

Her pulse quickened. The low timbre of his voice, the way her name slid like honey off his tongue, made her feel a little light-headed.

"Healing is my gift," she murmured, wishing her cheeks didn't feel as if they were on fire. "I couldn't let such a trivial wound carry off a man like ye."

"A man such as me?" His voice developed a wry edge. "I'm one of the hated English, remember?" He paused then. "And *you* are a very odd Scotswoman."

Nessa's chin kicked up, her gaze meeting his once more. He was challenging her, the reticence she'd felt when he'd first entered the cottage gone.

"English or not, it didn't seem fitting that a knight who has fought bravely at his liege's side for years … should die of a scratch to his hand," she replied.

Hugh gave a humorless laugh. "And yet even kings have choked to death on their supper. The Grim Reaper cares not for rank."

Nessa snorted, dropping her gaze to his hand. She reached for a clean bandage and started to wrap it. "Are ye mocking me, Sir Hugh?"

"Not really," he replied, his voice a low rumble. "If I'm honest, I don't know what to think of you."

Nessa huffed a laugh, even as her breathing quickened. "Is that why ye left so abruptly three days ago?"

Three days. Mother's milk, did she have to let him know she'd been counting the days since she'd seen him last?

Silence stretched between them for a few instants, and then Hugh reached out with his left hand, placing it over Nessa's. She'd just finished securing the bandage, although she hadn't yet let go of his hand.

"Aye," he said softly. "I don't trust myself around you."

Nessa stilled. The Three give her strength, she hadn't expected such an admission from him. Slowly, she raised her chin, meeting his eye once more. Hugh was studying her with an intent, hungry look. "And now?" she asked, her voice barely above a whisper.

"I still don't," he growled.

With that, Hugh caught her by the wrists and drew him to her.

The moment his lips grazed hers, relief slammed into Nessa. No, she hadn't imagined it. This man did indeed want her.

Hugh drew away slightly. His gaze held a pained edge as if he still fought his desire for her. Nessa's breathing caught. She'd cast no love charm on this man—the heat between them wasn't feigned, and he'd kissed her of his own free will. Nonetheless, that wouldn't necessarily stop him from deciding against taking things further.

Nessa swallowed. This moment was a crucial one; she wouldn't shatter it by speaking.

Their stare drew out, and then he dipped his head once more. His kiss was achingly gentle at first, teasing. Nessa leaned into him, breathing in the scent of clove on his skin. He'd recently shaved, and when she reached a hand to his cheek, she found it smooth, with just a faint rasp under her fingertips.

His tongue parted her lips then, and he pulled her up so that she straddled his lap. A chill draft from the shuttered window feathered across the exposed skin of her legs as her skirt rode up, yet Nessa barely noticed.

Linking her arms around his neck, she kissed him back.

Hugh de Burgh tasted of apple wine. And once he started kissing her, she lost herself in his embrace. Her tongue slid against his, teasing him. And when he groaned, his hands sliding down her back to cup her bottom, heat flared in the cradle of her hips.

She couldn't remember ever enjoying a kiss as much as this one.

At thirty winters, Nessa had taken a handful of lovers over the years, even if it had been a while now since she'd done so. The nomadic nature of her life meant that she had never been able to settle down with anyone.

She'd known some good men, and passionate ones, yet none kissed like Hugh de Burgh. He feasted on her mouth, tasting, teasing, and giving as much as he took. He unraveled her, and for a few instants, Nessa forgot that this was supposed to be a seduction. She was supposed to be in control, yet this kiss left her witless.

They drew apart, both breathless now. The need in his eyes made Nessa's heart pound a tattoo against her breastbone. It was clear what they both wanted. The sensitive flesh between Nessa's thighs ached. She sat upon his lap, but he hadn't pulled her hard against him. She thought he would merely lift her skirts, unlace his hose, and take her that way, yet he rose to his feet, letting her slide from his lap.

Nessa tensed, panic fluttering up. *He can't just leave—not now.*

8

HEALER, TEMPRESS

HUGH DIDN'T LEAVE.

Instead, he stepped close and began to unlace the front of her kirtle. He then reached down, caught both her kirtle and lèine by the hems, and drew them up. Aiding him, Nessa lifted her arms above her head, the draft pebbling her nipples and causing goosebumps to rise on her skin as Hugh tossed her garments away.

His gaze raked over her, devouring her nakedness.

Nessa shivered under the heat of his gaze. There was no wariness or discomfort on his face now. He wasn't going anywhere.

Wordlessly, Hugh unbuckled his heavy sword belt, tossing it aside. He pulled up his hauberk around his waist before leaning forward and shrugging out of it. He then stripped off his gambeson, revealing a broad, heavily-muscled chest covered in crisp light-brown hair. Nessa spied a number of scars upon his torso, many of them silvered and puckered with age. This man had clearly spent his whole life as a soldier.

Breathing quickly now, she watched him heel off his heavy boots before he stripped off his chausses and hose. She'd never seen such a beautifully muscled body, tempered to iron by years of hard use.

Her gaze settled upon his shaft: big, hard, and ready for her.

His chest rose and fell fast as they stared at each other. Then Nessa stepped forward, took Hugh's hand, and led him to the bed.

They fell upon it, kissing wildly, their hands everywhere. On her back, his big body moving over hers as his mouth traveled from her lips to her neck, Nessa gave herself up to his touch, to the hunger that now writhed within her.

Hugh cupped her heavy breasts, pushing them together and lifting them to his mouth. Her answering gasp mingled with the crackling of the hearth and the whisper of the wind against the stone walls of the cottage.

Hugh moved down her body, his lips and tongue leaving a trail of fire over the curve of her belly before he parted her thighs wide, cupped her buttocks, and raised her up to him. The feel of his mouth on her there made Nessa cry out, and without even realizing what she was doing, she dug her hands into his scalp, urging him on.

Nessa cried out again. Her limbs started to tremble, wildness rippling through her as she arched hard against his mouth.

A moment later, he released her. Breathing hard, Hugh parted her quivering thighs and positioned himself between them. Taking his rod in hand, he guided it into her—and Nessa spread herself wider still to accommodate him.

He slid deep, burying himself to the root, and then stilled there a moment, letting her adjust to him.

Sweat beaded across Nessa's skin as she stared up at Hugh. His face was a study in self-control, even if she noted how his strong jaw tensed, how his eyes glittered down at her in lust.

It had been a long while since she'd taken a man to her bed. Nearly five years if she was marking the time. She'd forgotten what it felt like to have a lover buried inside her: the intimacy, joy, and freedom of it.

Somehow it didn't matter that Hugh was English. Their identities didn't matter at that moment; she even had trouble remembering the reason she'd wanted him in her bed in the first place.

The mission.

It drifted into her consciousness before dissipating like morning mist.

She couldn't hold onto it at present, not when Hugh started to move inside her. He braced himself above her, sliding into Nessa in slow, even strokes. The slick heat between them made her groan, made her want. She hooked her legs around his hips, drawing him deeper into her with each thrust.

She felt a quiver in his powerful body as he struggled to hold himself in check.

He had iron-will this man, even lost in the throes of passion.

Nessa wasn't so strong. Aching pleasure built in her lower belly, and her eyes widened as it consumed her.

She gasped when wet heat exploded deep within her, a sensation she'd never experienced before during coupling. It was a wild, unraveling sensation. She trembled, her back arching off the bed as she sought to prolong the pleasure of it.

Panting, Nessa let her eyes flutter closed, her head rolling back against the pillow.

Maiden's blood, this English knight certainly knows how to please a woman.

Hugh eventually let himself go. Unlike Nessa, whose groans and gasps now filled the interior of the dwelling, he didn't make a sound. However, she felt the tension coil within him as he reached his peak. Eyes opening, she watched him take one last deep thrust—his head thrown back, eyes closed, his face a rictus of pleasure—and then the heat of his seed filled her.

Panting, Hugh lowered himself down onto the bed next to his lover. He reached out then, his hand sliding up from her belly, across her heaving breasts, to her flushed neck.

Nessa's body was slick with sweat, and he could still feel her trembling in the aftermath of the storm that had just spent itself.

Hugh reached up farther, brushing his knuckles along the soft curve of her cheek.

Nessa's eyes flickered open, and her gaze met his. A sensual smile curved that delicious mouth, and although he was still recovering from taking her, Hugh's groin tightened in response. It was folly, his lust for this woman, but at present, he couldn't think of any reason why he shouldn't indulge.

It was still winter; the army wouldn't be moving on for a while yet. The bitter cold would last for at least another month, and in the meantime, he could forget himself for a spell. Perhaps they both could.

"I liked that," she murmured, a sultry husk to her voice.

"So did I," he replied with a slow smile of his own.

Her eyes—moss green with a jade rimming the irises—gleamed then, and she raised a hand, letting her fingertips trace a line from his collarbone down the center of his chest. Her touch made him shiver, his shaft hardening further still.

This woman had lovely hands, healer's hands— temptress's hands.

"We both needed that, I believe," she murmured, her lashes lowering as a pretty blush stained her cheeks.

Hugh's mouth quirked. "Aye ... it's been a while," he admitted.

"Really?" She sounded incredulous.

"Aye, my wife died a few years ago ... and I've been too busy to take a lover since." It was the truth. Hugh had spent most of his adult life serving his king. His time with women over the years, although often passionate, had been brief.

"I suppose conquering Scotland leaves a man with little time for much else," Nessa replied. There was no missing the tart edge to her voice.

Ignoring the barb, Hugh nodded. His gaze traveled over Nessa's face. She had pretty, even features, and that mouth that had so enticed him from the very beginning was swollen from his kisses.

"It's been a long winter," he said, stroking her soft cheek once more, "and when a comely Scottish healer caught my eye, I remembered that I am, indeed, a man."

In truth, lustful thoughts had plagued him over the past days. Hugh hadn't planned to return to this cottage—in fact, as he'd stridden away days earlier, he'd sworn he wouldn't. But he just couldn't keep away. He'd stood there like a dull-wit before Nessa's door, gathering the nerve to knock, when she'd appeared from around the back of her cottage. There'd been no going back then.

"I'm glad ye came back." Nessa's voice softened. "This life gets lonely sometimes."

Hugh frowned. "You shouldn't really live alone, lass … it isn't safe."

She gave a soft snort, making it clear he should mind his own business. She then reached out and slid her hand down from his chest to his belly. Her fingers clasped around his rock-hard rod, and Hugh stifled a groan. "Will ye stay a little longer?" she whispered.

Their gazes fused then, desire sparking between them. Hugh had never met a woman like this. Enigmatic, sensual, and strong-willed—Nessa made him wish that winter was just beginning.

"Aye," he growled before he leaned down and claimed her lips with his.

9

TIME TO SPILL SECRETS

NESSA DREW A blanket around herself before she pushed her hair out of her eyes and cast a glance over her shoulder at the man sprawled upon the coverlet.

Hugh de Burgh *had* indeed stayed a little longer.

In fact, he'd remained overnight in her bed. He slumbered deeply now, after a largely sleepless night.

Nessa smiled. It was a tired, yet slightly loopy smile—the smile of a woman who'd been well bedded.

Rising to her feet, she stretched like a cat. Then, pulling the blanket tightly about her, she padded across to where the remnants of the brick of peat still glowed. It was close to going out. She added more fuel to it and then stirred the embers to life, before putting on some water to boil. The pale light of dawn peeked through the cracks around the shutters and doors. It was so cold this morning that Nessa's breath steamed. However, she didn't pay the chill any mind.

After the night she'd just passed with Hugh, the cold barely touched her.

She couldn't get the silly smile off her face.

Pull yerself together, a stern voice cautioned her. Suddenly, it was as if Fyfa and Breanna were standing next to her. *Remember why ye lured this man into yer bed.*

Nessa's smile did fade then. She imagined her sisters' steady gazes resting on her, reminding her of who she was. And who Hugh de Burgh was.

Glancing back at where her lover was starting to stir, Nessa frowned.

Aye, she had to remember what was at stake here.

The English were a blight on Scottish soil, and like some foul disease, they steadily marched north. Every year, more Scottish clan-chiefs bent the knee to The Hammer. Even the likes of William Wallace hadn't managed to stop them. The freedom fighter had currently gone to ground; no one knew his whereabouts.

Nessa turned away, her mood clouding.

The Guardians of Alba had watched over these lands since far back in the mists of time, when the Romans had tried to conquer the forests and mountains of Caledonia. The Romans had eventually failed—and so would the English.

Nessa's gaze flicked then to her work table. She had prepared a mix of herbs, Pennyroyal being the principal ingredient, which she would take, along with a charm whispered as the sun rose high into the morning sky.

The last thing she wanted was for her womb to quicken—especially with an Englishman's seed. One of the first things Colina had taught Nessa, after her moon flow began at fourteen winters, was how to prevent a bairn from taking root within her. A Guardian of Alba couldn't devote herself to protecting Scotland with a brood of bairns hanging from her skirts.

A murmured oath behind her drew Nessa's attention then. She turned once more, to see that Hugh had sat up.

"Is it dawn already?" he asked, his voice hoarse with sleep.

"Aye," Nessa replied, forcing a smile. "I'm about to make some broth. Would ye like some?"

"I'd better get back to camp," he replied, shifting off the bed and walking naked to where his clothing still lay upon the ground. "Before my squire sends out a search party for me."

Nessa's gaze tracked him. Did the man have any idea how beautiful his body was? Probably not—there wasn't much vanity in Hugh de Burgh. She wagered he cared little for his looks.

He retrieved his clothing and dressed deftly.

"Ye have a squire?" she asked lightly.

"Aye, Thomas has been with me for a few years now ... the lad fusses over me like a mother hen."

Nessa kept a smile firmly fixed in place. "Do ye have any bairns of yer own, Hugh?"

He straightened up then as he laced his hose. His eyes shadowed, his handsome face tensing. "Aye," he murmured. "A son. My wife, Anne, died birthing him ... it's been four years now, and I've not seen the lad since."

He didn't need to say anything more. His gaze said it all. This man harbored regrets.

Nessa pulled her scratchy blanket tightly around her. She suddenly felt exposed, uncomfortable. Enough of this. She was here to seduce him, not empathize. As yet she'd gained nothing useful from Hugh de Burgh. She had to make sure he returned to her bed.

Even so, she held her tongue as he dressed. This was a crucial moment. An overeager woman could ruin her chances in the cold light of dawn.

Hugh reached for his chausses, tying them on. Moments later, he'd also donned his gambeson and hauberk. Watching him dress, Nessa marveled at how easy he made it look. Then, retrieving his gloves, he approached her.

Nessa was a tall woman, yet Hugh towered over her.

Hooking a finger under her chin, he raised her face so that she met his eye. "Can I visit you again, Nessa?" he asked softly.

Nessa gazed up at him, triumph thrilling through her. Bless The Three, she was starting to get somewhere. Hugh was guarded and doggedly loyal to his king, but if he continued to visit her, she'd find a way to break down his defenses, a way to discover when and where the English would strike next. "Aye," she whispered back.

"Good." He leaned down then, his warm lips brushing against hers in a soft, sensual kiss that promised more. When he drew back, Hugh favored her with a slow, lover's smile. "I'll see you soon then."

Teeth gritted against the cold, Nessa urged Honey through the snow, steering the mare away from the high drifts. Her mount snorted, tossing her head. After days of being cooped up, the garron wanted to run. They'd left the outskirts of Dunfermline—squat cottages frosted with snow, icicles hanging from their eaves—and rode toward the dark line of trees north of town.

Nessa usually went into Dunfermline on foot, yet she'd had a number of supplies to buy at market this morning, and so she'd ridden instead. An icy wind whipped in from the north, stinging her cheeks and ruffling Honey's dark mane as they headed home.

Nessa's fingers, which gripped the reins, ached with cold.

She couldn't wait till spring.

Don't wish time away, lass. Colina's voice whispered to her. *Not when ye have yet to get anything useful from yer lover.*

"I don't understand it," Nessa muttered, voicing her frustration aloud. "The man's as tight-lipped as a clam."

In the weeks that had passed since Hugh de Burgh had first come to her bed, he'd visited her most evenings and always stayed the night—but he'd revealed nothing useful.

Instead, he'd told her more about Grosmont Castle, about the son he'd only seen once, and about his younger brother, Kit, who'd been a bit of a rogue in his early years. He'd even spoken of his widowed mother, who'd never been the same since the loss of her beloved husband. However, Hugh said little about the wife he'd lost, and less still about his king and the campaign Edward was in the midst of.

Muttering an imprecation under her breath, Nessa squinted ahead, at where her dwelling sat at the edge of the woodland, a thin column of smoke drifting from the turf roof. The sight of her home usually made her smile, yet this morning she was in ill spirits. It was the end of February now; this was likely the last snow before the thaw began. Eventually, the vast English army would heave itself off the valley floor east of Dunfermline, where they'd wintered, and march off.

But she had no idea when they planned to depart, or what their destination would be, and her frustration increased with each passing day. Frustration and nervousness—for each day she lingered here was one day her own people wouldn't have the advantage.

"I can't let Hugh get the better of me," she told her pony. Honey plodded on, ears pricked toward their destination, oblivious to her rider's words. "I should be done with my scruples and just use witching to get him to loosen his tongue ... the others likely would."

She didn't doubt it. She was being entirely too principled. She'd wanted Hugh to give up his secrets naturally, as the result of a night of passion. Some of their couplings had been torrid—yet de Burgh remained as reticent as ever to divulge the details she needed.

Still brooding, Nessa returned to her cottage. She stabled Honey and carried her leather satchels, bulging with supplies, inside. She'd bought some aged cheese, butter, and dried sausage. She'd also stocked up on some bottles of bramble wine, made during the autumn and left to age over winter.

Yet Nessa wouldn't need to dig into her stores until the following day. Hugh usually stayed for supper, but this evening he'd suggested they meet for a tankard of ale and a dish of roast mutton at an alehouse in town.

Nessa had readily accepted his invitation. Perhaps, after a few ales, the knight's tongue would loosen.

Stacking the wine bottles upon a shelf, Nessa stepped back. Her gaze lingered on them before her mouth compressed.

Aye, she'd waited long enough.

If she didn't get anything out of him at the alehouse, she'd have to take action. Next time he came to her bed, she would drug his wine. It was time Hugh de Burgh spilled his secrets.

"I have decided we will indeed strike Stirling next."

The king's words fell heavily in the warm air inside the tent. Hugh shifted upon his seat. He'd been expecting such an announcement. Edward's ice-blue eyes held a flinty look.

"Finally!" Prince Edward held up his silver goblet aloft in a toast. The prince sprawled on a nest of cushions, across from where his father reclined in his chair. "The men need a good scrap … and so do I." He cut Hugh a veiled look then. "Does the commander of our army agree?"

Hugh frowned. The three men were alone, except for two page boys, who stood unobtrusively in the corners, waiting to jump to the king's commands. It had been a long and bone-numbingly cold day. The afternoon was drawing on, and Hugh was keen to bathe before meeting Nessa in town. *The Abbot's Arms* put on a fine meal, and he wished to take Nessa out for the evening. However, the king had summoned him. "Aye," he replied. "Stirling makes sense."

Indeed, they'd spoken at length over winter of the various places they'd attack next. Stirling 'the brooch of Scotland' was a strategic choice. It was the bridge between the Lowlands and the Highlands. And, at present, the fortress was back under Scottish control.

It had galled Edward to lose Stirling in the past—and he knew the king was itching to take back the castle.

Hugh lifted his goblet to his lips and took a deep draft of wine. He then focused on the king. "And when do you propose to march?" He was aware his voice sounded flat.

The truth was he felt conflicted. Part of him was eager to move on, while another part dug its heels in—for he hadn't spent nearly enough nights in Nessa's bed.

Edward's cool gaze speared him. "In a month … if that's not too soon, Hugh?"

There was no mistaking the challenge in the king's voice, or the smirk upon the prince's face. Nonetheless, Hugh refused to rise to the bait. "No," he answered. "The worst of the weather will be over by then."

Edward grinned in response. "Good … I intend for us to lay siege to Stirling's walls by April."

10

CLAWS

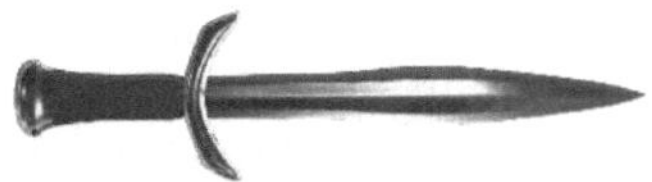

"SIR HUGH," A woman's voice hailed Hugh as he strode across the clearing between the king's pavilion and his own.

Hugh slowed his pace. He then turned, knowing without seeing who had spoken. Queen Margaret had a soft, musical voice that often carried the hint of a smile. Yet this one—although heavily accented in French like the queen's—was lower, with a slightly husky edge.

Lamia Delamare.

She stood a few yards behind him, swathed in a thick purple cloak. She'd pulled the fur-lined hood up, and it framed her pert features.

"Lady Lamia," he murmured, inclining his head politely.

Lamia approached him, boots crunching over fresh snow, an impish smile curving her lips. "We have seen little of you, of late, Sir Hugh." Her pale eyes fixed on him. "You haven't joined us for supper in weeks now?"

"I've been busy readying the men for the spring," he replied. It wasn't a lie. His days were spent organizing patrols, overseeing the camp, and ensuring that his men didn't lose their fitness and fighting ability.

However, his nights were spent with Nessa.

Thomas, who was a good lad and never asked awkward questions, had gotten used to having the commander's pavilion tent to himself. But, of course, others had noticed his absence as well.

"The men say you aren't spending your nights in camp," Lamia continued, her gaze never leaving his. She then inclined her head. "Have you found yourself a local lass?"

Hugh frowned. A rebuke simmered within him. It was none of this woman's business how he spent his nights. His behavior wasn't that unusual: no doubt a few of the other men here had found Scottish lovers.

When he didn't reply, Lamia glanced down, long eyelashes fluttering. She then toyed with the hem of her sleeve. "I counsel you to be wary, Sir Hugh," she murmured.

Hugh's frown deepened. "And why's that?"

"A man in your position might be targeted by unscrupulous Scots."

Hugh huffed a laugh. "I didn't get to this position by being a lackwit," he replied with a shake of his head. "But I thank you for your well-meaning concern all the same."

Lamia lifted her gaze to him once more. Her mouth pursed, and a faint blush stained her pale cheeks. Hugh was aware his reply came across as a trifle patronizing, yet it couldn't be helped. He had somewhere else to be. He needed to bathe, and he didn't want to keep Nessa waiting at the alehouse.

Hugh dipped his chin once more to the lady-in-waiting. "Good afternoon, Lady Lamia."

Not waiting for her response, he continued on his way.

The enemy surrounded her this evening.

Nessa raised the tankard to her lips, taking a sip. As she did so, she surveyed the room. It appeared she was the only Scot being served in here. Apart from the harried proprietor and his two apple-cheeked daughters, who carried tankards and platters of food across the rush-strewn floor, English soldiers filled the alehouse. They'd taken over the place, had driven the locals out—or maybe the men of Dunfermline had decided to drink elsewhere.

The rumble of male voices and laughter filled the dim interior of *The Abbot's Arms*. A fug of peat smoke hung under the low beams, so strong that it stung Nessa's eyes.

Leaning back against the booth she shared with her lover, Nessa noted the curious looks and smirks she and Hugh were attracting. None of the other soldiers in here were taking supper with women. Instead, they drank, diced, and played knucklebones at the round trestle tables.

Those smirks made Nessa's hackles rise. Of course, they likely were entertained by the sight of their commander taking supper with his Scottish whore.

Nessa clenched her jaw. Like the locals, she'd have preferred to dine elsewhere this evening. Nonetheless, her need to get Hugh to loosen his lips made her cast aside her discomfort.

Shifting her attention back to Hugh, she noted that he ignored his men. Instead, he appeared completely at ease, one arm slung across the back of the booth as he raised his tankard to her.

"Thank ye for inviting me out tonight," Nessa spoke up, meeting his eye with a smile. "Although I'm sure we'll be the talk of the camp by morn."

He gave a soft snort in reply. "I think it's too late for that."

Nessa arched an eyebrow, inviting him to elaborate.

"Gossip travels faster than the plague," Hugh said ruefully, shaking his head. "With little to do but wait, folk busy themselves in the affairs of others far too much."

Nessa laughed. "Then why add fuel to the fire by inviting me to dine with ye in a public place?"

Hugh held her gaze for a moment before his mouth lifted at the corners. "I suppose I just wanted to spend some time with you ... away from that drafty cottage."

Their supper arrived then, two dishes of mutton with oaten bread. The young woman serving them thumped the dishes down on the table and cast Nessa a baleful look before stalking away.

Traitor. Nessa had read the expression in the lass's face clearly. Irritation spiked within her as she tore her gaze from the girl's stiff back. Of course, it would look that way. The proprietor of this alehouse and his daughters had no idea who she really was—or that she'd dedicated her life to preserving their freedom.

Stifling a sigh, Nessa focused on her supper instead. The roast mutton smelled delicious, and she picked up her eating knife, readying herself to dive in.

"I was thinking today, Nessa, of how little I know of you," Hugh spoke up once more. "I've spoken of Grosmont, of my kin, and my life there ... but all I know about you is that you're a healer who lives alone here in Dunfermline. You have never even told me your clan's name?"

Nessa, who'd been about to take a mouthful of mutton, stilled. "I don't have a clan," she replied after a pause.

He cocked an eyebrow. "*Every* Scot has a clan. You must know who your people are?"

She shook her head, tensing. She was reluctant to reveal her past to him—but in doing so, she might get him to lower his defenses. Drawing in a deep breath, she replied, "I was a foundling ... abandoned by my mother shortly after birth. A woman ... a healer and wise woman ... found me and brought me up as her own."

Hugh swallowed a mouth of meat, his gaze never leaving her face. "And your childhood," he asked after a pause. "Was it happy?"

She nodded, favoring him with a smile. "Colina became my mother ... and I never missed the woman who'd abandoned me."

"Where did your birth mother leave you?"

"Upon a tree-stump ... for the fairies to take me. My adoptive mother believes I was likely born with a caul ... and so my parents thought me a changeling."

Silence fell between them. Hugh's mouth thinned. He'd likely heard of such practices. 'Fey births' were part of Scottish folklore. If a bairn was born with a caul—a piece of the birthing sac still in place over the face—folk believed that this meant the babe was a changeling. Such births were incredibly rare—the thin sac was harmless enough, and was pulled away straight after the birth. But that didn't stop people from believing it signified something was wrong with the child.

Seeing how his eyes shadowed, Nessa shook her head. "Don't look so concerned, Hugh. I was saved and brought up by a woman who loved me."

"Aye," he murmured. "But it's not the start in life you should have had."

Nessa shrugged. "No, it wasn't … but some have it much worse."

Aye, she'd been a foundling, but she'd grown up safe and cared for. Colina had never hidden the truth from her. As soon as Nessa was old enough to understand, the High Bandruì had explained her origins. All the druidesses of the order were foundlings. Some, like Nessa, had been left to die in the wilderness by superstitious folk. Both Fyfa and Breanna had been also. Fyfa had a large birthmark on her left thigh, and Colina had suspected her parents believed it was the sign of the devil. Breanna had been a strange infant, Colina had admitted. The bairn had hardly ever cried, and the High Bandruì suspected this had frightened her parents into abandoning her.

Other members of the order were orphans, abandoned on the steps of abbeys. Colina had simply crept in early and stolen away with the child before the nuns discovered them.

Nessa took a bite of mutton. Enough about her. It was time she got Hugh to talk.

"So," she said, reaching for the bread and tearing off a chunk. "I suppose I should ready myself for yer departure?"

Her lover raised his eyebrows yet didn't reply.

Undaunted, Nessa pressed on. "Ye *are* leaving, aren't ye?"

Hugh cast her a veiled look. "It sounds as if you are keen to rid yourself of me?"

"Of course not," she replied with a shake of her head. "But a woman likes to know how long her lover intends to warm her bed."

Hugh met her gaze squarely then, his strong jaw tightening. "And a man prefers the company of a woman who doesn't nag him, Nessa."

Silence fell between them.

Nessa frowned, anger igniting in her belly. "*Nag?*" Her voice hardened. "That's what ye think of me, is it?"

"No," he drawled, "but since you've asked me that twice already this week, you certainly risk turning into a fishwife."

Fishwife ... presumptuous English bastard, how dare he?

Slowly and deliberately, Nessa put her eating knife down. She then started to slide from the booth. Aye, she was a little vexed, yet his arrogance had given her an idea. Perhaps if he thought he'd offended her, he'd let his defenses down.

Hugh's gaze widened. "Where are you going?"

"Home."

"Why?"

"Agreeing to have supper with ye was a poor choice on my part." She paused then, glaring at him. "I've no patience with men who think themselves better than their womenfolk."

However, before she could slide out of the booth, Hugh's hand shot out, his fingers closing gently around her wrist. "Please ... don't go."

Nessa's jaw firmed. "And why not? Ye don't wish to be in the company of a *fishwife.*"

His gaze narrowed. "Are you really so easily offended?"

"It would appear so." She held his gaze, surprised to find her heart now thumping against her ribs. It seemed that he'd truly upset her after all. "I didn't grow up in yer world, Hugh. I'm neither yer wife nor yer chattel. I won't mind my place."

He stared back at her, surprise flickering in his eyes—surprise and something else.

"Sit down, Nessa," he said gently. "I apologize for offending you."

Their gazes held, the moments stretching out.

Letting her anger cool, Nessa did as bid. Aye, showing her lover that she had claws wasn't such a bad thing. Some men liked a woman with spirit, and she saw from the look on Hugh's face that despite his earlier comment, she now commanded his complete attention.

Slowly, Hugh let go of her wrist, and she sank back down into the booth.

A tense silence settled between them now, the easy camaraderie they'd enjoyed earlier gone.

Clearing his throat, Hugh leaned back against the back of the booth, his gaze searching her face. "We're leaving in four weeks," he said finally.

11

HARDEN YER HEART

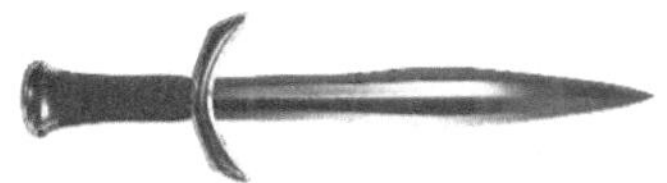

HUGH GRIPPED NESSA'S hips as he plunged into her from behind. Head hung low, her rounded bottom thrust up to meet him, she was an arresting sight. Her red-gold hair was mussed, spilling in heavy waves over the pillow. Letting go of her hips with one hand, he stroked the milky curve of one buttock before his hand splayed across the small of her back.

And then he undulated his hips as he thrust deep into her once again.

"H-u-g-h!"

God's teeth, he liked how she groaned his name. He liked how throaty her voice went when she gasped out words during coupling. He liked how she let herself go with him, how lusty she was.

He liked a great many things about Nessa: her spirit, her boldness, and her irreverence. He even liked it when she was angry with him—as she had been earlier that evening. No woman had ever stood up to him like that. But best of all, Hugh liked how it felt to be buried deep inside Nessa, for when he was, the rest of the world disappeared.

He gripped her then, fiercer than he usually did, and thrust into her hard.

Nessa gave a low groan, bucking against him. He felt her tremble, felt the walls of her womb tighten around his shaft. Heedless, he drove into her again.

Nessa shattered. Her cry echoed through the dwelling, trembling now wracking her body.

Gripping her hips, so that she wouldn't collapse, Hugh thrust once more. His eyes flickered shut, his head falling back as he let his own release barrel into him.

Afterward they lay together, sweaty limbs tangled, listening to the wind howl against the shutters. He wondered if more snow would fall during the night, and when the first signs of spring would start to show.

Hugh's breathing slowed. When they did, he would have to bid his Scottish temptress goodbye.

"What is it?" Nessa murmured, snuggling against his chest.

It pleased him that she did that after they'd lain together. She often lay her ear against his ribs as if she were listening to his heartbeat. He liked the feel of her cheek against his skin, how her soft, rosemary-scented hair tickled his nose. His wife, Anne, had never curled against him like a kitten. None of his lovers had.

"Nothing," he whispered back.

She lifted her head, her green eyes meeting his. The hearth, a few feet away, still burned bright, casting a golden light over the interior of Nessa's cottage. "Liar."

He snorted, holding her gaze. "How I shall miss your sharp Scottish tongue."

She gave a soft laugh. "I doubt that." She paused then, her eyes shadowing. "We have only a moon's turning before ye leave ... it will pass before we know it."

He reached up, his hand cupping her cheek. "Aye, nothing ever lasts, especially the good things."

It was true. Edward's campaigning in Scotland sometimes seemed interminable, yet a night in this woman's arms was over in an instant.

It wasn't fair—yet few things in life were.

Nessa stared into her lover's eyes, her mind racing.

Four weeks. March the twenty-eighth, to be exact.

She had the army's date of departure—now she needed to know where they were heading.

As the moments drew out, she considered questioning Hugh again—to ask him where the army would go. However, after their conversation at the alehouse, she decided against it. The time to go softly, to coax the knight to give up his secrets willingly, had passed. As she'd decided before meeting him for supper this eve, she'd have to use witching to get him to give up the rest.

Nessa needed answers, and she needed them tonight.

She stretched against Hugh, enjoying the feel of his strong body against hers. He'd been passionate this eve, had taken her with an urgency that had left her shaking and breathless. She'd miss the warmth of him in her bed, the feel of him buried deep inside her.

Longing spiked through her then, causing her chest to tighten. It wasn't just the coupling she'd miss though. Her cottage had felt empty and cold at night before Hugh de Burgh started spending his nights here. These days she barely noticed the chill. His company had filled a void she hadn't even known existed.

Nessa drew in a steadying breath. *Don't let yerself get distracted. Ye have a task to complete tonight.*

"My throat is dry," she murmured. "I'm going to pour myself a cup of wine. Would ye like one?"

"Very well," he replied, his mouth curving. "Thank you."

Relieved that she hadn't needed to convince him, Nessa rose to her feet, wrapped a blanket around her nakedness, and padded over to the table under the window.

The wind rattled the shutters, and damp tonight drilled into her bones. Ensuring that her body blocked her movements from view, she reached for a bottle of bramble wine and poured it into two cups.

And then she took three pinches of powder from a small pot and dropped it into Hugh's cup before stirring it with her finger. It was a truth-telling powder made from sweet pea she'd collected in the summer and a mixture of bitter herbs. She'd also blended in valerian so that he'd fall into a deep slumber after giving her what she needed to know.

Nessa picked up the cups. Tonight was the end of February's waning crescent moon—the last phase of the Storm Moon before the Chaste Moon would rise. A waning crescent signified surrender. There was no better night to loosen Hugh de Burgh's tongue.

And it had to be tonight. If she waited until the next full moon, it would be too late, for the English army would be on the move.

However, despite that Nessa's mind was already made up, her throat constricted as she carried the cups of wine back to bed. She really hadn't wanted to take this route with him, but the man was as stubborn as a mule. There was a reason why he was the English king's most trusted commander.

It didn't matter how much he lusted after her, for the passion between them seemed to burn more intense with each passing day, he would never lose his wits and blurt out his king's plans. He'd have to be coerced into doing so.

Nessa handed Hugh his cup and cradled her own as she sat cross-legged on the bed, the blanket wrapped around her shoulders.

They drank a few sips in silence before Hugh wrinkled his nose. "This wine tastes strange ... a bit bitter."

Nessa's belly flipped, although she took great care to keep her expression serene. She'd been sure he wouldn't taste the difference. "Ye are right," she murmured before taking another sip and feigning a grimace. "It's a new bottle ... perhaps it's starting to sour."

He shook his head, raising the cup to his lips once more and taking another gulp. "It doesn't taste 'off'."

"Well ... Scottish wine is rougher than what ye are used to," she replied, fighting to keep her tone unruffled.

He huffed a soft laugh. "You're probably right." He lowered his cup. "Nothing tastes quite right today. I will miss you, Nessa."

Nessa's gaze widened. The Crone spit in her eye, the working was a swift one.

Hugh wasn't a man to utter such things.

Nessa favored him with a tight smile, even as her pulse started to race. This wasn't the kind of admission she wanted out of him. "We'll just have to make the most of the time we have left," she replied, her tone gentle.

He nodded, his eyelids flickering.

Alarm coiled within Nessa. Maiden's blood, she hoped she hadn't added too much sedative to the wine. She needed him to reveal The Hammer's plans first.

"I don't know what's come ... over me," he murmured. "I'm exhausted."

His eyelids drooped once more, and Nessa gently took his cup from him and set both their wines aside. "It's late," she murmured, stretching out next to him. "Let us sleep."

Nessa nestled her head against his chest, even if her belly was now tied in knots. She knew she had to work fast. "Where is Edward taking ye, Hugh?" she asked him then, her voice low and urgent. Her heart was beating so fast she was sure he could hear it.

"Stirling," he mumbled. "For whoever holds Stirling ... holds Scotland."

Nessa's breathing hitched. *Finally.*

His news surprised her. More rumors had been circulating Dunfermline that Edward was planning to push north—to take Inverness and gain control of the Highlands. However, they were just whispers from locals, and it was just as well that Nessa had waited before taking word to her order.

The English had gained and lost Stirling a few times now. It seemed that Edward was determined to seize the castle once more.

"Lovely Nessa," Hugh murmured reaching up and brushing her face with his hand. "I don't want to leave you."

Nessa went still, forcing herself not to tense. Instead, she favored him with a smile, waiting until his eyelids fluttered shut. And even then, she didn't move, hardly daring to breathe.

Moments later, she felt his body relax, heard his breathing lengthen and deepen. He was asleep.

Nessa lay there a while. She then swallowed, in an effort to loosen the tightness in her throat. What was this—guilt?

Goose, she chided herself. *He's the enemy. Harden yer heart!*

Eventually, she propped herself up onto an elbow and stared down at her lover's sleeping face. Hugh's broad chest rose and fell gently. He would sleep like a bairn now and awake with a mild headache the following morning none the wiser.

Biting her bottom lip, Nessa slid off the bed and rose to her feet.

She wouldn't be here to greet him.

Stirling in a month it was, and Colina needed to know.

It was a week's ride north, and she would need to leave now if she was to deliver the news in time so that Colina could send word to their allies.

But with the howling wind and snow, Nessa wouldn't be able to leave until first light. She also had some packing to do—and that meant she would have to linger in her cottage a while longer. Wrapped in the blanket and shivering, she gazed upon Hugh's sleeping face.

He didn't want to leave her.

Reaching out, she trailed her fingertips down his strong jaw. "That's just lust talking, Hugh," she whispered. "In truth, we don't know each other at all."

Stepping back from the bed, Nessa cast off her blanket. Dawn was still a way off, yet she had much to prepare before then. She dressed in her heaviest woolen kirtle and her thick winter cloak, before stuffing two large leather saddle bags full of provisions.

Braving the biting wind, she made her way to Honey's stall behind her cottage. The mare greeted her with a snort.

"Aye, lass, I know it's not a night for traveling," Nessa murmured as she saddled the garron. "But as soon as there is enough light, we must go."

Although there was a crescent moon, the clouds had closed in, blocking out the silvery light that would have helped illuminate Nessa's way. It was so dark outdoors, she'd likely ride straight into a tree if she left now.

Once Honey was saddled and ready to depart, Nessa went back inside. The peat was burning low, and so she put on some more fuel.

Hugh slept deeply upon the bed, oblivious to her industry.

Nessa went to her work table then and made herself up more of the potion that would prevent her womb from quickening. She then packed away the rest of her herbs into a pouch that she carried upon the belt cinched around her waist.

It was just as well that she was a woman who traveled light. Despite that she'd lived in Dunfermline nearly six months, she'd been careful not to accumulate many possessions. When one moved around as much as she did, it wasn't wise.

Even so, as she took a seat by the fire and waited for the dawn, Nessa found herself not wanting to leave this warm and cozy cottage.

But leave it she would.

Nessa waited for as long as she dared before opening the door to her cottage and stepping outside. The wind still pummeled the walls, yet it wasn't snowing and she could see the sky was lightening to the east.

It's time.

Knowing she shouldn't, but unable to stop herself, Nessa went back inside. Standing next to the bed, she stared down at Hugh's face. He seemed younger in sleep, the hard edges of his handsome face softened. Leaning down, she stroked his brow before kissing him there.

"Goodbye, Hugh," she whispered. "May The Three bless ye and keep ye."

Her chest clenched then. Hugh was one of the enemy, but he was also her lover. She'd warmed to him over the past weeks, had grown to look forward to the lusty nights they'd spent together. She hadn't wanted to leave him without a proper farewell, but it couldn't be helped.

With a jolt, she realized she would miss him too.

Muttering an oath under her breath, and cursing her soft heart, she turned and strode from the cottage.

12

THE SAVIOR OF SCOTLAND

COLINA WALKED BAREFOOT through the mud, her necklace and bracelets of bone rattling. A wet wind caressed her cheeks, and heavy storm clouds hung overhead, turning the day dark. Thunder rumbled nearby, ominous.

Yet her gaze wasn't upon the approaching storm, or the distant mountains encircling this battleground, but on the dead that lay trampled in the dark, peaty mud.

So many of them—both Scot and English.

And as Colina picked her way across the field, her gaze scanning the corpses, she saw that there had been a clear victor.

Far more mail-clad men, their crimson surcoats stained dark with filth and blood, had fallen amongst the Scots in their quilted gambesons and iron helmets. Arrows and schiltrons—long Scottish spears—protruded from the bodies of the English soldiers and their hapless mounts.

The iron scent of blood and the stench of offal hung heavily in the air. Colina's gorge rose, and so she breathed shallowly through her mouth. She'd seen battlefields in the past, long ago, before her vision dimmed and her limbs grew stiff—but nothing on this scale.

How is it I can see so clearly?

Indeed, Colina's vision was so bad these days, it had reduced the world around her to a blur—and yet not so now. It was as if she were a lass again, and she could see every detail of her surroundings.

She halted then, her gaze going to where a banner lay trampled in the mud: three golden lions upon a blood-red field.

The Plantagenet banner.

And a few yards away, another standard flew high, snapping and billowing in the wind: a single red lion upon a sea of gold.

Gazing upon it, Colina smiled.

Wailing Widow Falls
Assynt, Scottish Highlands

A sigh of relief gusted from Nessa when she spied the falls.

Home.

Aye, it was, and yet over the past fifteen years, she had spent little time here. There was always information to be gathered, news to be spread, and rebellions to be organized.

Slowing Honey to a walk, she leaned forward and patted the garron's sweaty neck. The Highland pony wasn't the fastest of steeds, yet what she lacked in speed, she made up for in endurance. The pair of them had barely rested since leaving Dunfermline. And now, seven days out, as dusk approached, their destination finally rose before them.

They were in the heart of the Highlands now, with the grey, rock-studded sides of Glas Bheinn rearing up before them, and had just ridden up a steep-sided gorge, following a bubbling burn to its source.

High above her, Loch na Gainmhich gathered like an over-filled pail of water at the feet of the mountain before spilling over its lip into the gorge below.

Tumbling around fifty feet, the waterfalls threw out a heavy mist, and although she had grown up here, Nessa was struck as always at just how silent the falls were; she should have been able to hear their roar from a distance, and yet only a soft rumble intruded upon the twittering of roosting birds.

Drawing Honey to a halt, Nessa's gaze swept over the wall of water before her.

Inhaling deeply, for there was nothing like the sweet, fresh air up here, Nessa tried to cast off the heaviness she'd carried north from Dunfermline. Guilt had niggled at her during the journey, like a dull toothache, the sensation growing sharp whenever she thought of Hugh.

She tried *not* to think of him.

Nessa raised her chin, her gaze traveling up the gushing column of water to the top of the falls.

The Wailing Widow—a melancholy name for such a beautiful spot. Colina had told them a few stories linked to the name. However, the one that had remained with Nessa was that of the deer hunter who fell over the top of the falls while hunting during a thunderstorm. He hadn't heard the soft rumble of the falls over the noise of the storm and had toppled to his death. His wife, filled with grief, had thrown herself from the same spot the following morning.

Colina had told her daughters that, according to folklore, if one sat in the gorge upon a stormy night, the widow's cries could still be heard.

"Come on, lass." Nessa stroked Honey's neck once more. "Let's get ye indoors with a nosebag of oats." The garron snorted, tossing her head.

Nessa smiled. It had been an exhausting journey north; her limbs ached, and she was sure she stank, for there had been no time to bathe. She'd only stopped when her body cried out for rest, food, or drink. But Honey had been there with her the entire way, unflagging.

Reaching into one of the small pouches she wore upon her belt, Nessa's fingers curled around a smooth river stone. Withdrawing it, she held it out upon her palm, so that the last watery rays of sun could touch its surface.

A heartbeat later, she began a soft chant. The words were whispered, and yet the falls appeared to grow quieter still, and the chatter of birds in the surrounding trees died.

The world held its breath, and then the wall of water before Nessa parted, cleaving a path to the bank where she and her pony waited.

Nessa put the stone away, gathered the reins, and urged Honey down the bank. The garron crunched across wet pebbles, unperturbed by the strange sight. She'd entered the falls many times and knew that a warm stall and a good feed of oats awaited her inside.

And as such, she clip-clopped fearlessly into the darkness beyond.

"The High Bandruì has had a vision." Breanna's excited voice echoed through the cavern. "She knows who will be the savior of Scotland!"

Nessa, who'd just dismounted from Honey, looked to where her sister strode across the damp stone floor, dark hair flowing behind her. Breanna's proud face was flushed, her peat-brown eyes gleaming.

"Aye?" Nessa greeted her, excitement quickening in her belly. "Who?"

"Robert Bruce ... she saw his banner victorious upon a field of battle ... against the English."

Nessa's eyes snapped wide. This was the best news she'd heard in a long while. Ever since William Wallace, the Scots had been looking for someone to rally behind. Had they now found him?

"Which Bruce is it?" she asked. "The elder or the younger?"

"The younger ... the Earl of Carrick, and now seventh Lord of Annandale ... judging from the banner," Breanna replied. "His elderly father still lives, yet as eldest son, the Earl leads the clan these days."

Nessa's brow furrowed. *Robert Bruce.* She knew little of the man, apart from that he was one of the Scottish lairds who had submitted to The Hammer. Was he about to change allegiance?

Breanna reached Nessa, crushing her in a quick, fierce hug. "It's wonderful to see ye, sister."

Warmth washed over Nessa. "I've missed ye, Bree."

Stepping back, Breanna met her eye. "And I take it ye have news for us too?"

Nessa's mouth quirked. "I do ... although it will appear trifling compared to Colina's vision." She paused then. "The English will set off for Stirling on the twenty-eighth day of March ... to besiege the fortress."

Breanna's jaw tightened, her dark eyes gleaming. "Is that so?"

"Aye ... it took me longer than I'd hoped to gain the news ... but I got there in the end." Nessa glanced around her then, searching for Colina. She wished to inform the High Bandruì personally. "Where is our mother?"

"Sleeping," Breanna replied, motioning to the largest of the curtained alcoves at the back of the cavern. "The vision came to her in a dream ... and it seems to have drained her."

Nessa's frown returned. Colina had been such a dedicated, stalwart leader of the order that she sometimes forgot the woman was getting on in years. "She's not unwell, is she?"

"No." Breanna flashed her a reassuring smile, although her gaze was still sharp in the wake of Nessa's news. "Just tired ... she'll be awake soon enough." Her sister motioned to one of the four great hearths that burned behind her. A cauldron of what smelled like mutton and turnip stew simmered there. The aroma drifted through the cavern, mixing with the pungent scent of peat smoke and the musty odor of the fowl, goats, and horses that resided within. "Ye timed yer arrival well, sister ... supper will be ready soon." She then turned to the young woman who was stirring the stew pot. "Cadha ... open a fresh barrel of ale ... let's welcome Nessa home properly."

A short while later, with Honey fed, watered, and stabled in one of the large alcoves near the cavern entrance, Nessa settled onto a cushion before one of the hearths. Outdoors, the light had dimmed, while indoors, the ruddy glow of the hearths, and the cressets burning upon the walls, illuminated the cavern.

Breathing in deeply, as she let herself relax for the first time in a week, Nessa angled her chin up, taking in the cavern's vastness. It was higher than a cathedral in here. During the day, the slits in the rock above let in streams of light.

In daylight, the cavern appeared cluttered, but the night shadows hid bunches of drying herbs that hung on ropes from the ceilings, and hangings of bones, feathers, and desiccated animals and birds that crisscrossed the wide space.

The murmur of female voices rose and fell as dusk settled over the world. Clusters of blue-robed figures sat around the hearths, wooden bowls of stew perched on their knees.

A smile curved Nessa's lips. How she'd missed this place. The company of her sisters—old and young—the crackle of the hearths, and the ancient songs that were passed from generation to generation.

The sound of singing drew her attention now, a low husky voice that echoed through the cavern. One of the sisters began a song about the strength and wisdom of women—a beautiful refrain that Nessa hadn't heard in years.

Turning, she saw that the singer was Tara, a bandruì of around five years her senior. Tall and lean, Tara's angular looks contrasted with the richness of her voice. Until a few years earlier, she'd been an advisor to the

Scottish king—but now that Scotland had no king, she'd returned to the order.

Meeting Nessa's eye, Tara favored her with a nod. Warmth settled over Nessa then, a sense of belonging. They were a family, the Guardians of Alba. The singing and the company of her sisters were a salve to her tired body.

The song continued while Nessa turned back to her supper. She dug her wooden spoon into the stew and took a large mouthful of tender mutton. Hades, she was starving.

"It really is good to have ye home, Ness," Breanna murmured then, catching her eye.

"And it's good to be back," Nessa replied with a smile. "Everything seems right with the world when I'm once again inside these walls."

"And yet it's not," Breanna reminded her.

Nessa's expression sobered. Of course, Breanna was right. Nothing would be right until the English were driven from Scotland.

Tara's singing died away then, and Nessa shifted her attention toward the far end of the cavern, wondering why. A moment later, she heard the rattle of bones and spied a small figure emerge from the shadows, a crow perched upon her shoulder. Colina had mussed, greying walnut-brown hair and wore a sleeveless woolen tunic, dyed sky-blue, with a fur stole around her shoulders. Ropes of bone necklaces hung around her neck and bracelets covered her bare arms.

Nessa set aside her bowl of stew and rose to her feet. "Mother."

"Is that ye, Nessa?" The High Bandruì of the Guardians of Alba halted, squinting. A dreamy smile split her round face. Colina was now halfway through her sixth decade, and with the passing of the years, her eyesight had worsened. These days, her midnight-blue eyes had lost their sharpness. It was an irony that she was a gifted seer, for Colina's immediate surroundings had turned into a blur. Indeed, her unfocused gaze often made her appear as if she were leagues away.

"Aye." Nessa crossed the cavern to the High Bandruì, taking her hands and squeezing. "And I bring word from Dunfermline."

13

ANOTHER TASK

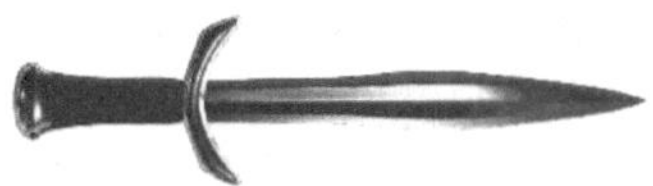

"YE HAVE DONE well, daughter," Colina's voice drifted across the hearth. "The details ye have gleaned will aid us greatly ... and tomorrow, we shall take action." The High Bandruì paused then, her soft features tightening. "But tonight, a more pressing task awaits. I must cast the bones."

Nessa frowned. She'd just finished telling Colina of what she'd learned at Dunfermline—and the High Bandruì's lack of excitement was a little deflating. However, looking at the woman's tired face, she realized that Colina was distracted.

"Shouldn't ye rest tonight, mother?" Breanna asked, her voice uncharacteristically gentle. "After yer dream, it's best that—"

Colina shook her head, raising a hand—bones rattling—to cut her daughter off. "This cannot wait. My vision of Robert Bruce's destiny was clear ... yet we must know more if we are to aid him in any way."

The High Bandruì swiveled on her heel then and started walking toward the rear of the cavern. "Come ... all of ye ... and bring candles."

Abandoning their suppers, the guardians rose to their feet and did as bid, gathering up candles and following their leader to the open space at the far end of the cavern. A few feet from the curtain that led into Colina's alcove there lay a pentagram—a five-pointed star inside a circle—drawn with chalk upon the stone floor. Each point of the star represented the elements: spirit, water, fire, earth, and air. Often the High Bandruì cast the bones upon the pentagram, for doing so gave her divinations more clarity.

Wordlessly, the druidesses set the candles down at the points of the pentagram before they all took their places in a circle around it. Colina knelt at the base of the star, Eclipse still perched upon her shoulder. She then reached into a pouch at her waist and withdrew a handful of bones—her 'telling bones'. Each yellowed lump of bone bore a symbol. There were many symbols: the moons in all their phases, the four elements, the five senses, and the four seasons, among others. Their meanings changed depending on how they fell and which bones lay nearby.

Colina's fist closed around the bones as she whispered ancient words. She then shook her hand gently, and the rattling of the bones filled the now silent cavern. Two figures flanked her, Sima and Crissa—the oldest and youngest members of the order. Sima was frail and bent, her eyes milky with cataracts, while Crissa had just passed her sixth winter. The trio stood together in honor of The Three: the Maiden, the Mother, and the Crone. When Colina undertook an important divination, she always asked for assistance from the goddesses.

Leaning forward, the High Bandruì cast the bones across the pentagram.

Nessa watched them bounce and roll—and, like her sisters, she craned her neck forward to gain a better look. All of the bandruì knew how to read the bones, yet none was as adept as Colina.

Growing up, Nessa had discovered that witching wasn't a 'gift' or a 'curse' but something that could be learned. Yet they all had their strengths, and Nessa had realized early on that hers was the healing arts.

"All women have witching in their blood," Colina had told her once. "They just have to learn how to bring it forth."

Nessa cast a glance at Breanna, who stood at her shoulder, to see her sister's face was taut with concentration, her gaze sweeping over the scattered bones. Like the High Bandruì, she was skilled in divination.

A heavy silence drew out, and then Colina sat back on her heels. A frown marred her brow, lines of tension appearing around her mouth.

"This wasn't what I'd hoped to see," she admitted softly.

Breanna shifted uneasily next to Nessa, a scowl marring her face. "Robert Bruce's path ahead will not be an easy one," she murmured. "Will it?"

Colina's attention snapped to Breanna, surprise lighting her dark-blue eyes. She clearly hadn't expected her daughter to read the bones as clearly as she had.

After a moment, the High Bandruì shook her head. "A shadow lies over him. The bones carry a warning."

Nessa stiffened, alarm flickering to life in her breast. Why was it that The Three gave with one hand and took with the other? "I thought he was to be our savior?" she whispered, voicing her worries aloud.

"He is," Colina replied firmly. "But the bones warn us to be vigilant ... he will need our help."

"Aye, we must help him fulfill his destiny," Sima spoke up then, her whispery voice echoing off the walls. "We cannot let the enemy prevail."

"But what of William Wallace?" One of the other sisters asked. "Can he not help us?"

Colina's mouth thinned. "The Wallace's time is ending. With no king at present, Scotland has never been weaker. Bruce is our only hope."

"Then we must do all we can to protect him," Breanna replied, her tone sharpening.

Silence followed these words, and then Colina rose to her feet. The movement was slower and stiffer than Nessa recalled. The bitter winter had taken its toll on their leader.

And yet, the High Bandruì's expression was determined when she squinted across at Nessa.

Tensing, Nessa stared back at her. She knew that look. "What is it, mother?" she asked warily.

A look of regret flickered across Colina's round face, but her attention didn't waver. "I know ye have only just returned to us, Nessa" —her voice was low yet with an iron edge of determination that they all knew well— "but I'm afraid I have another task for ye." The High Bandruì paused there, and Nessa's heart started to thud against her ribs. That pause and the tension that filled it told her she wasn't going to like what was coming next. "I must ask ye to mend things with yer English lover."

"Are ye not up the task, Ness?"

Glancing up from the glowing embers of the hearth, Nessa frowned across at where Breanna sat, watching her under veiled lids. It was late, and most of the bandruì, including their leader, had retired to their alcoves. Only Nessa and Breanna sat around one of the hearths as the evening deepened into night.

"Of course I am," she replied, her tone clipped. "I just hoped to have a breather for a few days ... that's all."

"None of us can rest at present," Breanna reminded her with a shake of the head. "Not while the English are busy making this land theirs."

Nessa's mouth thinned. She was well aware of that— but it didn't stop her feeling bone-weary in the aftermath of Colina's divination.

She felt sick at the thought of returning to Hugh de Burgh.

"Ye must go back," Colina had insisted. "Become our eyes and ears, Nessa ... any threat against Robert Bruce is likely to originate within the English camp. Ye must keep alert. I will send Eclipse every couple of weeks to ye ... so ye can pass word on quickly."

"Ye are one of our best, Ness," Breanna said then, intruding on Nessa's whirling thoughts. "And if ye are prepared, ye will be able to insert yerself back in the knight's favor without too much difficulty."

Nessa pulled a face. "He's a sharp one," she replied. "Even with witching, he won't be easy to fool."

A groove furrowed between Breanna's dark brows. She then gave Nessa a probing look. "Ye aren't soft on him, are ye?"

Nessa jolted as if stung. Crone's tears, why would Breanna suspect such a thing?

"Of course not," she replied, scowling. "What gave ye that idea?"

"I don't know." Breanna continued to watch her intently. "Ye are different … that's all."

Nessa huffed a deep sigh before rubbing a hand over her face. "I'm just tired, Bree." Heaviness pulled down at her at the admission. She'd hoped for a slight reprieve. Yet Colina was sending her—and others, Breanna included—back into the field the following day. There would be no rest after all.

Silence fell between the sisters, stretching out before Breanna eventually broke it. "So what's he like, this knight?"

Nessa shrugged, glancing at her sister once more. "Just a man."

Breanna arched a dark brow. "Was he a brute?"

"Not particularly."

"Handsome?"

"Aye."

Breanna flashed her a wicked grin. "That would have made yer task easier, I'd wager."

The following morning, Nessa stood by the fire, fingers wrapped around a cup of hot broth, while the High Bandruì allocated specific tasks to her daughters. Small brown fowl pecked around the hearth, in search of any spilled food from the night before, while goats bleated from their byre nearby, demanding to be milked.

A faint headache, a dull pain behind Nessa's eyes, made it difficult for her to concentrate this morning, yet she tried to ignore the lingering fatigue. She'd slept like the dead the night before, but it had been an effort to rouse herself from her alcove.

Watery dawn light now filtered in from the crevasses above, illuminating the High Bandruì's determined face. Colina's attention was resting upon two auburn-haired young women standing by the fire. Alike in form and features, the twins had just passed their seventeenth winters. "Erica and Cadha … ye are to ride south to Ardvreck Castle … ye know what must be done."

"Aye, mother," Erica murmured before casting her sister an impish smile. Cadha grinned back.

Watching them, Nessa suddenly felt old—as old as their 'grandmother', Sima, the oldest living member of their order. Once she too had bubbled with excitement when Colina charged her with a mission. Once she'd been eager to prove herself to the order. But this morning, she felt like a candle that had burned down to its stump, as if she had little left to give. The sensation was new to Nessa—and it bothered her.

"Only three weeks remain. We must move quickly," Colina continued, oblivious to Nessa's unease, while Eclipse surveyed the blue-robed women gathered around the fire with unnerving intensity. The High Bandruì's sight was failing, yet her familiar had become her eyes of late. "Someone must warn Fyfa about what is afoot." Squinting, Colina looked to Nessa. "Pay her a visit … on yer way to intercept the English."

Nessa nodded, warmth spreading across her breast. She hadn't seen Fyfa in years. It would be good to catch up with her, even in the current circumstances.

Colina's attention then flicked to Breanna. "Travel to our allies in Inverness. Alert the warriors who have been wintering there, awaiting our call."

Breanna's dark gaze gleamed. "I will see it done," she promised. Nessa viewed her sister for a long moment, silently in awe of her unwavering strength. Breanna was the toughest of them all: stubborn, spirited, and as adept with a longbow and dirk as any man.

Raising her cup to her lips, Nessa took a measured sip of broth. They *all* had to be strong. It didn't matter how tired she was, the order came first. It always had.

Nessa understood why. So much was at stake. For years they'd been keeping the lines of communication open with the Highland clans who'd agreed to support them. Few knew of the Guardians of Alba's existence—only of the mysterious blue-robed women who brought word from the south and then disappeared like morning mist. Their allies had been awaiting this moment for a long while—a chance to strike back against the English, a chance to liberate the lowlands.

"We are fortunate this time, my daughters," Colina spoke once more, her voice carrying across the cavern. "For years now, the English have always been one step ahead of us. But now, thanks to Nessa's hard work, we have the advantage. We know where and when they will attack next ... and if we move fast, we can thwart them." The High Bandruì's unfocused blue eyes turned even more distant. "Invaders have long plagued these lands," she murmured. "It started with the Romans. They marched into Caledonia in their red-crested helmets and forced our countrymen to kneel to them." Colina drew in a deep breath. "But Bedelia, our founder, helped bring down the fated Ninth Legion ... and she then cursed the last three survivors of that army to immortality."

Colina halted there, and the fine hair on the back of Nessa's forearms prickled. Of course, she'd heard this tale many times, yet Colina told it periodically, to remind them of their beginnings, of the purpose they carried from generation to generation. It seemed fitting that she would repeat it this morning.

Like all those of the order, Nessa knew of their founder, Bedelia. But unlike the others, even Colina, Nessa had actually *met* the men the Pict bandruì had cursed. Three years earlier, in Stonehaven, just outside the fortress of Dunnottar, on Scotland's northeastern coast, she'd encountered Draco Vulcan—one of the three cursed centurions—and advised him. And then, once the curse was finally broken, she'd saved his life.

All three men now lived mortal lives at Dunnottar.

But Nessa had told none of her sisters, or the High Bandruì herself, of what she'd done. At the time, she'd wondered if her actions could be seen as disloyal. Yet when she'd met Draco, and seen the desperation and unhappiness in the man's eyes, she'd decided that one thousand years was long enough for him to wander lost and alone in the world.

The Romans were long gone from Scotland's shores. She bore them no hate—not like the English. Not like the man she'd set out to seduce.

Only, did she really hate Hugh de Burgh?

Oblivious to the turn of Nessa's thoughts, Colina pressed on. "Years later, we were behind 'The Barbarian Conspiracy' … we helped unite warring tribes against the Romans. Next, the Angles pushed north to harry the Kingdom of Fortriu … but when they were forced to pull back to Northumbria, we were there." Colina halted once more, her features tightening. "When the Norsemen arrived in their great ships to burn and pillage, we did our best to thwart them … but their numbers were too many … and now Norse blood runs through our veins."

Silence fell then, while the gathered druidesses waited for their mother to finish her tale. The High Bandruì favored them with a tired smile. "Through the ages, the Guardians of Alba have always been here … watching and waiting in the shadows," she said softly. "Our own Tara" —Colina motioned to the bandruì standing to her right— "provided worthy counsel to John Balliol … although the man was too weak to heed it."

Nessa tensed at the mention of Scotland's last king. Indeed Balliol or *Toom Tabard*—Empty Coat—as he was derisively known, had been chosen to rule Scotland by a group of men hand-picked by The Hammer himself. Tara had inserted herself into the king's inner circle, and had done her best to help Balliol develop a backbone, yet the English king had undermined him at every turn, and eventually, the Scottish nobility deposed Balliol and appointed a Council of Twelve to rule instead.

"Never have the Guardians faced such a challenge," Colina concluded. "The Wallace has disappeared … our people no longer have a freedom fighter to rally behind. The Hammer will make us all kneel … make every Scot a vassal of England. We must stop him."

14

WE HAVE BEEN

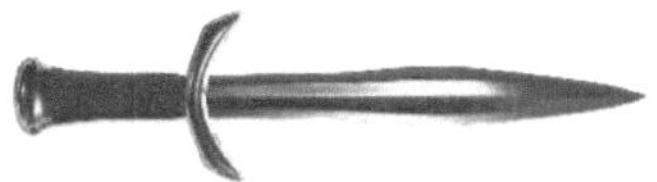

The same morning ...

LAMIA DELAMARE SAT up in bed, her heart pounding. It was dark inside the tent, although she could hear the rumble of men's voices, the clang of iron, outdoors. The camp was awaking.

Pushing her unbound curls off her face, Lamia closed her eyes in an attempt to keep the dream in her head. She couldn't forget that word—for it held the key.

"Fuimus," she whispered aloud. It was Latin—a tongue that Lamia was fluent in. "*We have been* ... what do you think it means, Fantôme?"

Something warm and dry shifted against the skin of her right arm, and then a tiny scaled head appeared from the sleeve of her night-rail. A forked tongue darted out. Witch and familiar looked at each other.

"Is it a message of some kind?" Lamia mused, "or maybe a warning?" Moments passed, and then she frowned. "Perhaps it is a clan motto?"

Ants marched over her skin as she threw back the bed covers and rose to her feet. "I had a dream, Fantôme," she announced, depositing the small white snake onto the bed and wriggling out of her night-rail. "And in it, I saw the English defeated." Naked, she reached for a clean chemise and shrugged it on. Then, seating herself on the edge of the bed once more, she rolled on her hose. "We can't let that happen."

Indeed, the vision of that dream still lingered.

A great battlefield.

Trampled gold and red Plantagenet banners.

Bodies of English soldiers strewn across the muddy ground.

And the whispered word: Fuimus.

If it were indeed a clan motto—and she wasn't sure it was—Lamia had to find out which clan it belonged to. She also needed to do so without alarming the king and queen.

Lamia's mouth firmed as she donned a silver-blue cotehardie and fastened a heavy belt around her slender hips. She then twisted her unruly flaxen hair into a tight bun at the nape of her neck. However, as always, wayward curls escaped, framing her face. One man in this camp knew more about Scottish clans than any other. She had to seek him out.

"Come, Fantôme," she murmured, reaching out her hand and allowing the tiny albino grass snake to slither up her wrist and under the bell-sleeve of her cotehardie. Fantôme—whose name meant 'Ghost' in French—went everywhere with her. Her familiar had been with her a while now, nearly eight years. Since before she and Margaret had traveled from France to England so that her mistress could wed the English king. "We shall find Sir Hugh."

Ducking out of her pavilion, Lamia straightened up and cast her gaze about her. The last of the snow had melted, turning the camp into a bog. A grey sky stretched overhead this morning, and a damp breeze caressed her face. Lamia wrinkled her nose; although she resided in the inner perimeter, this morning's breeze carried in the stench of the privies and the reek of stale sweat, along with the pungent odor of horse.

The shouting of men at sword practice drifted across the camp. The army was less than three weeks from departure now. Shortly, they would march on Stirling.

Lamia's brow furrowed. Of course, if she wanted to hunt down Sir Hugh, she would have to venture out of the sanctuary of the inner perimeter. The knight usually spent his mornings overseeing combat training.

Lifting the hem of her skirts, Lamia picked her way across the muddy ground. A sigh escaped her. How she tired of this dirty, drafty camp. Once they took Stirling, she could live in comfort again. Lamia imagined steaming baths scented with musk, her favorite perfume. She fantasized about sinking down into the hot water, a goblet of rich French wine at her elbow.

Now, *that* was living.

Passing through the gate into the camp and ignoring the curious gazes of the guards, Lamia struck off toward the training arenas. Men clad in hauberks battled with swords—the blades wrapped with cloth—while a bald knight bellowed instructions at them.

Nicholas Harrington halted his shouting when he caught sight of Lamia approaching and cast her an appraising grin.

Lamia ignored him. Sir Nicholas wasn't the one she'd ventured out to speak to this morning. Instead, her gaze shifted to where Hugh de Burgh stood a few feet back, his brow furrowed with concentration as he scrutinized his men's technique. Robert le Breton stood with him. Like Sir Nicholas, the dark-haired knight favored Lamia with an appreciative look as she neared.

"Good morning, Sir Hugh ... Sir Robert," she greeted them with a bright smile.

"Lady Lamia," Robert nodded to her. Lamia inclined her head to him before she focused wholly on his companion.

To her surprise, her pulse quickened as she met Hugh's eye. Ever since she'd joined the queen on campaign, Edward's commander had fascinated Lamia. Big, stoic, with unquestioning loyalty to his king that she appreciated, Sir Hugh was a man of many layers.

She'd learned that he'd been married once, although he'd lost his wife to childbirth. Hugh's manner could be dour, although she'd noted the change in him this winter. His handsome face seemed younger, his hazel gaze less guarded. She'd also noted that he disappeared most evenings.

The whole camp knew of the lover he'd taken in Dunfermline.

Lamia had been keenly disappointed, for she'd hoped to entice the knight to her bed one day. Hugh was exactly the sort of man—of high rank, wealth, and standing—that she sought for a husband. Jealousy had twisted her belly when she'd learned of the Scotswoman he was seeing. She'd even considered casting a hex upon his lover. However, one morning, just over a week earlier, Hugh had returned to the camp with a face like thunder. Lamia had been out taking a turn around the perimeter, arm in arm with Margaret. The women had watched the knight storm past.

"What ails Hugh this morn?" Margaret had murmured.

"I'd say things have soured with his woman," Lamia had replied, relief and a little vindictive pleasure spiking through her.

And she'd been right—for Hugh de Burgh no longer left the camp in the late afternoons.

This morning, his face wore a shuttered expression. Nonetheless, it didn't put Lamia off. Her gaze lingered on his broad shoulders before sliding down his powerful body. Of late, this man had become something of an obsession, one she couldn't shake. Lamia had taken a few paramours over the years, yet the lure of a man who wouldn't succumb to her easily was too tempting to ignore.

Especially a man of Sir Hugh's caliber.

I won't give up, Lamia promised herself. *By summer, Hugh de Burgh will spend his nights in my bed.*

"Good morning, Lady Lamia," he greeted her gruffly. "How are you faring?"

Lamia reached up, twirling one of the ringlets that framed her face. "Very well, thank you. How are preparations going for our departure?"

"Well enough."

"So, we'll be ready to leave at the end of the month?" she asked, boldly holding his gaze.

"Aye," he replied, giving her an assessing look. "I take it that you are as impatient as the men to see us take Stirling?"

"I certainly am."

She inclined her head then. "Sir Hugh ... I have a question for you."

He arched an eyebrow. Meanwhile, Sir Robert was watching them with a knowing smile upon his lips and Sir Nicholas had resumed his bellowing. "Watch yourself de Chertney ... that was a sloppy feint!"

Lamia ignored both other knights. "You are familiar with the mottos of the Scottish clans, I take it?"

"Aye," he murmured, his brows drawing together. "Why?"

"Have you ever heard of them using 'Fuimus'?" she asked.

Hugh inclined his head. "*We have been* ... aye, it's the Bruce motto."

Lamia's belly fluttered. So it was a clan motto after all. She'd heard of the Bruces—a powerful and ambitious Scottish family. Had the dream been a warning?

Margaret must learn of this.

She realized then that Hugh's gaze was searching her face, perhaps noting her reaction. "Why do you ask?"

"Oh, just a wager the queen and I were having," she replied with a shrug, twirling the lock of hair once more. "Nothing important."

Hugh's brow furrowed as he watched Lady Lamia Delamare walk away. It was a sensual walk, the sway of her hips causing most of the men nearby to stop and gawk. Her cotehardie hugged the slender lines of her body. Nearby, he heard one of the men murmur something appreciative.

Turning back to the training arena, Hugh was surprised to see that both Nicholas and Robert were watching *him* rather than the comely lady-in-waiting.

His frown deepened. "What?"

Robert smirked. "*That* was a pretense if ever I saw one."

"Aye," Nicholas added with a rueful grin. "*Sir Hugh … I have a question for you,*" he mimicked with a saucy French accent.

Hugh snorted. However, he had to admit his friends had a point. It seemed odd that Lady Lamia would venture out into the training arena, braving the mud and lustful stares of his men, to ask him something so trivial.

He hadn't missed the way she'd boldly held his eye, utterly ignoring Robert, as she played with one of the curls that had escaped her bun.

She desired him.

Hugh's mouth thinned. After Nessa, he was done with women for the time being.

The reminder of his lover made his belly clench. He tried not to think of her these days. Yet his encounter with Lamia had brought the memories back.

He'd awoken late that morning, just over a week ago, with a dry mouth and a pounding headache, to find the cottage empty. Rising from the bed, he'd hauled on his clothes and called out to Nessa, thinking she'd gone next door to see to her pony. However, when he'd ventured out to the lean-to, he'd discovered it empty. A search inside the cottage itself revealed that she'd taken provisions and clothing with her.

Nessa had disappeared.

Head still pounding, Hugh had stood by the smoldering hearth and tried to recall the events of the night before. They were strangely hazy, and his pounding temples didn't make remembering any easier. But he managed to recall that she'd poured them both wine then, and they'd talked.

Hugh tensed then as he recalled the scene, a chill stealing over his body. He'd then growled the filthiest curse he knew.

The wine … she drugged me. Christ's blood, what did I tell her?

Even now, he couldn't remember.

Nicholas turned back to watch the men as they resumed their training. Grunts and the muffled thud of bound blades punctured the damp air.

Hugh clenched his jaw, seeking once more to recall the things he and Nessa had spoken about as they'd sipped wine, yet his memories were muddled.

"All's well with you, Hugh?" Tearing his gaze from the men, Hugh glanced then at Robert. The watery morning sun glinted off the crucifix the knight wore around his neck. His friend was watching him with an assessing look that made Hugh's hackles rise.

"Of course," Hugh replied, his tone terse. "Why?"

"You haven't been into Dunfermline in days."

"Aye, and what of it?" Hugh injected a warning tone into his voice, yet Robert continued to watch him steadily.

"What happened to that woman you were seeing?"

Hugh drew in a slow breath, trying to bank his quickening temper. He'd known Robert le Breton a long while—it was the only reason he didn't bite the man's head off.

"It ended between us," he bit out between clenched teeth.

Robert inclined his head. "She got upset about you leaving?"

"You should frequent whores ... as I do," Nicholas piped up with a grin. The bastard had been eavesdropping rather than concentrating on overseeing the training. "They're less complicated."

Hugh scowled. "We're terminating this discussion now," he growled, "And wipe that grin off yer face, Nicholas ... before I do."

15

BRINGING WORD

Stirling, Scotland

One week later ...

"NESSA!"

FYFA COMYN flew down the steps of the keep and raced across the outer-bailey toward Nessa. Standing at the gates—next to the scowling guards who'd been reluctant to send word to the steward's wife that she had a visitor—Nessa smiled at the sight of her sister.

Fyfa enfolded her in a fierce hug. "I've missed ye!"

Blinking back tears, for indeed it had been too long since the pair of them had set eyes on each other, Nessa drew back. She then cast a look over Fyfa, taking in her vibrant auburn hair, winsome face, and twinkling blue eyes. "Marriage must agree with ye," she murmured. "Ye look well."

Fyfa's blue eyes shadowed suddenly, like a cloud passing over the sun on a windy day. But as quickly as her brilliance dimmed, the shadow was gone. She then gave a soft snort. "Aye, well, Hume is a bit dour at times, but he treats me well enough," she replied, hooking her arm through Nessa's. She then flashed the guards a smile, and Nessa didn't miss how one of them blushed. Fyfa hadn't lost her ability to turn men tongue-tied and witless, she observed. "Come on ... ye look exhausted. Let's get ye some food and ale, and we can talk."

Nessa sighed, falling into step with Fyfa. Indeed, she'd reached a new level of exhaustion this afternoon. Likewise, poor Honey was done in. She'd left the garron at *The Golden Lion* in town, where she was lodging at present. The stable hands had been fussing over the mare when she left her, yet Nessa had felt guilty nonetheless. The pony's head had hung low during the last part of the journey, her gait sluggish.

Nessa hated driving her so hard. She didn't want to push the pony further, not for a couple of days at least. She had time, surely. The English would be on the eve of leaving Dunfermline now, yet an army that size didn't move quickly—and it would take them a few days to reach Stirling.

However, she needed to intercept them en route, which meant that she couldn't linger too long at Stirling, even if her mind and body cried out for rest.

The keep of Stirling Castle loomed above her, its grey stone bulk blocking out the windy sky. The sight of it momentarily distracted Nessa from her exhaustion, and from the dread that weighed in the pit of her belly like a lump of granite—she really didn't want to face Hugh again.

This was her first time inside the walls of Stirling. She'd been in awe of it as she'd ridden in, for the castle perched high upon a rocky outcrop above Stirling town, with the glittering waters of the River Forth spanning beneath it. She'd ridden by the merchants hawking their wares at Riverside and up the cobbled thoroughfare leading to the upper town.

But now she stood within those massive curtain walls, inside a fortress that was Scottish once more, and her breath caught at its majesty. Fyfa led her from the outer-bailey, where the stables and barracks were housed, and through an archway into the inner-bailey. Nessa's boots crunched across fine white pebbles, and when she glanced to her right, she spied another archway—this one covered in budding roses—that led through to a knot garden.

"What a bonny place," she murmured, voicing her awe.

Fyfa cut her a look and smiled. "Aye ... I've been here a while, and I never tire of it."

Nessa met her sister's eye. Indeed, it had been at least five years since Fyfa had wed Hume Comyn. Nessa hadn't set eyes on her sister during those years. The order had kept them both busy, and Fyfa's position in Stirling was vital.

Fyfa had been instrumental, a few years earlier, in helping rid Stirling of English occupation. She and John Comyn, the then Guardian of Scotland, had sent word to their allies for help while Edward Longshanks marched north to Dunnottar to capture William Wallace.

The Hammer hadn't succeeded in finding the Wallace, and while he was gone, John Comyn had organized an attack on Stirling, to take it back from the English.

The women entered the keep, passing two heavily armed guards. Fyfa called out to them cheerfully, and they responded, although Nessa didn't miss the sideways glances *she* was receiving.

Nessa's lips thinned. She imagined she looked a fright.

Fyfa should have led me in by the back door.

However, that wasn't Fyfa's way. She strode into the keep as if she were Queen of Scotland and led the way across a wide entrance hall to the stairs, taking Nessa up to her apartments.

Nessa sank down into a high-backed chair by the fire, allowing her sister to fuss over her. Fyfa brought in fresh bread, cheese, and some salted pork, along with a large jug of ale and two cups, and pulled up a low table between them.

She let Nessa eat and drink her fill before interrogating her.

The heat of the fire had a soporific effect on Nessa. The chair was more comfortable than it looked, and the food and wine in her belly made her feel drowsy.

Mother's milk, what she would give to be able to soak up to the neck in a hot bath right now. She just wanted to wash away the grime of her long journey and sleep—yet she was aware of Fyfa's keen gaze upon her face.

Leaning forward, Fyfa met her eye. "What news?"

"Where to start?" Nessa replied with a sigh. A groove appeared between Fyfa's eyebrows, yet Nessa didn't keep her in suspense. "Colina sent me to Dunfermline over the winter, to make contact with one of The Hammer's men … and seduce him to find out where and when they would strike next."

Fyfa's arched eyebrows shot up to her hairline, and she murmured an oath under her breath. "Were ye successful?"

Nessa nodded. "I gained the trust of a knight named Hugh de Burgh, the king's right-hand." She paused then, for the mention of Hugh's name made a strange ache rise under her breastbone. "He was understandably tight-lipped, but in the end revealed that they will leave Dunfermline at the end of the month. I used witching upon him and discovered they plan to lay siege to Stirling."

Fyfa's mouth pursed at this news, although she hardly seemed surprised.

Of course, Fyfa had resided within Stirling Castle long enough to see the English come and go.

"I wondered when that carrion crow would return to Stirling," she muttered.

"Aye … the army will depart Dunfermline on the twenty-eighth day of March … ye have little time."

Fyfa nodded, a fierce expression settling upon her winsome face. "And has Colina sent word out to our allies?"

"Aye … everyone is ready." Nessa helped herself to more wine. "Ye will receive aid."

"And William Wallace?"

Nessa shook her head. "He's disappeared … I doubt he will stand against the English this time."

Fyfa's blue eyes narrowed at this news. The Wallace was a symbol of Scottish hope. Like many, she likely believed that if he didn't reappear to continue the fight against the English, The Hammer would find it all the easier to crush them.

"That's not all though," Nessa continued, holding Fyfa's gaze. "Colina had a vision come to her in a dream just over a week ago ... she saw a golden banner with a red lion flying victoriously upon a battlefield against the English." When Fyfa frowned in confusion, clearly not recognizing the crest, Nessa pressed on. "It's the banner of Robert Bruce the younger. Colina believes he will be instrumental in defeating our enemy."

Fyfa's eyes went the size of moons at this admission, yet Nessa pressed on. Unfortunately, not all her news was good. "But when Colina cast the telling bones after waking from her dream, they presented her with a warning." Nessa paused there, a chill feathering down her spine. "Robert Bruce is in danger ... and must be protected if he is to fulfill his destiny."

Fyfa scowled. "Of course ... The Hammer will want him dead." She spat the hated name like a curse.

"Aye ... he's the most obvious threat. But we mustn't rule out others. There's rivalry between clans, after all."

Fyfa grew still at these words, her gaze shadowing.

Nessa frowned at her sister's odd reaction. "What is it?"

Fyfa's lips compressed. "Hume tells me that things are strained ... between his cousin John and Robert Bruce of late."

Nessa inclined her head. "Aye ... and?"

"They both suspect the other of collusion with the English. John complained to Hume recently that he believes Robert Bruce is ambitious enough to betray his countrymen."

Nessa digested these words, her frown deepening. John Comyn, Baron of Badenoch, was known for his fiery temper. Although the fact that he was known as John 'The Red' was due to his distinctive red hair and beard rather than his character.

"Well, Colina believes Robert Bruce has Scotland's best interests at heart," Nessa replied cautiously. She could tell from Fyfa's tone that she was fond of her husband's cousin.

Her sister now wore a tense, worried expression. "Our mother has never failed us before."

"No," Nessa admitted. A sigh gusted out of her then, weariness pressing down.

Fyfa cast her a sharp look. "What's wrong?"

"Colina has another task for me," Nessa replied. "I'm to return to the English, win back the trust of Hugh de Burgh ... and report back if I discover that The Hammer has any plans to move against Bruce."

Fyfa gazed at her for a long moment. It was a probing, assessing look. Although they hadn't seen each other in years, the bond between them hadn't weakened. They both read each other's moods well. "And ye don't think ye can manage it?"

Nessa frowned, tensing. Crone's tears, Fyfa was as bad as Breanna. She didn't appreciate her sisters questioning her abilities. They never had before. But then, Fyfa had sacrificed much for the order. She'd assumed a new identity and wed a man whom she likely didn't love. All for Scotland.

"Of course I can," Nessa replied tightly. "I'll just have to be a bit heavier-handed with my witching this time, that's all."

Fyfa cocked an eyebrow. "And ye weren't last time?"

Nessa's frown deepened. "Ye know I'm hesitant about using our abilities in that way."

Fyfa's gaze veiled. "So, ye didn't use the craft to lure the king's commander into yer bed ... to loosen his tongue?"

Nessa pulled a face. "Aye, to loosen his tongue ... eventually ... but not to seduce him." She paused then, suddenly embarrassed. "I didn't need to ... things developed between us naturally."

Fyfa's gaze narrowed. "I don't know how ye could have found a man like that attractive," she replied with a shake of her head. "He's one of the *enemy*."

Heat washed over Nessa. She hadn't thought Fyfa would judge her for being so candid, yet she'd been mistaken. Clearing her throat then, she focused on her sister. "And what of ye and Hume ... did ye use witching to lure him to yer bed?"

Fyfa's jaw tensed, revealing that Nessa's question had hit a nerve. "The man was cripplingly shy," she murmured. "As such, I might have used some candle witching to give him some gentle persuasion." Her brow then knitted together, her gaze hooding once more. "Yet Hume Comyn is a Scot ... a man I wished to make my husband. I didn't want to be heavy-handed."

Nessa's brow furrowed. "But he—"

The 'whoosh' of the door opening interrupted them.

An instant later, a tall, muscular man with short dark-red hair strode into the chamber.

Nessa stiffened.

Without needing to be introduced, she knew this man was Hume Comyn, Steward of Stirling.

The man was younger and more attractive than Nessa had expected. However, he had a solemn face that gave him a grave presence. Cool, moss-green eyes swept the chamber, widening as they moved over Fyfa and rested upon Nessa.

"Who's this, Fyfa?" he asked.

Unruffled, Fyfa cast her husband a tight smile. "A cousin of mine, husband ... she's visiting from Dunfermline."

The steward frowned, although his gaze remained on Nessa. "Aye, and what brings ye to Stirling?"

Nessa's lips parted, as she readied a suitable reply. However, Fyfa beat her to it. "As ye know, the English have been wintering just outside Dunfermline ... Nessa brings word that they are about to march upon Stirling." Hume's gaze narrowed at this—for he was likely wondering how his wife's cousin had discovered such a thing—yet Fyfa pressed on. "We shall need to ready ourselves for another siege."

16

THE LIVES WE HAVE CHOSEN

NESSA SANK DOWN into the hot water with a deep sigh, her eyes fluttering shut. It had been years since she'd had such a bath.

Her earlier wish had come true.

Servants had brought up pails of hot water to her chamber and filled the iron tub by the hearth. One of the lasses had then added a little rose oil to the steaming water. The sweet scent now wrapped itself around Nessa, soothing her senses.

She hadn't expected to lodge inside the castle itself, yet Fyfa had insisted.

Hume had sent a man down to collect Honey from the inn. The garron was now stabled within the castle.

Outdoors, night had settled over Stirling. Fyfa and Hume had gone off to speak to the governor of Stirling—William Oliphant—of the impending siege, leaving Nessa to the solitude of her bed-chamber.

A solitude that Nessa welcomed.

Sinking up to her chin in the hot water, she closed her eyes. She needed to wash her hair, yet she couldn't summon the will. It had been a long day, and her conversation with Fyfa had exhausted her. The look in her sister's eyes, when Nessa had revealed that she hadn't used witching to seduce Hugh de Burgh, still lingered—still stung.

Nessa's belly clenched. She hated the English as much as Fyfa did, yet she'd been in closer contact with them than her sister had. Fyfa thought she should despise Hugh, should have found it easy to manipulate and trick him.

But she hadn't.

Nessa murmured an oath under her breath. *Bleeding-heart.* She needed to harden herself toward Hugh before meeting him again, or she'd be done for.

Whenever she thought about the task that awaited her, queasiness stole over her. Even the steaming bath couldn't soothe the trepidation that writhed within her. She didn't want to go before him again. Although she planned to do so armed with her witch-will, she dreaded locking gazes once more with her former lover.

Hugh would likely remember little of his last evening with her, yet he'd *know* he'd been tricked.

Nessa's eyes flickered open. She took in the protective stone walls of her chamber and suddenly felt loath to leave Stirling. She was safe here within this castle, surrounded by her countrymen. She didn't want to live amongst the English.

Jaw tensing, Nessa reminded herself that the folk residing within this castle were no safer than she was. War was coming to Stirling. She had to do this. She couldn't let the Guardians, or Scotland, down.

"I won't fail ye," she whispered to the silent chamber, before releasing a deep sigh and sinking deeper into the tub.

Nessa had been at Stirling Castle for just two days. She couldn't risk delaying her departure, despite that the weariness of the journey south still lingered. She'd spent most of her time in Stirling catching up on sleep and resting her exhausted body.

The evening before her departure, she took a walk with Fyfa. She would set off at first light the following dawn, riding east to hopefully intercept the English army that now advanced toward them. But before Nessa did, she wished to spend time with her sister.

The two women circled the garden, their boots crunching on the fine pebbles before they halted in front of the statue at the heart of the space. Delicately trimmed hedges, herbs, and trellises of flowers surrounded them, and a large stone kelpie reared up, head thrown back, mane blowing in the wind.

"That's quite a statue," Nessa murmured, awed as she stared up at the kelpie's wild face.

"Aye," Fyfa murmured. "Hume's grandfather sculpted it."

Something in Fyfa's tone made Nessa glance her way. Fyfa was gazing up at the statue, her usually impish face tense.

Dusk was approaching, and this would likely be their last walk together for a long while. Around them, sounds of industry drifted across the fortress: the ring of iron against stone and the shouts of men as they shored up the castle's defenses.

Hume had spread word that the English were on their way, and Stirling was readying itself for their arrival.

Nessa's breathing slowed as she realized she might not see Fyfa again for years. A certainty deep in the marrow of her bones told her that both their lives would be very different the next time they met.

"Hume seems a good man," Nessa said when the silence stretched out between them. "Although things appear a little … strained … between ye."

Fyfa's face tensed as she tore her attention from the kelpie and focused upon Nessa.

Watching her sister, Nessa waited for Fyfa to deny her observation. She'd dined with the couple twice now and had observed the brittle formality between them. Fyfa was usually so carefree. Nessa had missed her laughter over the years. But there was no laughter when Hume was in the room, not even a knowing smile.

The couple were oddly polite and distant with each other and avoided each other's gazes most of the time.

"Things have been this way for a while now," Fyfa
murmured. She favored Nessa with a half-smile then,
although the expression didn't reach her eyes. They were
unusually veiled. "Hume and I" —she broke off there as if
searching for the right words— "we were never really
suited ... I wed him to further our cause, and I think that
... deep down ... he's always known my heart isn't in our
marriage. He's even grown a bit suspicious of me of late."

Nessa tensed. "He doesn't suspect who ye really are,
does he?"

Fyfa drew in a slow breath before answering. "I hope
not ... I keep my use of the craft confined to a disused
storeroom under the kitchens and have been careful over
the years."

Nessa's gaze remained upon her sister's face. She'd
always thought Fyfa the most resilient of the three of
them in many ways. She had an irrepressible side to her,
a mischievousness that had been ideally suited to the
task the High Bandruì had charged her with.

But a little of her fire seemed dimmed this afternoon
as the pair stood together in the knot garden.

Nessa sensed there was far more to Fyfa's marriage to
Hume Comyn than she was letting on. The tension
between them, the distrust on the man's face whenever
he glanced his wife's way, had a depth to it.

"It's not easy sometimes," Nessa said after a pause.
"Pretending to be someone ye are not ... is it?"

Fyfa gazed back at her, and Nessa sensed her
struggle. She fought between her unwavering loyalty to
the Guardians and the situation she now found herself
in.

"Ye can admit it, ye know?" Nessa continued softly.
"It doesn't diminish ye to tell me that the lives we have
chosen carry sacrifice with them."

Fyfa drew in another breath and glanced away, her
shoulders tensing. "Aye," she murmured. "Sometimes ...
I look at Hume, and I feel ... sad. For him. For me."

Fyfa's voice trailed off there, and both women lapsed
into silence.

A moment later, however, Fyfa rallied. Her jaw firmed, and her shoulders drew back, as her chin lifted, and she turned to meet Nessa's gaze once more. "But enough of that … I've done what was necessary … as have ye."

Nessa favored Fyfa with a tight smile. "Aye … and let us see how much further I can take things."

"Just rely on yer witching, Nessa," Fyfa replied. "When ye approach the English camp, don't try to use clever words or lies to gain entrance … use the craft." She paused then, her blue eyes hardening. "And when ye stand before that English knight once more, ye will need to wield a strong charm if he is to ever trust ye again."

Nessa snorted. "Aye."

"Do ye have one prepared?"

"I've been weaving a charm into my cairn stone … I was hoping—"

Fyfa made an impatient noise in the back of her throat before stepping forward and linking her arm through Nessa's. She then steered her away from the kelpie statue and back toward the archway leading from the garden.

"*Hoping* isn't good enough. If ye don't want to be skewered on an English blade, ye need to be canny. We shall go down to my storeroom right now. I think ye are in desperate need of some of my candle witching."

17

MY BUSINESS IS MY OWN

"I'M GOING TO need more than candle witching, Fyfa," Nessa murmured the words aloud, even if she knew her sister couldn't hear her.

Fyfa Comyn remained within Stirling's curtain walls, safe for the moment at least. But fortunately, she'd sent Nessa on her way prepared for what was to come.

Nessa had saddled Honey in the early dawn and ridden east, as the mist lifted from the River Forth and curled across the green hills around Stirling. The first signs of spring were upon them now: crocuses, snowdrops, and daffodils poked through the soil, their friendly faces greeting Nessa as she traveled the highway. However, even the spring flowers, which usually put a smile upon her face, couldn't ease the nervous knot under Nessa's ribcage.

Fyfa had done her best to aid her. The women had sat together in the storeroom while Fyfa drew a pentagram upon the stone floor with a nub of charcoal. Drawing the pentagram was a ritual that honored the elements and opened them up to witching.

"It's a good time of year for bold moves," Fyfa had murmured. "For the Horned God rises, and we are at the beginning of the Egg Moon, a time of growth and renewal." She'd glanced then over at Nessa, who'd barely spoken a word since they'd entered the chamber together. "Are ye ready?"

Nessa had nodded, and Fyfa handed her a candle— red for passion and strength—and the nub of charcoal.

"Write the name of the man whose trust ye must regain, from top to bottom."

Nessa had done as bid, knowing that to write the thing one focused on, from top to bottom, would draw it to her. She then placed the candle at the heart of the pentagram and watched as Fyfa lit it. Candle witching on a new moon was strong.

"Close yer eyes," Fyfa had instructed then. "Think of him."

Ever since leaving Dunfermline, Nessa had deliberately forbidden Hugh de Burgh from creeping into her thoughts unless absolutely necessary. Yet she needed to cast the reticence aside. Her jaw had clenched as she recalled his hazel eyes, the rough timbre of his voice, and the strength of him.

Honey stumbled, jolting Nessa out of her thoughts. Blinking, she glanced around her. They rode up a hill, Stirling now far behind, and the morning mist had all but burned away. The sky stretched overhead like a washed-out blue sheet, and the sun was a hot pinprick in the center of it. Warmth was returning to the world.

Nessa's fingers tightened on the reins as she urged her garron on. She'd lingered a long while in that storeroom with Fyfa the evening before, had focused on Hugh de Burgh while Fyfa murmured a soft chant, invoking the craft. And eventually, when her knees ached from kneeling for so long, Nessa had opened her eyes and blown out the candle. Fyfa had then produced a knife and swiftly cut the pad of her sister's thumb so that Nessa could write out a mind-bending charm upon a piece of parchment. She now carried the scroll tucked into the bodice of her kirtle, against her heart.

The working was done, but would it be enough?

Nessa also carried the lump of smoky quartz in a pouch upon her belt, her cairn stone of protection and persuasion that she would use to gain access to the camp.

A wry smile stretched Nessa's lips then. Fyfa had done her utmost to ensure Nessa was prepared and had even risen at first light to see her off.

"Trust in yer witch-will," she'd murmured to Nessa as they hugged outside the stables. "And remember what's at stake if ye fail."

Nessa's mouth flattened, and she kicked Honey into a brisk canter. She would, on both counts. *The craft will see me through.*

Nessa sighted the English vanguard first—a long, glittering serpent that inched its way west. Pennants fluttered in the afternoon breeze, the red and yellow of the Plantagenet banners alongside the white and red Saint George's cross.

It had taken her another day to reach the English army. As she'd suspected, such a large force moved slowly. A day out from Stirling, she'd deliberately left the highway and skirted north, ensuring that she kept the road in sight while making herself as unobtrusive as possible.

Nessa's mouth thinned as she surveyed the vanguard. *Those bastards don't belong here.* The anger that warmed her belly galvanized her and settled her nerves. If Colina's vision came to pass, then those banners would one day be trampled in the mud.

English blood would be spilled.

And so will Hugh's.

The thought made her belly knot. Nessa's ire subsided, anxiety rising once more. She shook her head, in an attempt to quell her reaction. *He's the enemy, Nessa,* she reminded herself sternly. *Ye don't care what happens to him.*

Reining in Honey under a yew tree upon the brow of the hill, she watched the vanguard rumble along the highway. Her gaze narrowed as she peered at the riders out front.

Hugh would likely be up there, riding with the king's bannermen.

She could go down now to see him, but such an act would be foolish indeed.

She'd likely receive an arrow through the throat for her trouble.

The Hammer's infamous Welsh archers had a long reach, and they wouldn't question her before loosing their arrows.

Nessa drew in a deep breath, counseling patience. No, she'd better wait till the army made camp for the day. The shadows grew long now, and the sun was dipping toward the tree line to the west.

She wouldn't have to wait long.

It was almost time for her to move.

Nessa sat astride Honey, looking on from a hillock as horses pulled in armored wagons around the perimeter of the camp and supply wagons formed an inner circle. And as she watched and waited, nerves danced in her belly.

While she kept moving, it was easier to keep the dread at bay. But now that all she had to do was bide her time, she was starting to feel a bit sick once more.

Hugh wasn't going to give her a warm welcome—she would have to work fast once she faced him. There wouldn't be time for hesitation or sentiment.

Nessa had followed the army for the rest of the afternoon, careful to keep as far back as possible. Although she viewed The Hammer's army as a blight upon the landscape, she had to admit that the soldiers setting up camp was an impressive sight. Every man seemed to have a role. Not one appeared idle.

Within the hour, both perimeters were raised and a sea of billowing pavilions popped up like white and red toadstools on the valley floor where the English now camped.

She waited for as long as she dared, until the torches and hearths were lit and the valley twinkled gold as if a swarm of fireflies had settled there. And then, her body stiff with cold and tension, she urged Honey down the hillock and toward the entrance to the camp.

The soldier peered up at Nessa as she drew up her garron before him, his expression incredulous. "What do you want, woman?"

Next to him, another soldier sniggered. "You know what Scotswomen are like ... they can't get enough English *iron*."

This comment drew rough laughter from the small group of men gathered before the gates.

Halted before them upon Honey, Nessa gritted her teeth.

She'd like to give all of these fools some Scottish *steel*. Her dirk sat at her side, hidden under her blue cloak. She'd love to draw it across the sniggering soldier's throat and watch his smirk fade.

Instead, her grip tightened around the lump of smoky quartz that she now palmed. She needed to keep her focus.

"I'm here to see Hugh de Burgh," she replied in English. "Please take me to him."

This comment drew surprised looks from the soldiers. They exchanged glances before the soldier who'd greeted her frowned. "What do you want with him?"

"My business is my own," she answered with a demure smile. She felt the heat of the cairn stone pulse against her palm.

My business is my own.

The soldiers stared at her, and then one by one, they went slack-jawed.

"Take me to Sir Hugh," she murmured. "Now."

"He'll be too busy to see you," the soldier, who wasn't sniggering any longer, growled. However, there wasn't any force to his voice. He wore a dazed look as if he were struggling to focus.

The charm was working.

"He *will* see me," Nessa insisted before she shifted her attention to the first soldier who'd spoken to her.

She'd sensed less resistance in him. "Take me to his tent."

Nodding numbly, the soldier motioned to his companions to stand aside, before he gestured for Nessa to follow him. "This way."

Nessa urged Honey on and focused on keeping her breathing deep and even. The quartz now burned hot against her skin; she could feel its power crackling in the air around her.

She and Fyfa had done an admirable job with this one. Fyfa had always been particularly gifted at candle witching and charm casting, whereas Nessa had a knack for working with elemental objects such as earth and stone. Together, they'd created a potent charm.

She rode into the English camp, following the soldier as he led her down a narrow thoroughfare, through the tents and flickering torches, toward the inner perimeter. Around them, the camp bustled with industry. The rumble of men's voices, and the snorts of horses, blended with the clang of iron pots as soldiers went about heating their supper.

A few curious gazes turned Nessa's way when she rode by—but both she and her escort ignored them. The line of supply wagons appeared before her then, as did another gateway and more guards.

As she approached, Nessa closed her eyes and tightened her grip on the rapidly cooling cairn stone. She then murmured the charm once again. "My business is my own."

The stone flared hot once more against her palm, and a soft witch-wind, bringing with it the scent of pine and freshly turned earth, whispered through the camp, causing tents to billow and torches to gutter.

Nessa breathed the witch-wind in, gathering strength from it.

The guards at the inner perimeter drew back without a word, letting the soldier and the woman cloaked in blue, riding upon a sturdy dun pony, enter.

The main camp was dirty, noisy, and crowded compared to the inner circle. Large pavilions, their sides decorated with colorful banners, dotted the grassy space while a fire burned at the heart of it.

Honey snorted then, tossing her head. The garron side-stepped, her stocky body tensing. Nessa soothed her with a murmured word.

Something had unsettled the mare.

Nessa glanced around her, looking for the source of upset. Apart from the odd soldier crossing the space, there were few folk about.

And then Nessa saw her.

The woman stood by the central hearth, her slender form bathed in golden light. Finely dressed, with white-blonde hair coiled around the crown of her head, the woman's unnerving stillness caught Nessa's eye.

Honey snorted once more, and this time, Nessa stroked her neck. As she did so, her gaze never left the woman.

The garron wasn't her familiar, but the pony had been with her for many years. She was used to Nessa's witching, to the strange wind it brought with it.

But this evening, Honey sensed something different, something unnerving.

And Nessa felt it too. Cold washed over her limbs, and suddenly she found it difficult to focus on the task ahead. Her pulse started to race.

Maiden's blood—what was another witch doing in this camp?

18

LIAR

LAMIA WATCHED THE blue-robed woman ride into the inner perimeter, and as she did so, Fantôme shifted against her arm.

But she'd already sensed something 'amiss'. There had been a gentle breeze that evening, one rich with the scents of spring, and Lamia had been warming her hands over the crackling flames of the fire. And then, without warning, a strange wind had sprung up, one that smelled as if she stood deep in a pinewood.

It was a smell that Lamia recognized instantly.

They were two days from Stirling now, and soon the break in hostilities that winter had brought with it would end. Lamia would join Margaret and the king for supper shortly, yet she always liked to have some solitude first. She'd been savoring the quiet before the storm, while at the same time anticipating what would come.

Margaret longed for her husband to achieve dominion over Scotland, something he'd worked so hard for over the years—and Lamia shared her desire. Not only that—but Lamia wished to be part of history in the making. Her destiny was calling to her, she could sense it. Why else would she have received that warning about the Bruces?

But then a stranger had ridden into the midst of the inner circle, a woman of around thirty, with long red-gold hair tumbling over her shoulders, bringing with her the scent of pine and peaty earth.

Fantôme coiled around Lamia's wrist in warning.

Lamia needed no cautioning. She knew what this woman was. She was the first of her kind she'd encountered in Scotland: one of the bandruì who'd once held so much sway in these lands.

Witch-will emanated from her, a gentle, earthy power, yet something that Lamia marked nonetheless. It was as different from her own aura as winter was to summer. She knew this kind of woman as an 'earth witch'.

One that was no match for her.

The woman spied her, as did her mount. The pony tossed its head and sidestepped. However, Lamia sensed there was no connection between them. This witch wasn't powerful enough to draw a familiar to her.

Lamia didn't take her gaze from the witch. Instead, she watched as the newcomer swung down from her pony's back and handed the reins over to the soldier who'd led her in here. The man wore a stunned look. He said something to the woman and then gestured to the tent beside him.

Hugh de Burgh's pavilion.

The woman nodded to the soldier. Lamia could almost taste her nervousness, could almost hear the drumming of her heart, yet she held herself with the easy self-confidence of someone who knew her own worth.

All witches did. Their lives weren't like those of other women. They did not need to become wives or mothers. They didn't have to follow their fathers, their brothers, or their husbands.

The soldier led the garron away, to be unsaddled and fed, leaving the blue-robed woman standing alone before Sir Hugh's pavilion.

Fantôme's grip on Lamia's wrist tightened. Her familiar demanded to know what this witch was doing here.

"I don't know," Lamia whispered back, as she watched the stranger enter Sir Hugh's tent. She frowned then, jealousy coiling within her. *What does that witch want with Sir Hugh?* "But I intend to find out."

Hugh stared at the woman who'd just stepped inside his pavilion.

She stood there, her pale face and golden hair illuminated by the candles flickering inside the tent, her expression imploring.

Thomas, who'd been cleaning Hugh's chainmail, let out a gasp and leaped to his feet. The squire stood in the center of a sheet upon which he'd spread out the knight's helmet, gauntlets, greaves, and plate armor. He was always meticulous about keeping them clean and polished, but as Stirling approached, the lad had become even more diligent. "Who the devil are you?"

"My name is Nessa," she said in English, her low voice filtering through the pavilion.

"How did you get in here?" The squire took a step forward, his cheeks reddening. Nessa paid him no mind. Her attention didn't move from Hugh. "Good eve, Sir Hugh."

Thomas pulled up short, his gaze flicking between his master and the blue-cloaked woman who'd just ducked into the tent. "You know her, Sir Hugh?"

"Aye." The admission tasted bitter upon his tongue.

"I apologize for appearing like this," Nessa murmured, continuing in English. "I didn't want to alarm you."

Hugh merely watched her for a long moment, clenching his jaw. It had been a wearing day. His belly was empty, and he'd been about to sit down to his supper. Bread, cheese, and cured sausage sat upon the trestle table behind him. This unexpected visitor was the last thing he needed at present.

Hugh glanced at Thomas. The lad was watching Nessa with naked suspicion. "Leave us, Thomas," he murmured.

The squire glanced at him, his blue eyes full of questions. But, perhaps judging the look on Hugh's face correctly, he nodded, cast Nessa one more probing look, stepped over the armor he'd been polishing, and left the tent.

Alone, Hugh and Nessa watched each other. Then Hugh went to the table behind him and poured himself a goblet of wine. He'd been planning to have a tankard of ale with his supper yet now felt in need of something stronger. "Can I ask how you managed to get through both gates and find your way to my pavilion unchallenged?" he asked coldly, shifting to Gaelic.

He lifted the goblet to his lips and then froze, remembering that night nearly a moon earlier when Nessa had drugged his wine. Lowering the goblet without taking a sip, Hugh's mouth twisted.

She took a step toward him, her green eyes luminous in the candlelight. "I told the men at the gate that I wished to speak to Hugh de Burgh, and one of them agreed to lead me here," she replied.

His mouth twisted. "Aye, that straightforward, was it?"

He knew his men. None of them would agree to lead a strange Scotswoman through the camp and to their commander's tent without express permission from him.

His gaze searched Nessa's face. Who was this woman really?

He too moved forward, closing the gap between them so that he loomed over her. Nessa raised her chin, holding his gaze. "Did you get the answers you were seeking?" he demanded. "When you laced my wine?"

Her expression gave little away, yet he noticed a nerve flickering on one cheek, betraying her tension. He also saw fear shadow her eyes.

Aye, she was wise to fear him, after what she'd done.

"It was just a sedative," she answered him, her voice husky. "Valerian ... to make ye sleep."

Fury kicked to life in his gut, although when Hugh replied, his voice was steady. "And why did you give it to me?"

Her throat bobbed, and her eyes glittered. "I was afraid, Hugh," she whispered. She cast her eyes down then, as if she could no longer bear to hold his gaze. Her cheeks were now flushed. "After we lay together that eve, and ye told me ye would depart Dunfermline within the month, I panicked."

Hugh went still, his gaze narrowing. "And so you fled? It makes no sense, woman. Don't take me for a witless knave, some fool you can wrap around your little finger."

"It's the truth," Nessa replied, her voice barely above a whisper. She wouldn't meet his eye. "I knew ye would leave, and I couldn't bear it. I thought it would hurt less if I went first, during the night while ye slept." She drew in a trembling breath then before raising a hand and placing it upon her breast. "But I was wrong ... it hurt more. I've missed ye, Hugh ... more than ye can imagine."

Hugh's lip curled. He didn't believe her in the slightest, and yet her nearness was doing strange things to him. His mind felt as if fog were drifting across it, and the sudden urge to reach for this woman, to haul her into his arms and kiss her, was almost overwhelming.

"I should have kept my distance from you." He bit out the words, as he fought himself. "Right from the beginning, I knew you weren't like other women ... that your way of healing was ... *unnatural*."

She glanced up then, her eyes shadowed. "And yet ye let me heal ye. That wound on yer hand would have been the end of ye."

"So you say." He took another step toward her, so close now they were almost touching. It was an act of intimidation, yet he didn't care. Fury pulsed through him, warring with the wooliness in his head and the desire that heated his veins and spiked through his groin.

Curse the woman, his rod was now rock-hard, just at the sight of her, and the soft lilt of her voice drove him insane.

She's working some kind of spell upon me. Aye, that was it. Had she done so right from the beginning?

"What did I tell you that night?" he growled, his gaze pinning her to the spot.

She stared up at him, her eyes glistening. "Nothing," she whispered.

"Liar."

She swallowed again before licking her lips. It was an anxious gesture, and yet it made Hugh fixate on her mouth, on those soft, sinful lips that he'd once so enjoyed kissing.

"Ye told me ye loved me," she whispered.

Hugh scowled. He certainly didn't remember saying such, although his memories once he'd started to sip that wine were hazy at best.

"And that's why I couldn't stay away from ye," she continued, her voice husky now. "I realized that what we have is special ... and I *had* to return to ye."

Hugh's pulse thundered in his ears. This was nonsense. The hard, pragmatic side of his character, the side that had always protected him, jeered at this woman's words.

She was trying to manipulate him, enslave him, yet she wouldn't succeed.

But the rawness of her words, the way her throat bobbed as she spoke, the gleam in her eyes, and the scent of rosemary and sunshine that emanated from her, drew him in.

"We had *nothing*," he said roughly, fighting his need for her with every ounce of will he possessed. This woman was a witch. She had cast an enchantment over him and would bring him to his knees if he let her. "You were a fool to come to me tonight, Nessa."

With that, he reached out, his hands fastening around her wrists. "Thomas!" he called out, his voice lashing across the tent. "Fetch me some shackles and a chain."

19

GREETINGS, SISTER

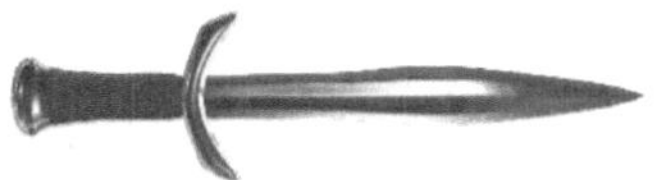

THE CHARM HADN'T worked.

Nessa couldn't believe it. The man had resisted the powerful witching she and Fyfa had woven into that scroll. He'd known what she was—and that had prevented her from bending him to her will.

Failure tasted like vinegar on her tongue.

Hunched near the fire, Nessa watched as the flames died to embers and those embers slowly dulled with the passing of the night. Knees drawn up under her chin, she leaned back against the pole that had been driven into the ground overnight—the pole she was chained to.

Around her, the camp slumbered; only the occasional cough or murmured conversation from guards punctured the stillness. The night lengthened, and she tilted her chin, fixing her gaze upon the star-sprinkled void. The moon's absence from the night sky—for it was a new moon—made the stars stand out in relief against the inky blanket beyond.

They were all looking down upon her: the Maiden, the Mother, and the Crone. All watching the mess she'd made of things.

Nessa swallowed to ease the tightness in her throat. She'd seriously underestimated Hugh de Burgh.

What will become of me now?

Would he have her imprisoned? Executed?

She'd used every bit of her witch-will in that tent—as well as a slew of honeyed words and fabrications to get him to yield to her. The Three Curse her, she'd even told the man she couldn't bear to be without him.

She hadn't been able to meet his eye when she'd said that, for such declarations shouldn't be bandied around—yet it had all been for nothing.

Hugh de Burgh had resisted the enchantment and slapped iron shackles on her wrists. He'd then led her outside before calling for two of his men to fetch a pole. A few soldiers gathered, looking on in interest as the pole was driven into the ground and Hugh fastened Nessa to it.

"Who's this, Sir Hugh?" One of the men called out.

Hugh had initially ignored the question. However, he looked around at the curious faces and scowled. "No one is to talk to her," he'd ordered. "The woman is a witch." Then, ensuring that Nessa was secured, he swiveled on his heel and stalked back to his tent without a backward glance. Only his squire had lingered, his gaze flicking from Nessa to the man he followed, confusion upon his boyish face.

And so, Nessa was left alone with the dying fire.

Murmuring an oath, Nessa opened her eyes once more, taking in the canopied outlines of the pavilions against the twinkling sky.

Lost in thought, she didn't see the cloaked figure that emerged from one of the tents at first. However, as it moved across the dew-soaked grass toward her, Nessa's skin prickled in warning.

Her gaze settled upon the woman she'd spied earlier.

Nessa's heart started to flutter like a sparrow caught in the cage of her ribs.

Mother's blood, who was she? The sight of her had so unnerved Nessa before she'd gone into Hugh's tent that it had been hard to fully focus on gathering her witch-will. Was that why she'd failed? It certainly hadn't helped matters.

Fur-lined hood pulled up, framing a heart-shaped face, the woman drew up before Nessa. She had pale blue eyes that almost appeared silver in the firelight.

"Greetings ... sister," she greeted her in soft, melodious French.

Nessa tensed.

Sister.

So, her instincts hadn't tricked her. This woman *was* a witch, yet not of the same kind as Nessa. Scottish witches left the scent of pine, crushed herbs, and freshly turned earth behind them. This one emitted the odor of hot iron, blended with a darker, muskier scent that Nessa couldn't place.

Nessa stared up at her, unspeaking.

The witch favored Nessa with an arch look. "There's no need to look so wary, sister. I mean you no harm."

Nessa's mouth thinned. She wasn't so sure about that—and when the woman raised an arm and pushed aside her cloak, revealing the wide-sleeve of her cotehardie, Nessa spied the silvery head of a small snake emerge.

A chill washed over her.

Crone's tears, this witch has a familiar.

Colina was the only druidess she'd ever known who'd drawn a familiar to her—and she was reputed to be one of the most powerful bandruì their order had been blessed with. Her recent vision and divination were proof of the skill she wielded.

Was this woman as strong?

A beat pulsed between them before Nessa murmured in French, "Who are you?"

"I am Lamia Delamare ... lady-in-waiting to the English queen ... and you?"

Although this woman had given up her name easily, Nessa was loath to do the same. Names held power. And yet, she found herself answering. "Nessa."

"And what *are* you ... some foolish hedge-witch who's fallen in love with an English knight?"

Nessa drew in a slow, deep breath, anger quickening within her. The mockery in this woman's voice was vexing. Aye, she'd failed in her task, yet she wasn't the idiot Lamia Delamare seemed to think she was. The iron shackles around her wrists prevented Nessa from summoning her witch-will. If not, she'd have shown this woman she was no hedge-witch.

Even so, it was probably best Lamia didn't consider her a threat—best let her think she'd allowed her infatuation for Hugh cloud her good sense.

"I'm a healer from Dunfermline," she replied after a pause, choosing her words carefully. "Sir Hugh and I ... formed an attachment over the winter. But I didn't want to be parted from him ... and so I followed him here."

"Ah, Sir Hugh's 'mystery lover'," Lamia murmured.

Nessa didn't answer.

"Clearly, Hugh doesn't want you back," Lamia said, breaking the silence between them. "He looked mightily vexed when he chained you up."

"Lady Lamia," a gruff voice intruded then from behind the witch. "Sir Hugh has given orders for the prisoner to be left alone." The bulky outline of a big, chain-mailed figure stepped from the shadows. "Please retire to your pavilion."

A heartbeat passed, and the small white snake wrapped around the witch's wrist slithered back into its hiding place. Lamia Delamare's pretty red mouth tightened.

"Lady Lamia?" the guard rumbled, his voice more insistent now.

The witch drew her cloak tightly about her and stepped back from Nessa. The moment she did, Nessa felt the air about her lighten. "Very well," she murmured. She then cast Nessa a veiled look. "We shall talk again soon, *sister*."

Lamia Delamare swiveled then, favored the hovering guard with a nod, and walked away toward one of the pavilions that ringed the central fire pit.

Nessa watched her go. Her brow furrowed. There was no mistaking the subtle threat in Lamia Delamare's voice—yet in revealing that she too was a witch, the woman had unwittingly made herself vulnerable.

It was something that Nessa would keep in mind, if and when the woman approached her again.

20

DANGEROUS TRUTHS

"WHO IS THAT woman? The men are saying she's a witch."

Despite that he'd been waiting for the question, Hugh immediately tensed. Dawn was breaking across the valley in which they'd camped, and the army was preparing for departure. He'd just ducked into the king's tent, hailed by Edward himself.

Edward Plantagenet stood, battle-ready, in a glittering hauberk and long, blood-red surcoat, his hands wrapped around a steaming cup of broth. His grey-blond brows knitted together as he surveyed his commander, awaiting a response.

Hugh drew in a deep breath. He'd slept fitfully overnight, and the time had allowed him to think over the folly of what he'd done. In chaining Nessa up in the middle of the camp, he'd drawn attention to her—and him.

He'd have been wiser to keep her hidden. Yet he'd been so angry the night before, he hadn't been able to think straight—and he hadn't wanted her in his pavilion. She might have tried to bewitch him again.

He'd already fielded several questions about the woman who, still chained, had been escorted over to one of the supply wagons, in which she'd travel during the day. As such, Hugh knew what he would say to his king.

"She's my lover, sire."

Edward's eyebrows shot up to his hairline, while his son, who'd just stepped into the tent behind them, barked out a laugh. "Not a witch then?"

"No ... I only called her that out of anger. We didn't part on good terms last time." Hugh didn't shift his attention from the king. "We met at Dunfermline ... but she followed me here."

"She's a comely one too," Prince Edward piped up once more, moving to his father's side. "I certainly wouldn't chain her up outside." He shot Hugh a wolfish look. "She can warm my bed, if you don't want her in yours?"

The king frowned, irritation flashing in his cool blue eyes as he glanced at the prince. He then fixed Hugh with another searching look. "My son has a point ... why have you brought a lovers' quarrel into my camp? I don't want the men distracted."

Hugh's jaw clenched. Neither did he. It galled him that the king and prince both thought he'd argued with some besotted woman who'd chased him from Dunfermline. He could see the disappointment on the king's face and the wry amusement on the prince's.

Letting everyone think that was the case was making a fool out of him.

But the truth was too dangerous.

If Edward discovered that he'd let a witch-woman drug his wine, and extract God-knew-what from him, his rage would be blistering. Such carelessness on Hugh's part could cost him his spurs. No, he couldn't risk telling Edward the truth.

He was doing this for Nessa's sake too. Damn the woman to the pits of hell, he shouldn't want to protect her. She'd lied to him, tricked him. He should throw her to the wolves—yet he couldn't.

If he told the king Nessa was a witch, chaos could break loose.

Who knew how Edward would respond? Some folk were suspicious about witch-women. Edward had been on Crusade; he knew what folk did to witches abroad. Would he have her burned, hanged, or drowned?

Hugh had no idea—but he couldn't have Nessa's blood on his hands.

"I don't know what *issues* lie between you and this woman," Edward continued, fixing Hugh with a stare that was growing icier by the moment. "But I give you two choices, Hugh: send her away this morning or keep her out of sight." He paused then, letting the weight of his words sink in. "Is that clear?"

Hugh nodded.

Next to the king, Prince Edward was grinning. Hugh's mouth thinned. The pleasure the young man was taking at his expense was starting to vex him.

"Aye, sire," Hugh finally replied, dipping his head.

"Right." The king's tone turned clipped. "Enough of this nonsense. Have your patrols spied any Scots lurking in the woods nearby, ready to ambush us en route to Stirling?"

Hugh shook his head. Although humiliation burned like a hot coal in his belly, he was relieved to focus on military matters once more. "I've had men out scouting overnight," he replied. "There's no sign of trouble."

"Good," Edward grunted. "Let's keep it that way."

A short while later, Hugh exited the king's pavilion. He strode toward where Thomas had just finished saddling Ajax, Hugh's destrier.

Casting a glance in the direction of the supply wagons that were now being hitched to horses, ready to continue their journey west, Hugh's pace slowed, and he halted.

Nessa.

He'd saved that treacherous woman's neck and chosen the latter of the king's two choices—to keep her close, yet hidden from the king's eye.

Muttering a curse under his breath, Hugh continued on his way. He needed to find out what he'd revealed to her on that fateful night in Dunfermline. Who was she really, and did she work alone?

That scheming witch will answer me, he told himself, his jaw clenching. *Or she'll never taste freedom again.*

"Who is that woman?" Margaret, queen consort of England, finished a neat stitch before holding out the embroidery she was working on so she could admire her progress. "The camp's in an uproar about her."

Lamia glanced up from her needlework. They both risked pricked, bloodied fingers, sewing in the liveried carriage that trundled westward toward Stirling. Yet the journey passed much quicker when they kept busy. And both women enjoyed spending time together, sewing or weaving.

Pale Scottish sunlight filtered into the carriage through the open window, bringing the scent of grass and rich, damp earth with it.

"Apparently, she's Hugh de Burgh's lover," Lamia replied. "She followed him from Dunfermline."

Margaret's finely arched eyebrows lifted. "Vraiement?"

Alone together, the two women always spoke French, their native language. Much to the chagrin of the other ladies-in-waiting, Margaret preferred to share her carriage with her favorite and no one else.

A smile tugged at Lamia's mouth. "Oui ... the woman is clearly infatuated."

Margaret cast her an arch look. "I thought you had your eye on Sir Hugh, Lamia ... did you not?"

Lamia's smile faded. "Perhaps," she admitted, meeting the queen's eye. She and Margaret were close, so close that they shared most things. However, she wished she hadn't confided her interest in the knight to Margaret.

The queen's brow furrowed then. "My handmaid tells me the woman is a witch ... is she?"

Lamia nodded.

The queen's brown eyes widened, and she leaned forward, her dainty hands clutching at the tunic she was embroidering for her husband. "Are you certain?"

Lamia quirked an eyebrow. Margaret knew who she was. In fact, she'd encouraged Lamia to develop her natural abilities over the years. They'd grown up together outside Paris. Lamia was an orphan, the daughter of a nobleman who'd fallen on hard times before taking his own life. She'd been raised as Margaret's companion and then had become one of her court ladies, but the bond between them had never waned.

"That's how she gained access to the inner perimeter," Lamia replied, glancing back down at her own sewing project and making two neat stitches. "She used a mind-addling charm to convince the guards to bring her to Sir Hugh's tent."

Margaret frowned. "Is she dangerous?"

Lamia shook her head. "More of a nuisance than anything."

"But ... does she know who you are?"

Lamia nodded. "I introduced myself last night." She then stroked her right arm, where her familiar now slept. "And I introduced her to Fantôme."

Margaret's worried look intensified. "Is that wise?"

Lamia shrugged. "The witch is in iron ... and I doubt Sir Hugh knows what she really is either."

"And he isn't sending her away?"

Lamia shook her head. "I saw her being bundled into one of the supply wagons just after dawn." She paused then, dwelling on this fact. She didn't like that Nessa was traveling with them. The woman didn't pose a threat to her, but Lamia didn't trust her nonetheless. She would have to keep an eye upon her over the coming days.

Leaning back against the upholstered seat of the carriage, and abandoning her needlework for the moment, Lamia fixed Margaret with a level stare. "It's best if you say nothing of what we've discovered to Edward," she advised the queen. "We shouldn't bother him with such trifling matters."

Margaret nodded, although her brow furrowed. "Of course, I won't say anything," she replied. The queen generally refrained from mentioning anything related to witchcraft to the king. Best he remained ignorant of such things—especially with Lamia residing in his court.

Lamia smiled back at Margaret. She'd answered her mistress's questions—but now she had one of her own. "Have you managed to convince the king that clan Bruce could be a threat to this campaign?"

Margaret sighed. She then put down her sewing and folded her hands over her rapidly growing belly. "I've brought the subject up with him twice now ... delicately, of course."

Lamia inclined her head. "And?"

"He wanted to know where I'd obtained such a warning."

"What did you tell him?"

"That you'd taken a lover in Dunfermline, a man who'd recently arrived from Annandale. He'd once been in the employ of Robert Bruce the younger but had been cast out after an argument. As such, he'd been only too happy to spill the news that Bruce the younger believes his family are the rightful rulers of Scotland. I told Edward that although the clan appears to have bent the knee to him, it is but a ruse."

Lamia nodded, impressed. "A fine tale ... I don't think I could have invented better myself."

The queen flashed her a grin, her pretty face turning impish. "I learned from you, of course, my dear Lamia. I've always remembered what you said to me once ... before we left France. Do you remember it? You said that men may rule the world, but women are the ones in the shadows, the puppeteers pulling the strings. A clever woman can wield her influence over her husband."

"I do remember." Lamia smiled back. "We women pay attention to details that slide by most men. And you are proof of how even a king's ear can be bent ... by the right woman." Lamia paused then. "Yet Edward wasn't swayed by your story?"

Margaret's grin disappeared. "He listened to me, yet I could tell the news didn't bother him. The second time I mentioned it, he muttered something about bitter men spreading rumors and then changed the subject." Margaret's gaze clouded. "He is friends with Robert Bruce the elder … the pair of them campaigned together in the Holy Land."

Lamia frowned. She hadn't realized Edward had such a connection to the Bruces. It would make convincing him difficult but not impossible. "He *must* take this news seriously," she murmured.

Margaret nodded, picking up her sewing once more. "Edward is England's warrior king … and he's supremely confident." Her brow furrowed as she peered down at her needlework. "Yet he is a good husband … a man who respects women." She paused then before clearing her throat. "I was worried when we wed that I would never be able to equal the affection he held for his first wife … but ever since I joined him in Scotland, he has opened himself to me. I never thought I could fall in love with a man forty years my senior … and yet I have."

Margaret glanced up then, her gaze meeting Lamia's once more.

Lamia favored her with a soft smile. All of Europe had heard of the great love between King Edward of England and his first wife, Eleanor of Castile. The queen consort had even accompanied her husband to the Holy Land on Crusade. There was a tale that she'd once sucked the poison from a knife-wound when an assassin attacked him at Acre. And when Eleanor had died at Lincoln, he'd ordered a stone cross to be erected at each stopping-place on the journey to London, ending at Charing Cross, in her memory.

Edward of England was indeed a fascinating individual. A warrior, a conqueror, a king—and yet a man who doted on his wives.

Lamia's smile faded then. "Careful, Margaret," she murmured. "It's not wise to love one's husband."

The queen huffed a laugh, even if her brown eyes shadowed a little. "Why not?"

"It clouds our judgment ... leads us to make ill-advised decisions."

Margaret shook her head, negating her friend's cynical words. And they *were* cynical. Apart from Margaret, Lamia had let no one into her heart over the years—especially none of the lovers who'd warmed her bed. How could she realize her many ambitions if she let a messy emotion like love cloud her judgment?

"My place is at Edward's side," the queen pointed out with a shrug. "If I love him, I can do my utmost to help him, can I not?" She paused then, her features tensing. "That is why I rely on you so heavily, my dearest Lamia. Edward is a warrior, yet he is getting on in years. I want Scotland to be a success for him ... and for him to return to Westminster in glory so that he can enjoy his twilight years in peace. Together, you and I can help ensure that happens."

Lamia nodded. She intended to be instrumental in that glory. History would remember Lamia Delamare. She reached over and placed a hand over Margaret's, squeezing gently. "And we will," she promised. "But to do that, you must ensure he heeds my warning."

21

LOYALTY

THERE WAS A nervous energy in the air this evening—a hum of tension and excitement. Hugh could taste it, could see it on his men's faces.

After months of waiting, battle finally loomed on the horizon.

They camped at the bottom of a wooded vale, near where a burn bubbled over smooth grey stones. The army was less than a day from Stirling now; they'd reach it by the following afternoon.

Hugh talked with the guards at the gate, and then, once he'd checked the outer perimeter was secured, he rode to the enclosure where he'd stable his destrier overnight. There he gave his stallion a decent rub down, shooing his squire away when Thomas tried to take over the task.

Anticipation of the coming siege coiled within him. This eve, his nerves were taut, and restless energy made it difficult to settle. Rubbing down his horse helped ease the tension. They hadn't encountered any hostile forces on the highway, yet with every furlong west, Hugh's senses sharpened.

After seeing to his warhorse, he joined Nicholas and Robert for supper in Nicholas Harrington's pavilion. Conversation between the friends was usually light, but with Stirling close by, all three were in sober moods. They ate, drank, and talked of the siege that was to come. With his mind on the upcoming battle, Hugh successfully avoided thinking about the prisoner who awaited him in his tent.

It was only when he bid Nicholas and Robert 'good eve', and ducked out of Nicholas's tent, that he remembered who awaited him in his own.

Hugh's brow furrowed. He was tired and distracted tonight, yet Nessa had to be confronted.

He strode across the clearing at the heart of the camp, passing the fire glowing there, and was around ten yards from his pavilion, when a slender figure moved into his path.

"Sir Hugh," Lady Lamia greeted him with a warm smile. "How goes it?"

Irritation spiked through Hugh. He wasn't in the mood this eve to bandy words with one of the queen's ladies. However, he remembered his manners and dipped his chin to Lamia. "Well enough ... and you, Lady Lamia?"

"I'm excited." She stepped closer, lifting her chin to meet his gaze squarely. "For soon Stirling will be ours."

Hugh arched an eyebrow. The lady certainly was confident. "Aye, let us hope the defenders yield it easily this time," he replied. "They don't always."

Lamia's brow furrowed. "Are you expecting trouble?"

"Aye, where the Scots are concerned ... always."

Their gazes held for a moment, and then Lamia stepped nearer still, gazing up at him under lowered eyelashes. The light from a nearby torch gilded her face.

To his consternation, the woman reached out then, placing a small, finely-boned hand upon his forearm. "You carry much responsibility, Sir Hugh," she murmured, her voice a seductive purr. "Come to my tent, and I will ease your cares."

A strange warmth emanated from Lamia, enveloping them both in the scent of heady musk.

And for an instant—despite that he'd never once entertained lustful thoughts for her—Hugh was tempted.

Blinking, he stared down at Lamia, his body stirring in response.

Favoring him with another sultry smile, Lamia held his gaze. "Your tent is drafty and cold," she crooned. "Whereas mine is warm and welcoming." She stroked his arm. "Come."

Hugh stood there for a few instants as if his feet had just grown roots. And then a chill washed over him.

What am I doing?

He blinked. "No," he said roughly. "I can't."

Lamia Delamare's pretty face tensed, her gaze shadowing. She then removed her hand from his arm and drew back. "Very well, Hugh," she murmured, favoring him with a sensual smile that didn't quite reach her eyes. "I shall see you later ... remember you are always welcome." The lady-in-waiting then walked away, in the direction of her tent.

Hugh twisted, watching Lamia disappear. He felt oddly woolly-headed. What had just happened?

Disquiet settled over him then, a sense that his world was starting to unravel. Was he losing his wits? Had years of military campaigning turned him into some lust-crazed fool?

Hugh shook his head. He clearly needed to stay away from women at present.

He then closed the gap to his pavilion. Stooping to enter, and steeling himself to face Nessa, Hugh dismissed Lamia Delamare from his thoughts. Now that she'd departed, he felt in control again.

Straightening up inside the tent, Hugh's gaze went to where Thomas was dutifully sharpening his master's longsword. It was yet another reminder that battle was on the horizon. Thomas's gaze gleamed when he glanced up and greeted Hugh. "This blade is sharp enough to cut through iron, Sir Hugh."

"Glad to hear it," Hugh grunted before he turned his attention to the woman who'd lied to him, tricked him—and who'd tried to bewitch him the evening before.

Nessa sat in a corner of the tent upon a low stool. Her stance was demure, her shackled wrists clasped together. She shifted her gaze up, her green eyes alighting on him.

For a long moment, the pair of them merely stared at each other. Then Hugh looked over at where Thomas was still sharpening the blade upon a whetstone, the rasp filling the tent's interior.

"Leave us for a spell, Thomas."

The lad glanced up, meeting his eye. A look passed between them before the squire nodded. Picking up his things, and casting a wary look in Nessa's direction, Thomas departed the pavilion, leaving the pair of them alone.

Hugh let silence settle after Thomas left. He moved to the table, where the squire had set out a clay bottle of wine and a pewter goblet. Pouring wine into it, Hugh then crossed to Nessa, passing the goblet to her.

She took it warily, eyeing the dark liquid with suspicion.

Hugh's lip curled. "If I wanted you dead, Nessa, you'd already be so. Drink up."

A nerve flickered upon her pale cheek, and her throat bobbed. Yet she wisely didn't answer him. Instead, she tentatively raised the goblet to her lips and took a sip of wine.

Shifting back from her, Hugh pulled out a chair from beside the table and lowered himself onto it.

Then, he waited.

Nessa took another sip of wine and cleared her throat. "What are you going to do with me?" she asked, her voice husky.

"That remains to be seen. It all depends on how honest you are with me."

She stared back at him. There was a vulnerable look to her expression, one that Hugh had never seen before.

When she didn't reply, he continued. "You told me nothing of value last night, woman. But now, I want the truth out of you. *Who* are you ... really?"

Nessa's fingers tightened around the goblet of wine. The wine itself was delicious, rich and spicy—better than any she'd ever tasted. It warmed her throat and belly, yet it didn't ease the nerves and fear that twisted within her.

She'd known this confrontation would come, had spent the day trying to prepare for it. She concocted various answers, some of them more plausible than others. But having Hugh seated before her, no warmth upon his handsome face, his eyes hard with suspicion, she knew there was no getting out of this.

I can't betray my order.

The Guardians of Alba was part of her; she'd grown up inside it. She knew no other life. She'd sworn, on her own blood, that she'd forever keep its secrets safe.

However, no plausible excuses came to her—no tall tales that he'd accept.

Of course, she was now seeing a different side to Hugh de Burgh. Previously, she'd known him as her lover. She'd likely seen aspects of his character that he'd revealed to very few people over the years—the tender, passionate side to him. But the ruthless, iron-willed knight who watched her under hooded lids, his hazel eyes flinty, was the Sir Hugh most folk knew.

He felt betrayed on many levels, and she didn't blame him.

"I can sit in silence for hours, Nessa," Hugh said eventually when she didn't answer. "But I swear I'll get the truth from you."

Nessa swallowed. "Ye still haven't said what will happen to me."

"As I told you before ... that depends."

Nessa raised the goblet to her lips, taking a large gulp. Hugh's squire had brought her some bread, cheese, and ale earlier, yet the wine took the edge off the fear that now shivered through her.

"Ye are a loyal man, are ye not?" she asked then, forcing herself to raise her chin and meet his eye once more.

Hugh's brow furrowed. "Aye ... and?"

"So ye know what it is to devote yer life to something?"

His frown deepened, yet he didn't reply.

Heaving in a lungful of air, Nessa continued. "I cannot tell ye of my people, for they are cloaked in secrecy." She gulped in more air, aware that Hugh had tensed. He leaned toward her, his elbows resting on his muscular thighs. She could almost taste his simmering anger. "Ye must know that there are many who fight for Scottish freedom," she said, holding his eye. "And I am one of them."

He inclined his head, although his expression didn't change. "Like William Wallace?"

Nessa nodded. It wasn't quite the same, but the comparison was a safe one; it steered them away from her order, while at the same giving her an idea.

She sat before an astute man, one who was now watching for lies. Yet the best falsehoods were blended with the truth, and she could intermingle the two.

"The woman who brought me up was part of a group of outlaws," she said, forcing her voice to remain steady. "I discovered early in life that I had skills ... not just as healer, but with the ancient ways of the bandruì ... the druidesses who once guided the folk of this land."

His lip curled. "So, you truly are a witch."

Nessa's lips compressed. "Name me what ye will, Hugh. The fact remains that my skills were of use to my people, and I have spent my entire adult life traveling Scotland, spying for them."

Silence fell then, and Hugh went still. His quietness made dread slither through Nessa's bowels, made her skin prickle in warning.

"You're a *spy*?" he eventually ground out, his voice roughening.

Nessa nodded. The Three protect her, he'd have her hanged for this. "I was sent to Dunfermline to gain the confidence of one of the king's knights, and to gain news of Edward's plans from him."

Hugh's face hardened. His hands were clenched, and a muscle ticked in his jaw. "So it was a *seduction*?"

Nessa nodded, guilt constricting her throat. "It was," she whispered.

"Everything was false then?" he ground out. "You cast an enchantment on me from the very beginning."

Nessa swallowed. "No ... I could have used the craft to make ye succumb to me from the first time we met, but I didn't." She inhaled sharply. Maiden's blood, why was she even admitting this? He wouldn't believe her anyway. "But I've always been against using my abilities to manipulate others" —he snorted at this comment, yet she pressed on— "instead I let the attraction between us build ... and hoped ye would inadvertently reveal yer king's plans to me."

"But I didn't." His voice was a growl.

"Aye ... and so when ye told me the army was to move on within the month, I panicked. I added some herbs to yer wine ... and used witching to loosen yer tongue."

He leaned forward further still, his face hard, eyes blazing. "And what did I tell you, woman?"

Nessa stared back at him, her heart hammering now. "That Edward intended to lay siege to Stirling."

A heartbeat passed, and then Hugh's mouth twisted. He leaned back, viewing her with open contempt. "And so you rode off in the night to warn your ... *people*." He said that last word with such scorn that Nessa's hackles rose.

Arrogant English cur. He didn't understand what it was to have his lands marched upon by invaders, his towns and castles sacked, and his countrymen forced to kneel.

Careful, Nessa, she counseled herself as the urge to snarl at him arched through her, cloaking her fear and shame. *Leash yer tongue.*

Straightening her spine, Nessa's gaze didn't waver. "I did."

Hugh rose to his feet and crossed to her, gripping Nessa by the shoulders and hauling her up. Wine sloshed over the rim of her goblet, soaking her cloak, yet neither of them noticed.

His fingers bit into the flesh of her upper arms. Their faces were just inches apart now, yet the fury that burned in Hugh's eyes made it clear this was no lover's embrace.

"What are they doing with that news, Nessa?"

"They have warned Stirling already," she whispered back. "Ye will not catch the castle by surprise … there will be a much stronger defense than ye expect."

"What else?" he ground out, his grip on her tightening.

Nessa didn't wince. She merely stared up at him. "Word has spread among our allies."

"And they will come to Stirling's aid." Hugh ground out the words. She could feel the slight tremor in his grip, not from fear or upset, but rage. Silence stretched between them then, and when Hugh spoke once more, his voice was flat, cold. "But you sought me out again … to what purpose?"

She heaved in a deep breath then, still holding his gaze. What did it matter now if he knew the truth? She was done for anyway. "I was supposed to regain yer trust in case ye offered up any other information that could be of use to us," she said softly, deliberately omitting to mention Robert Bruce. "I knew ye wouldn't trust me … but I decided to use an enchantment on ye this time … one ye resisted."

22

ENEMIES

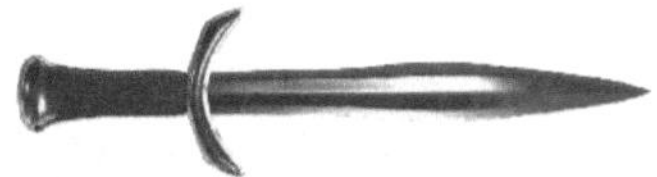

HUGH STARED DOWN at her, unspeaking, unmoving. Something dark moved in the depths of his eyes, and Nessa suppressed a shudder.

"I know it's too late," she whispered, "but I *am* sorry."

"What for?" he snarled. "For failing at your task?"

Nessa winced. Aye, she was sorry about that—but also for so much more. "I lied to ye, tricked ye, used ye ... for ye and yer kind are my enemy ... but I *did* like ye, Hugh. Some things weren't feigned."

Nessa's heart was pounding now. She wasn't sure why she was saying all this to the knight. None of it mattered anyway—but the words just flowed out of her. And it was the truth. The passion between them hadn't been a lie. And, somehow, it was important that he knew that.

Another heartbeat passed, and then he released her and stepped away. Nessa stumbled slightly, for she'd been leaning into him, before regaining her balance.

She saw then that Hugh's chest was rising and falling sharply, despite that he'd barely moved since she'd started speaking. "You are good, Nessa, I'll give you that," he said roughly. "You have a way of drawing men in ... the outlaws were wise to send you to do their bidding."

"I'm not lying to ye at this moment," she said, even as a sinking feeling dragged at her belly. "And I really am sorry."

He shook his head, taking another step back. "Enough." His voice developed a harsh edge then. "Keep your witch's tongue behind your teeth."

Nessa swallowed. "Will ye hand me over to the king?"

Hugh growled a curse under his breath. "Luckily for us both, Edward believes you to be some spurned lover," he muttered. "He'd string me up … and rightly so … if he knew that I'd been idiotic enough to let a woman trick me into giving up details of our campaign."

Nessa's breathing caught at this admission. She hadn't realized he'd held his tongue and allowed Edward to believe this was just an infatuation that had gone sour.

Hugh's mouth twisted. "Thanks to you, I now keep secrets from my king. Thanks to you, this camp could be in danger tonight." He swept his arm around. "For all I know, Scotsmen are surrounding us right now."

A chill feathered down Nessa's neck at these words. He was right. It was a possibility.

"So ye will keep me prisoner?" she asked, her voice barely above a whisper.

Hugh dragged his gaze from her, his strong jaw bunching. "Aye," he said, reaching for his cloak and strapping on the longsword his squire had left behind. "I'll not have you running back to the outlaws with news of our numbers, of how our camp is structured, or any other information you have gleaned since traveling with us." He cast her a hard, penetrating look. "I'd prefer to keep my enemy where I can see her."

Enemy.

A cold knot tightened in Nessa's throat. Aye, that was what she was. And when he'd ascertained that she couldn't do him any more harm, Hugh de Burgh would rid himself of her. Exactly how she wasn't sure—yet she didn't imagine her end would be pleasant. The best she could hope for was to rot in an English dungeon for the rest of her days.

Whatever tenderness the knight had once held for her, it was gone.

Without another word, Hugh swept out of the tent, leaving Nessa alone.

Curse that woman to the depths of Hades, what had she done?

What had *he* done?

Hugh strode through the camp, his cloak billowing behind him.

"Good eve, Sir Hugh!" There were plenty of guards at watch tonight, especially this close to Stirling. Men called out to their commander as he passed, and Hugh acknowledged them with a brusque nod, even as his gut twisted.

None of them knew what he'd done. They weren't aware that the Scots had been forewarned about where and when the English would strike next.

A sickly sensation washed over Hugh then. *We could be riding into an ambush.*

He walked on, his hands clenched by his sides. The sickle of a waxing crescent moon rode high above him, although the light of hundreds of flickering pitch torches illuminated the tightly-packed sea of tents around him. Many soldiers were still up, hands cupped around mugs of ale as they shared stories by the numerous hearths that burned low throughout the camp. Of course, they were too on-edge to sleep, what with Stirling so close. Muffled laughter reached him.

Hugh gritted his teeth. They wouldn't be laughing soon. Somewhere, out in the night, the Scots were readying themselves for the English assault.

A short while later, Hugh reached the perimeter. "All is well?" he asked the soldiers at the entrance. He was careful to keep his tone neutral—not to let on that something was amiss.

"Aye, Sir Hugh." One of the men replied, his helmeted head shining dully in the torchlight. "It's a quiet night ... not a breath of wind." He flashed the knight a grin. "We'll hear a Scotsman if he makes as much as a fart."

The soldiers behind him laughed at this, yet Hugh quieted them with a stern look. "I've received word that Scottish rebels are on the move," he told the group.

"They may attack us before we reach Stirling. Keep alert."

All smiles and looks of mirth faded at this news.

"Do they know where we're headed?" Another soldier asked.

Hugh nodded. "Expect a rousing welcome at Stirling."

He left the soldiers with grim expressions and walked to the other side of the camp, where he repeated his warning to the men there. However, even after delivering it, Hugh couldn't settle.

And he couldn't bring himself to return to his pavilion.

He couldn't bear the sight of Nessa.

Devious, lying bitch.

Her betrayal made him so angry that he'd bitten his tongue earlier. He could still taste the coppery tang of it in his mouth.

And yet, he'd felt himself weakening toward her. He knew her words were poison, but when he stared into those luminous green eyes, it was hard not to drown in them. She'd told him she hadn't cast an enchantment on him in Dunfermline—that the passion between them had been real—and he'd actually wanted to believe her. Fortunately, he'd had the wits to shove the temptation aside.

It's all lies.

If he told himself that often enough, perhaps he'd eventually believe it, deep down in the marrow of his bones where her words had touched him.

Standing in the midst of the slumbering encampment, Hugh halted, dragging a hand through his short hair.

Nessa was dangerous—he would need to be on his guard with her at all times.

Hugh resumed walking, pacing the perimeter of the camp. He was putting off his return to his tent—but he wouldn't be going to Lamia Delamare's.

However, eventually, he circled back to his pavilion. The candles burned low, and many of them had gone out, casting the interior largely into shadow. Thomas huddled under his blankets a few feet from the gently glowing brazier, while Nessa had curled up on the mat next to the stool she'd been placed on.

No blankets or furs covered her, and although she didn't look up when he entered, Hugh sensed she was awake.

He also saw that she was shivering. Winter's bite had eased, yet the nights were still cold.

Let her shiver, a nasty voice whispered inside his head. *Let her suffer.*

Clenching his jaw, Hugh strode to his bedside and stripped off his heavy clothing before crawling into his cot.

Indeed, it was silent tonight, as the men at the gates had mentioned. Too silent. He could hear Thomas's gentle snoring and the soft, tremulous murmur of Nessa's breathing in the pauses in-between.

God's teeth, he could hear her chattering teeth from here. How was he going to be able to sleep?

Just ignore it.

Hugh pulled the covers up around his ears and turned over, facing away from Nessa. Long moments passed, and still, he couldn't relax. He couldn't ignore her. Eventually, teeth still gritted, he sat up and pulled off one of the heavy blankets upon his bed. Sliding off the cot, he padded over to where the shivering woman lay.

Hugh watched her for a long moment, and then wordlessly, he leaned over and placed the blanket over her.

Nessa didn't speak, didn't look his way—and yet he heard her breathing hitch. A heartbeat later, her shivering eased.

A little of the tension knotted within Hugh's chest eased before he caught himself.

Satan's cods, you're a soft-hearted fool.

This woman didn't deserve any kindness, not after what she'd done. Silently cursing himself, Hugh turned and went back to bed.

23

EYES AND EARS

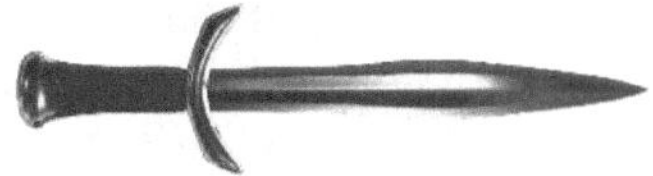

NESSA ROLLED OUT of the supply wagon, chains rattling, collapsing upon the ground in an undignified heap. Clenching her jaw, she clambered to her feet. Such a move was difficult with her wrists shackled, and she winced as her cramped and stiffened muscles cried out in protest.

It had been another long, tense day of travel.

She hadn't spoken to a soul, not since her exchange with Hugh the night before. She'd lain awake until late, shivering from cold, and had heard him return to the pavilion. When he'd lain a blanket over her a short while later, she'd stifled a gasp.

Hugh de Burgh was English. He was everything she'd been brought up to hate. And yet even when he was furious with her, he could still find it within himself to show her kindness.

He'd been up before daybreak though, and out of the tent long before she stirred. She hadn't seen him since.

Nessa was grateful for the reprieve. She had been far more honest with him than she'd intended the night before—and she'd spent most of the day going over their conversation in her head, checking to see if she'd revealed too much.

She hadn't, yet she had to be more careful in future. One careless word could land her in deep trouble. She needed to refocus on her purpose here.

Stretching her aching back, and attempting to ease the stiffness in her shackled wrists, Nessa glanced up, her gaze alighting upon the vast stone fortress perched above her, its grey bulk the same hue as the dull afternoon sky.

Stirling Castle.

As she stared up at it, worry clenched in Nessa's gut. *Fyfa.*

Her sister had been adamant that she would remain at the castle, along with her husband, the steward. Sir William Oliphant still governed Stirling at present, and the castle had held a garrison of no more than one hundred and twenty men when Nessa had departed less than a week earlier. She hoped that the reinforcements her sisters had been rallying had arrived.

Nessa swallowed hard. She hated the thought of Fyfa being trapped within those walls.

Glancing around, Nessa saw that the army had made camp on the slopes east of Stirling. The town itself sat huddled on the southern slopes, under the shadow of the fortress.

Nessa's gaze rested upon the town, where dark, oily smoke drifted up from the thatch and slate roofs. She then heard faint shouting and the clash of steel. Her pulse quickened. They'd only just arrived, and already the English had set about taking control of the town.

The castle itself would be much harder to take.

Pulling her cloak tight, for the afternoon was damp and cool, Nessa couldn't take her gaze off that smoke. She hoped her warning had ensured the folk of Stirling had fled long before the arrival of the English. However, from the sounds of battle, they'd encountered someone there.

Aware then that she was being watched, for the skin on the back of her neck prickled in warning, Nessa tore her gaze from the burning town and glanced left.

Lamia Delamare stood a few yards distant, swathed in a silver-grey cloak that matched her eyes. The lady was richly dressed, making Nessa feel drab and filthy in comparison. Her own cloak and kirtle were stained from sweat and travel, and she hadn't bathed in days.

As if making note of this, Lamia's gaze raked over her from head to foot.

Nessa tensed. There no mistaking the condescension in the woman's gaze. What did she want?

Favoring Nessa with a knowing smile—an expression that made her nerves stretch taut—Lamia turned and walked away, swallowed into the sea of men, horses, and wagons.

A chill feathered down Nessa's spine. If she had to be careful with Hugh, she had to be doubly so with Lamia. She wasn't sure how much sway the woman had with the king. Despite that Hugh had taken her prisoner, it appeared that he was also protecting her identity. She wasn't sure why he hadn't yet dragged her by the hair before his king and denounced her as a witch—but she was grateful he hadn't. She wondered what Lamia Delamare was planning to do.

Jaw clenched, Nessa turned her attention back to the majesty of Stirling Castle rising above her.

Look after yerself, Fyfa, she thought. *I wish I could help ye ... but I have a few problems of my own to deal with.*

Moments passed before her attention returned to where the English were setting up camp a safe distance from the castle, far enough that catapults and crossbows couldn't reach them. The thump and creak of pavilions being erected drifted through the camp, mingling with the rumble of men's voices and the odd horse's whinny.

Before traveling with the English, she hadn't realized an army made so much noise. It was a moveable town, a highly organized one.

And of course, like their camp outside Dunfermline, this one would be built to last for a few weeks at the very least. Already, Nessa could see signs of greater permanence. A wooden perimeter was going up, hemming her in.

Standing there, watching the soldiers hard at work, Nessa felt exposed. She was also gaining unwelcome stares—most of them inquiring, yet one or two were lewd. Over the past two days, Hugh's squire, Thomas, had come to fetch her as soon as they'd begun making camp, yet the lad hadn't yet appeared this evening.

And Nessa was starting to feel nervous. She had little to defend herself with, for Hugh had taken her dirk from her on the night he'd taken her prisoner. He'd left the various pouches she carried on her belt though, although with her hands bound and her witch-will muzzled, Nessa couldn't defend herself using the craft.

One of the soldiers called out something obscene as he sauntered past. Nessa glowered at him, her heart pounding a tattoo against her ribs. Drawing in a deep breath, she then scanned the milling crowd, watching for Thomas.

Where was that thrice-cursed squire when she wanted him?

She glanced down at the chain that connected her shackled wrists to the supply wagon she'd traveled west in. Hugh had taken no chances with her; he'd ensured the chain was bolted to one of the wagon struts.

Nessa couldn't make use of the confusion and distraction around her and attempt an escape. But escape she must—as soon as the chance presented itself.

No ... ye must remain here, Colina's voice whispered to her then, as if her mother stood at her side. *Even if ye are prisoner, ye have yer eyes and ears still.*

Nessa swallowed. Aye, the High Bandruì would send her familiar south soon, in the hope that Eclipse would bring back news. But, as yet, Nessa had nothing to give the crow.

No, she wouldn't seek to flee—she would stay put and gather anything that could aid them.

Shouts echoed across the camp then, and she glanced up to see the crowd part before her—as a knight upon a warhorse rode toward the heart of the camp.

Nessa's breathing slowed.

The knight's face was helmed, yet she knew, even without seeing his face, who he was. She'd know Hugh de Burgh's proud bearing anywhere.

His steed was huge, one of those enormous beasts called destriers. Such warhorses were rare and expensive in Scotland, and they'd been bred specifically for battle. Even so, its muscular bay form was protected by armor that gleamed, despite the dull afternoon.

As horse and rider neared, Nessa spied blood splattered across the destrier's breast plate and armor covering its face. Likewise, its rider's blood-red surcoat was filthy and tattered.

Nausea lurched through Nessa. They'd just arrived at Stirling, and already Hugh had spilled Scottish blood.

Bile stung the back of her throat, and the wrenching feeling in her chest was so strong that she raised her bound hands and rubbed at her breastbone with her knuckles.

Why can't I hate him?

Hugh de Burgh, bloodied and faceless in his armor, was a symbol of everything she'd been fighting against. After drugging his wine back in Dunfermline, she should have used her dirk on him while he slept.

But she hadn't.

Hugh drew up his destrier a few yards away and swung down from the saddle. In an instant, Thomas was at his side. The squire appeared from nowhere, deftly taking the helmet that Hugh yanked off.

"How did it go?" Thomas asked, his voice tight with excitement.

Of course, to a squire who'd never yet tasted battle, this was thrilling. Hugh's face didn't share his eagerness.

"The town is ours," Hugh replied, his voice terse. His cheekbones were flushed, his skin damp with sweat, and his short hair mussed. "However, we found no *locals* there," he continued. "Someone likely warned the folk of Stirling that we were on our way." His gaze shifted then, past Thomas's shoulder, to Nessa. She hadn't thought he'd seen her standing there, yet he had.

Of course, those words were meant for her.

"A host of Scotsmen were hiding in the homes instead," Hugh added, his gaze still spearing her. "They ambushed us as we rode in."

Nessa stopped breathing. Their allies had gathered.

Her belly lurched in an odd blend of elation and dread. She was standing in the most dangerous place imaginable for a Scotswoman. And despite that Hugh so far had shown her surprising mercy, she wasn't sure how much longer it would last.

His face was hard this afternoon, his gaze glinted.

Splattered in Scottish blood and gore, he looked dangerous indeed.

"So now we can focus on the castle," Thomas replied, his eyes shining.

Hugh tore his attention from Nessa and huffed a humorless laugh. "Aye, lad. The easiest bit, eh?"

Nessa lowered herself onto the low stool Thomas had placed in the corner of the tent. Catching a whiff of herself, she then wrinkled her nose. After days without bathing or changing clothes, she was starting to smell ripe indeed.

In a camp full of sweaty, dirty men, it didn't matter much, although Nessa longed to bathe and scrub away the grime of the past days.

Trying to distract herself from her itchy scalp and skin, she glanced around her. Quite frankly, she felt as if she had entered a foreign land. On the journey here, she'd thought the interior of Hugh's tent luxurious, but now that they'd made a more permanent camp, his pavilion looked fit for a king.

Use yer eyes and ears, Nessa, she reminded herself. *If ye aren't going to escape, ye need to start paying close attention.* Not only that, focusing on externals helped settle her nerves—and so she took in every detail of her surroundings.

At least three layers of mats and furs covered the ground, to keep out the damp, while heavy hangings covered the pavilion walls, stoppering chill drafts. A large wooden bed, piled high with fine blankets, now replaced the narrow cot Hugh had been sleeping on en route to Stirling. A long scrubbed wooden table sat next to it, instead of the small trestle he'd used previously. Banks of candles lined the space, and a brazier burned in the center of the tent, casting a warm glow over the interior.

It was more comfortable than any home Nessa had ever lived in—and yet another reminder that she and Hugh de Burgh came from vastly different worlds.

As if summoned by her thoughts, the man himself swept into the tent, chainmail clinking and armor rattling, his squire at his heels.

Hugh didn't look Nessa's way as he stood, allowing Thomas to remove his armor. He removed his blood-splattered gauntlets before stripping off the knight's red surcoat. The once lovely garment was a ruin.

Still ignored, Nessa looked on as Thomas removed the plate armor from the knight's arms and the greaves that protected his legs. Hugh then leaned forward and shucked off his heavy hauberk before stripping off the sweat-soaked gambeson beneath. Clad in hose and a loose tunic, Hugh then turned to his squire and motioned to the ruined surcoat on the ground behind them.

"Throw it away," he ordered, "and fetch me a new one for tomorrow."

"Aye, Sir Hugh," Thomas replied, scooping up the surcoat. "Anything else?"

Hugh paused, his gaze swiveling to Nessa for the first time. "Did you bring any belongings with you?" he asked in English, his voice toneless and clipped.

"Aye," Nessa replied in the same tongue. "Two saddlebags with clothing ... and some food that will be spoiled now."

Hugh nodded to his squire. "Fetch them too ... and a second bowl of hot water." His mouth pursed as he glanced back at Nessa. "I'm not the only one who needs to bathe."

24

LOYALTY'S PRICE

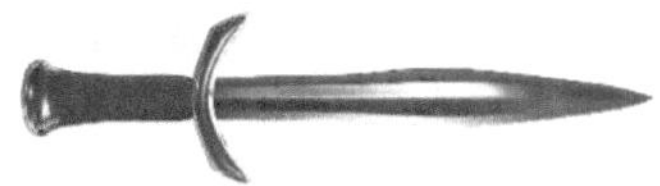

ONCE THOMAS LEFT the tent, Hugh went back to ignoring Nessa.

Pulling off the loose tunic, he strode to where a steaming bowl of water sat upon a washstand next to the bed. Picking up a cake of lye soap, he then started to wash.

Nessa couldn't help but watch him.

She knew she shouldn't, yet her gaze was riveted upon his broad back and the muscles that rippled there as he washed. However, when he stripped off his hose and braies, Nessa did avert her gaze, her heart hammering against her ribs.

He didn't care she was there and wasn't the least perturbed about standing naked before her.

Heat rose to Nessa's cheeks as she stared down at her shackled wrists. Although she longed to bathe as well, she didn't want to strip off before him and his squire. Just a few weeks earlier, she'd been eager to disrobe before her lover—yet how things changed.

Hugh was brisk in his ablutions, and so by the time Thomas re-entered the pavilion, a saddle bag over each shoulder, and a fresh bowl of hot water in his arms, Hugh had donned fresh hose and a clean tunic.

"I just saw Prince Edward, Sir Hugh," Thomas announced, setting the items down carefully. "The king wishes to speak to you before supper."

Hugh nodded. He pulled on a clean gambeson and reached for his boots. "I shall go to him now." He then cast the squire a meaningful look. "Go and get yourself fed and watered ... I'll take care of things here first."

Nessa stiffened at his tone. She wasn't sure what he meant by that.

Neither did Thomas evidently, for the squire's glance flicked between the two of them. His lips parted, as if to question the knight, before he thought better of it. With a nod, the lad collected the cooling bowl of water Hugh had just used and left the tent.

Nessa's gaze tracked Hugh as he picked up the fresh bowl of water and placed it on the stand. He then produced a key from a pouch on his belt and advanced toward her.

And although he'd never lifted a hand to her, Nessa flinched.

Hugh's step faltered. "Do you really think I'd harm you?" he asked gruffly.

"I don't know," she admitted. "Despite everything, we are little more than strangers after all."

Hugh's mouth thinned. "Aye," he murmured, drawing close. "That's the first thing you've said of late I'd agree with."

Nessa couldn't help it; she gave a soft snort. Hugh's brow furrowed in response, yet he didn't answer her. Instead, he hunkered down, took hold of her wrists, and released the iron shackles.

They fell to the mat with a dull thud.

"Don't get too used to freedom," he said, his gaze spearing hers once more. He then gestured to the saddlebags Thomas had placed at the foot of the bed. "You have a little time alone now, and I suggest you use it to wash and change." His brows drew together then. "However, if you try to escape ... or make any mischief at all ... I won't be removing those shackles again. Is that clear?"

Nessa frowned. The man's commanding tone was starting to grate on her nerves. "Aye," she replied, her tone clipped. "I'm a woman, Hugh ... not a lackwit."

His gaze widened, and Nessa could have sworn she spied a glimmer of grim amusement spark in his eyes.

Yet the spark vanished as quickly as it appeared. "That's a relief to hear," he replied, his tone dry. He then stepped back from her and gestured to the still steaming bowl of water. "And I'd hurry up if I were you … I doubt Thomas has seen many naked women … he'll be eager to change that."

Nessa frowned, deliberately biting her tongue as her captor strode from the pavilion without a backward glance.

Yet she heeded his words.

She wasn't going to waste this precious time alone.

The first thing she did was remove the scroll, still tucked away in her bodice. Crossing to the brazier, she dropped it into the flames. The charm had been useless against Hugh de Burgh. Nonetheless, it was dangerous to keep the scroll—she didn't want the knight finding it.

Then, digging around in her bags, she retrieved clean clothing before stripping off her soiled lèine and kirtle and approaching the washbowl.

The water was still deliciously hot, and the lye soap was scented with rosemary. Breathing in the cloud of steam that surrounded her, she washed carefully, ridding herself of the sweat and grime of the past days.

She even forgot to glance over her shoulder, to make sure the squire hadn't returned for a peek.

Frankly, the hot water and soap were such a pleasure, she couldn't have cared less.

A short while later, she was seated upon her stool once more, dressed in a fresh blue kirtle, and combing out her damp hair, when Thomas re-entered the tent. He carried a platter of food and drink, and Nessa's belly growled loudly at the sight. It was simple fare, for there had likely been no time for the army's cooks to prepare anything hot, yet the bread, cheese, and cured sausage all looked delicious.

Setting the platter down upon the table, Thomas's gaze flicked to the washbowl. "Have you finished with that?" he asked.

Nessa nodded. "Aye, thank you." Unlike Hugh, Thomas didn't speak a word of Gaelic, and so he and Nessa communicated in English.

The squire's gaze met hers an instant before he glanced away. A dark-blond fuzz covered his chin, revealing that he was in the midst of the passage between boy and man. As such, there was an odd vulnerability about him.

Thomas glanced up again, his eyes full of questions. "The men are saying you're a witch," he said awkwardly. "Is it true?"

A humorless smile stretched Nessa's mouth. "Aye, and if you aren't careful, I shall turn you into a toad."

The lad's blue eyes widened, the look on his face was so startled that Nessa immediately regretted her flippant reply. She didn't want to frighten him. However, an idea took root in her mind then. Hugh was immune to her witching, yet she wagered Thomas wouldn't be. Perhaps she could work a charm upon him so that she could ask him questions about the army. Any information she could glean would help the order.

"Does Sir Hugh believe you're dangerous?" the squire asked, taking a step back from her as if she were about to spring at him.

Nessa snorted a laugh, even as her hand moved toward a pouch on her belt. She wished to retrieve her cairn stone—and she needed to move fast before Hugh returned. "Aye, that'll be why he shackled my wrists."

Thomas's gaze dropped meaningfully to the said shackles, which were currently sitting at her feet.

"A temporary reprieve," she answered his unvoiced question.

"Aye, that it is," a low male voice intruded.

Thomas jumped as if prodded with a red-hot poker, while Nessa dropped her hand from her belt.

Curse the man for returning so soon.

Her gaze slid past Thomas to where Hugh straightened up after ducking into the tent.

"Stop pestering the woman, lad," Hugh continued. "Ajax could do with a proper rub down ... go and see to him."

"Aye, Sir Hugh." Blushing as scarlet as the English surcoat, Thomas hurried from the tent.

Irritation thrummed through Nessa as she held out her wrists to Hugh. "There ye go." As always, when they were alone, she shifted into Gaelic. It was the language that flowed the easiest between them.

Hugh cocked an eyebrow before making his way to the long table. He then started to set out the food and two wooden dishes. "You might as well eat first," he replied, his voice off-hand. "Take a seat."

Watching him warily, Nessa rose to her feet and walked to the table. After the events of the past days, she didn't trust this man any more than he did her. She wondered if his gentler treatment of her this evening had a purpose behind it.

Now ye are starting to think the man's as devious as ye, she chided herself, sinking down onto the bench seat opposite him.

Hugh placed the food between them before helping himself to a large chunk of bread and cheese. He then poured them both goblets of wine. His expression was carefully shuttered, and he seemed to be taking great care not to look at her.

Even so, Nessa's mouth filled with saliva at the sight of the food. Eagerly, she took a large bite of bread, forcing herself not to stuff it into her mouth. Even so, she grabbed a sausage as if she expected it to sprout legs and run off.

Hugh glanced up. "Have we been starving you?"

Nessa nodded, swallowing a mouthful before replying. "I've been given little more than a crust of bread and a cup of hot broth all day."

She expected a growled rebuke, yet Hugh frowned. "An oversight, Nessa. I'll see that doesn't happen again."

Surprised by his reaction, Nessa picked up the goblet of wine and took a gulp. "And now we're in Stirling ... have ye decided what to do with me?"

He gave her a probing look. "Well … I might keep you my prisoner … or I could hand you over to the king?"

"Or ye could let me go?" Nessa inserted a hopeful edge to her voice. Of course, she wished to remain in the camp as a spy, yet she couldn't risk Hugh suspecting that was her plan.

He inclined his head, yet didn't answer.

Nessa swallowed the wine. "I heard ye earlier," she said, feigning a casual attitude. "Stirling town is taken."

"Aye, but that was always the easiest part." He paused then, his mouth twisting as he picked up his goblet. "And, of course, your *friends* were here to greet us."

Nessa's mouth thinned. She wasn't going to apologize for that.

"How many more of them will crawl out of the shadows?" Hugh asked, meeting her eye squarely.

Nessa put down the piece of bread and sausage she'd been about to bite into. "I don't know. I was sent to spy on ye, not to rally warriors." She paused there, deciding that, thanks to her, this man knew too much already. "I have no idea how much resistance ye will find here."

Hugh regarded her over the rim of his goblet. He didn't need to say a word; she knew he didn't believe her.

"It's a hard life you've chosen, Nessa," he said after a long pause. "Such loyalty always comes at a price."

Nessa stared back at him—unbalanced by the sudden change of topic. A moment later, her jaw clenched. "That's rich … coming from ye," she muttered. With that, she stuffed the bread and sausage she held into her mouth, to prevent herself from saying anything else.

Hugh cocked an eyebrow. "Excuse me?"

Nessa swallowed her mouthful. "Ye and I aren't so different."

He snorted. "We aren't alike at all."

"Really? Whenever ye talked to me of yer home at Grosmont Castle, yer eyes misted over with longing," she countered with a frown. "Yer marriage was empty … ye have a son ye have hardly seen … and ye sacrificed yer life for yer king."

Hugh lowered his goblet to the table with the thud, his jaw tightening. He wouldn't appreciate her reminder that he'd confided in her. "Following Edward has been a privilege, not a sacrifice," he said coldly.

Nessa frowned. She knew she was vexing the man, yet she couldn't help herself. His arrogance was galling. "Aye … and I feel the same way about my own cause." She paused then, her gaze fusing with his. "See, Hugh … we are more similar than ye'd care to admit."

25

HEALER'S HANDS

THE RAIN PELTED down, its patter so loud on Hugh's helmet that he could barely hear himself think. Squinting up at the dark clouds that had settled over Stirling, and the veil of rain that obscured the top of the fortress walls, he frowned.

Not the weather to begin a siege.

Ajax snorted, pawing the ground. Reaching forward, Hugh soothed the stallion with a gauntleted hand. The destrier was eager for a fight; they all were.

Yet before hostilities could begin, they needed to hear from the castle's governor, Sir William Oliphant.

Casting his glance left, Hugh's gaze alighted on where the king sat upon his own great warhorse. Prince Edward was mounted next to him; the younger man's shoulders were hunched under the driving rain, although his disgruntled expression was largely hidden by his helm.

Both men were warriors, and although the king was getting on in years, he remained in the thick of things. A line of them waited at the foot of the castle, behind wooden fortifications that the king's men had built. Catapults were being erected behind them.

The party continued to wait in silence, tension etched into their faces. And still, the rain pattered down.

Edward's wintry blue gaze never wavered from the road leading into town—from the direction a messenger would come.

A missive had been delivered to Oliphant the night before, demanding his surrender. They now awaited his response.

Hugh's gaze narrowed then, as he spied a figure on horseback appearing from the murk.

"Someone's coming," he announced.

As if sensing his anticipation, Ajax shifted under him, tossing his head.

The lone rider slowed his horse as he approached the English front line. He was a tall, broad-shouldered man, wearing a rain-slicked cloak and chainmail vest. The man's short dark-auburn hair was plastered to his skull, his expression stern.

The newcomer's gaze swept the line of armored men and horses, alighting upon the crowned figure in the midst.

"What news from Oliphant?" the king called out in French, impatience edging his voice. Although Edward conversed in both English and French with his kin and family, the latter tongue was used when dealing with the Scots. Few of them spoke English.

The lone rider urged his mount forward, drawing it up before Edward. "I am Hume Comyn, Steward of Stirling," he introduced himself in heavily accented French, "and I indeed bring word from the governor." Hugh watched the steward, silently impressed by the steadiness of his voice. After all, he was a Scot alone before a large English force. That mail shirt he wore wouldn't help him if things got nasty.

"Out with it then," Edward rumbled.

"The governor will not surrender Stirling at this time," Hume Comyn replied, his gaze never wavering. "He informs you that he will need to ask permission from his superior, John de Soules, before making such a decision. Sir William asks that you wait until we hear from him."

Silence fell after these words.

"John de Soules is in France at present, is he not?" Edward asked finally, his tone cool.

"Aye," the Steward of Stirling replied. "We will send a missive to him without delay."

Edward stilled, watching the steward under hooded lids.

Recognizing it as a sign his liege's temper was quickening, Hugh tensed, waiting for the storm to break. However, Edward managed to rein it in this morning. "So, he has made his choice?"

"Aye," Hume Comyn replied. "There will be no surrender today."

Edward's lip curled. "Very well ... let him consider whether he thinks it better to defend the castle than to surrender it to us." He then flashed the steward a hard smile. "Oliphant will come to regret this."

The 'whoosh' of catapults loosing drew Nessa from the tent. It was audible, even over the drumming of the rain on the pavilion roof.

She wasn't supposed to show her face in the camp; in fact, Hugh had left her with express orders not to, yet as soon as the noise started, she'd been unable to remain inside. He'd also left her wrists shackled, a wise choice since Thomas wouldn't remain with Nessa that morning. Instead, the squire had been tasked with hauling ammunition to load the great catapults the English were erecting.

Frustration thrummed through Nessa. How could she gather details about the English siege plans while being chained up in this tent? Yet the dull rattle of the shackles as she moved to the entrance of the pavilion was a reminder that she wasn't going anywhere.

Peering outdoors, through the murk, Nessa viewed projectiles flying toward the great walls of Stirling: huge chunks of stone that had been brought from a nearby quarry flew through the air before smashing against the walls.

But Stirling Castle was strong. It had endured other attacks before now, and Nessa was impressed to see that even the largest of the stone missiles barely dented the walls.

Drawing in a deep breath, she wished she could work a protection charm for Fyfa—but these cursed iron shackles prevented her. She hadn't wanted her sister to stay in the fortress.

But stubborn to the last, Fyfa had remained.

Nessa's attention shifted down, from the castle itself to the edges of the English camp. The army had been camped here less than a day, and already it appeared part of the landscape.

Stirling wasn't without its own defenses. Fyfa had shown her the number of trebuchets assembled on the walls. Thanks to her warning, they would have had time to gather ammunition.

Nessa's brow furrowed then. But how long could they wait the English out?

As she looked on, lead balls flew from the top of the walls, scattering the enemy lines on the hillside below. To protect themselves from the missiles, the English had erected mantlets, large wooden frames. However, she watched as one of them shattered, and shouts and cries of the soldiers taking cover behind it drifted across the hillside.

Remaining there, as rain splattered against her face and wet her kirtle, Nessa vowed she'd find a way to convince Hugh to let her out of this tent. She needed to get a look at this camp and possibly find a weakness her allies could exploit.

Eclipse was due to visit any day now too—and the crow wouldn't find her if she remained indoors.

Hugh said little that eve when the siege finally ceased with the setting of the sun and he returned to his pavilion. He wore a distracted expression. Watching him, Nessa reflected on the shadow that battle cast over men. She'd seen plenty of warriors in the aftermath of a skirmish over the years. They often seemed weary and dislocated from their environment, as if their minds were still fighting on the battlefield.

But, of course, this man carried much upon his shoulders. He was the king's commander—and if the siege went ill, the responsibility would be his.

Nessa wondered how the day had gone. Judging from Hugh's shuttered gaze, she imagined the defenders were putting up a good fight.

Pride warmed her belly at the thought.

After supper, Hugh sent Thomas off to clean his armor—quite a task as dark mud now encrusted his greaves and plate armor, and hauberk.

Hugh bathed, and then, clad in his gambeson and hose, he padded over to the table and poured himself a goblet of wine, wincing as he did so.

Watching him from the corner of the tent, Nessa frowned. "What is it?"

Hugh glanced up and scowled as if he'd forgotten she was even there. "Nothing," he replied brusquely. "I just pulled a muscle in my shoulder today." He reached up, attempting to massage the offending muscle.

Without being asked, Nessa rose to her feet and crossed to him.

He'd removed her shackles, so she could eat and drink, and hadn't yet put them back on.

Hugh watched her approach, his gaze wary.

"Och ... don't look at me like that," she admonished, forcing herself not to roll her eyes. "I'm not going to cast a hex upon ye ... I just want to help."

"I don't need your help."

"Aye, ye do."

Hugh's brows crashed together, and Nessa thought he'd argue with her. However, after a pause, he lowered the hand he'd been using in an attempt to loosen the knotted muscle, allowing Nessa to step up behind him.

The moment she laid her hands upon him, Nessa wondered at the wisdom of her actions. She'd made the offer in an attempt to rebuild trust between them—she was never going to get out of this cursed tent otherwise—yet she now regretted taking this route to achieve her goal.

The heat of his skin, evident even through the quilted gambeson, made her breathing quicken. She inhaled the warm, spicy scent of him, mixed with the perfume of rosemary from the soap he'd used to bathe.

A giddy, light-headed sensation filtered through her, as memories of those heated nights they'd spent in her drafty cottage in Dunfermline returned to her.

Stop it, she inwardly chided herself. *Focus.*

Pushing aside her misgivings, she probed his right shoulder to find out where the problem lay. This shoulder needed to function well, for it wielded his sword arm.

It didn't take her long to find the knot of muscle, and when she started to knead it, Hugh muttered an oath between clenched teeth.

"It's not that bad," she murmured, with a wry smile he couldn't see. "Just relax into it."

She then started to massage that knotted muscle harder.

Hugh cursed again, yet he did as bid, and she felt the tension in his shoulders loosen under her hands.

Moments passed as she worked, and then Hugh's chin dipped, a sigh escaping him.

Heat fluttered to life in the pit of Nessa's belly as she recalled how she'd made him sigh like that before—although for an altogether different reason.

She looked down at his broad shoulders, her gaze alighting on the nape of his neck. Hugh wore his hair cut short and so the back of his neck was exposed.

The urge to lean down and kiss him there welled within her, the impulse so strong that Nessa bit down on her bottom lip to quell it.

Some acts were pure folly, and succumbing to such an urge would only destroy the trust he'd extended to her by allowing her to help him this evening. And she needed Hugh to lower his guard if she was ever going to learn anything useful.

"You have strong hands," Hugh murmured after a spell.

Nessa huffed a soft laugh. "Healer's hands," she replied.

The muscle beneath her fingers was slowly unknotting, and so she softened her massage so as not to bruise it.

"Do ye have any clove oil?" she asked. "I should rub some on so that your shoulder doesn't stiffen overnight."

"Aye," he replied. "There's some on the stand next to the bed ... in the small brown bottle."

Nessa stepped back. "Take off yer tunic then, and I'll rub some on."

Hugh hesitated for a moment, although his face was still hidden from view, so she couldn't see his expression. Pretending not to notice his discomfort, she moved to the side table, picked up the bottle, and unstoppered it. The spicy scent of clove drifted up to greet her. Clove was often used on sore muscles; as such, she wasn't surprised Hugh carried some with him.

When she turned back to Hugh, she saw that he'd indeed stripped off his gambeson and the thin tunic he wore under it, revealing his heavily muscled shoulders and back.

Mouth dry, Nessa returned to him. Then, trying to ignore the heat from his body that reached out and wrapped itself around her like a lover's caress, she poured some clove oil onto her palm and began rubbing it into his shoulder.

Hugh issued another soft groan then, his head dipping once more.

Heat started to pulse between Nessa's thighs. Maiden's blood, she wished he wouldn't make sounds like that. It made her ache for him.

Treacherous body—he was her enemy, her captor, yet she found him as attractive as ever.

She rubbed in the oil, and was just smoothing the last of it across the top of his shoulder, when he reached up with his left hand, his fingers covering hers and stilling her progress.

"I think that's enough." His voice had a slightly strangled edge to it, betraying that the intimacy of the massage had aroused him as much as it had her. "Thank you."

Nessa stilled, reveling in the strength and heat of his hand over hers. Yet he didn't lift it, didn't release her from his grasp. The moments drew out, desire shimmering in the narrow space between them.

Heart pounding, Nessa drew in a slow, steadying breath. What was he doing?

And then, Hugh twisted on his seat, pulling her onto his lap.

An instant later, his mouth claimed hers.

Nessa gasped, although the sound was muffled by the kiss. His tongue swept her lips apart, plundering her mouth. With another gasp, Nessa melted against him.

The Three Curse her, she shouldn't want Hugh de Burgh this much—but she did.

The feel of his powerful hands as they slid down her back to grasp her hips made her tremble. Deepening the kiss, he lifted her up, so that she sat astride him. He then possessively cupped her backside and hauled her against him.

Wild excitement swooped low in Nessa's belly when she felt the rock-hard length of him pressing against her core.

Whimpering low in her throat, she kissed him back with equal fervor, the embrace turning hungry, desperate. And when she ground herself against him, the growl he issued made her forget herself. Gently, she bit his lower lip.

A draft of chill, damp air gusted into the pavilion.

Hugh's body went rigid against hers. Breathless, Nessa tore her lips from his and looked up. Thomas

Charlton appeared, his arms filled with Hugh's clean armor. Spying his master and the woman he'd taken prisoner in such proximity, the squire skidded to a halt, his blue eyes snapping wide, his face flushing deep red.

"S—sorry," he stuttered. "I was just—"

"Don't apologize, Thomas," Hugh said roughly, cutting the squire off. He rose to his feet, letting Nessa slide from his lap, depositing her on the ground. Still not looking her way, Hugh reached for his tunic. "We're done here."

26

FALL BACK

CHAOS REIGNED ON the hillside below Stirling Castle.

The spring rains had ceased for a spell, although the heavy deluge of the past days had turned the ground into a bog. The siege was in its fifth morning.

Ajax sank up to his fetlocks in mud as the destrier lunged forward, meeting the howling Scotsmen who raced toward them, claidheamh-mòrs—their great Scottish broadswords—swinging.

The warriors had appeared from nowhere, seeming to sprout from the ground beneath the volcanic outcrop on which the castle perched.

Hugh's blade bit into flesh, and cries and grunts of agony followed. Yet he plowed on, jaw set.

He'd been waiting for this attack.

Hugh had said nothing to the king of Nessa's compatriots gaining word of the siege weeks before they arrived at Stirling—he couldn't do so without giving himself, and her, away. Nessa's warning had given the Scots a chance to rally, to spread the news throughout Scotland. In the meantime, Hugh had increased the guards around the perimeter every night and urged the king to send for more artillery.

Edward thought him overly cautious. Yet all the while, Hugh knew all the small attacks would be building into something much bigger. And here it was.

These Scottish warriors didn't belong to the garrison at Stirling Castle. They wore Highland sashes. Some of the colors, Hugh recognized: MacLeod, Sinclair, and

Mackay. They'd been waiting for word from their allies in the south.

And now the time had come for them to unleash their fury.

There was no time to think about the woman he held prisoner now—or the searing kiss they'd shared just three days earlier. Hugh's world narrowed. Nothing existed but steel, blood, and death.

One of the Scotsmen came howling toward Hugh, long dark hair flying behind him, claidheamh-mòr arcing toward Hugh's armored thigh. Ajax was in danger from these warriors fighting on foot.

Hugh leaped down from his destrier, bringing up his shield just in time to ward off the heavy blow that vibrated down the length of his left arm.

The warrior was good. Unlike Hugh, who wielded a lighter English longsword, he gripped his claidheamh-mòr two-handed and so carried no shield. Hugh's shield shuddered a second time under the impact of a blow before he used it to shove his opponent backward.

Hugh stabbed then, driving the Highlander back farther.

Edward fought to his right, still on horseback. The king roared curses as he swung his sword at the men who challenged him. His crown, which sat atop the raised coif of his hauberk, gleamed in the watery morning light.

A few feet from his father, Prince Edward gutted an opponent. The man's howls rent the air, echoing down the hillside.

An instant later, Hugh slashed his own opponent across his exposed throat, taking advantage of the moment the Highlander stumbled in the mud.

They fought on, driving their attackers back—and then, suddenly, the remnants of the originally savage force of Scots turned tail and ran.

"Cowards!" Prince Edward roared after them.

Hugh swung up onto Ajax's back once more. As always, the destrier had waited farther back from the fighting and came when the knight whistled to him.

Sweeping his gaze around him, Hugh's brow furrowed. *Cowards, indeed.* He couldn't believe those attackers had given up so easily.

An instant later, a shadow fell over them.

Hugh's chin kicked up, to see a huge boulder sailing toward them, launched from a trebuchet on the walls.

Cursing, Hugh shouted to the others, reining Ajax back.

There was little time for any of them to avoid the rock, and it took down a knight on horseback, just feet from the king.

Edward's bearded face went rigid, as his attention snapped to the walls. "Retreat," he boomed. "It's a trap!"

Hugh realized it too at that moment.

The Highlanders had attacked with great savagery. It had taken a number of English to repel them—and to do so, they'd pushed them back toward the foot of the cliffs.

But now their attackers had fled down the steep rock-studded slopes either side of the battlefield, Edward and his men were exposed to the walls.

Thud.

A crossbow bolt embedded in the cantle of the king's saddle.

Fury pulsed through Hugh. They were all in the sights of the row of archers wielding crossbows, their helmeted heads outlined against the washed-out blue sky.

"Shit-eating bastards!" Prince Edward roared.

"Fall back!" Hugh shouted, reining Ajax around. "Fall *back!*"

His order echoed across the hillside, reaching every man there. But it was too late.

Crossbow bolts flew through the air, descending upon them in a deadly hailstorm. And they were stuck in the midst of it.

Hugh raised his shield high and urged Ajax to his king's side. Nicholas Harrington and Robert le Breton followed suit. They closed their shields around Edward, while all four men turned their mounts and drew back toward the safety of the camp below.

Some of the bolts clattered off shields or thudded into the earth, yet others found their mark. Screams ripped through the air, and Hugh was dimly aware of men falling around him.

Somewhere close by, he could hear Prince Edward's curses ringing through the air.

Next to Hugh, Robert grunted.

The knight then toppled off his horse. Hugh snarled an oath, torn between going to help his friend—a man he'd known since they were both squires—and remaining at the king's side.

He never got to make a decision either way though, for two crossbow bolts hit Hugh.

Thud. Thud.

The force of them threw Hugh off Ajax and onto the muddy ground. Hot pain lanced through his right thigh and down his back. He was vaguely aware of shouting, although a strange roaring in his ears dimmed out the sounds.

Hugh clawed his way through the mud to Robert's side. His friend lay on his back, his helm raised, a bolt embedded through the throat. Blue eyes gazed sightlessly up at Hugh. Robert's lips were parted as if he were about to call for help.

Hugh collapsed next to his friend, his vision dimming. Pain ripped down his back, heat pulsing through him.

Robert was dead, and it looked as if he too would soon be.

They carried Hugh into the tent, insensible and covered in mud and blood. Two crossbow bolts protruded from him.

Rising from her stool, Nessa stifled a gasp of horror.

At first, she thought Hugh was dead.

He was so pale, so still.

However, the care the men were taking with him, as they placed him on the bed and gently removed his armor, told her that Hugh de Burgh still breathed.

Moments later, the camp physician—a harried-looking man with a red face—hurried into the pavilion. Thomas Charlton followed close behind.

The squire's face was taut, his cheeks wet with tears.

No one looked Nessa's way or acknowledged her. Their attention was wholly upon the knight, now clad in hose and gambeson, who lay upon the bed, his blood soaking into the sheets.

Nessa's belly twisted, and she realized then that she was trembling.

It had been a strange last few days. Things had been awkward in the aftermath of that kiss. Hugh's face had been set in stern lines as he'd quickly pulled on his tunic and gambeson. She hadn't been surprised when he'd approached her, retrieved her shackles, and replaced them around her wrists.

The knight had been withdrawn ever since. He'd spoken to her only when necessary and kept their exchanges short and formal. Likewise, Nessa had been uncomfortable in his presence. The kiss had indeed muddied things further between them.

But there was no awkwardness now, only concern.

I have to help him.

The physician had already gotten to work. He clipped off the end of the two bolts and slowly drew them from the wounds; one had lodged in the meat of Hugh's right thigh, and the other in the upper right of his back.

The physician then set about staunching the wounds and bandaging them.

"Will he live?" Thomas asked, the quaver in the lad's voice giving his dread away.

"I think not," the physician grunted as he wrapped the bandage about Hugh's leg. "He's still losing a lot of blood ... and the bolt in his back has likely pierced something vital."

Not his lung though. Nessa had noted that blood didn't stain Hugh's pale lips.

"Can you do something for him?" The plea in Thomas's voice cut Nessa deep. The lad looked to Hugh like a father.

"Not at present," the physician replied with a weary shake of his head. "The best thing you can do for him now, lad … is to stay by his side." He then met the squire's pained gaze, his voice softening. "No man should die alone." Without another word, the physician gathered up his things and headed for the tent's entrance.

Nessa watched him go, her brow furrowed. There was no mistaking the fatalism in the man's voice. He thought Hugh was done for.

And he likely was.

Alone in the tent with Hugh and his squire, she made a decision.

"Thomas," she murmured. "Free my hands … and let me treat Hugh's wounds."

The squire turned to her, knuckling away tears. He'd clearly forgotten she was even there. "What?" he rasped.

"I'm a healer," she replied, nodding toward the saddlebags of her belongings that sat against the wall of the tent. "I have salves and herbs that could save his life."

Thomas stared at her, yet he still hesitated. "I can't," he said after a pause, his voice hardening. "You're Hugh's prisoner."

"I won't be for much longer," Nessa shot back, her anger quickening. "If you don't let me aid him, he'll most certainly die." Her belly tightened as she said those words. Hugh was seriously injured. It would take more than just her healing skills to save him.

She'd have to use witching.

"Please, Thomas," she said, holding her bound wrists up to him. "If you wish for Sir Hugh to live, release me … let me help him."

The squire stared at her a moment longer before his eyes guttered. With a nod, he retrieved a key from a pouch upon his belt and stepped forward.

The heavy iron shackles fell away, dropping to Nessa's feet.

Moving quickly, she went to her bags, withdrawing her pestle and mortar and a few cloth bags of dried herbs.

"I need freshly boiled water," she said, carrying her items to the bedside table. "Can you get me some?"

Thomas didn't move, and Nessa glanced toward him, her gaze narrowing. "Thomas, I must work fast if I am to save his life. And I'm going to need your help. You need to make a decision."

The squire stared back at her, conflict playing across his young face. He was clearly divided.

Frustration welled within Nessa. They didn't have time for this. "Thomas?"

"Aye," he said roughly, his gaze darting to Hugh's deathly pale face. "I'll get that water."

She nodded. "Hurry."

The squire raced from the tent.

Alone with Hugh, Nessa drew in a deep, steadying breath. She reached down, placing her hand upon his brow. It was damp and clammy. His breathing was shallow and fast, and his pallor worried her.

Indeed, she needed to work fast.

She poured dried herbs into her mortar before adding a few pinches of other ingredients she had in pouches upon her belt. She then began to pound the items into a powder.

The Egg Moon was still in its first quarter—a time for decision-making, for resolve.

"Ye won't die, ye stubborn English bastard," she muttered, casting the unconscious man a stern look. "I refuse to let ye."

Moments later, Thomas burst back into the tent carrying a pot of steaming water. "Is this what you need?" he asked, his eyes pleading.

"Aye." Nessa motioned for him to bring the water to her. She needed it for the poultices she'd make for Hugh's injuries—and for the witching that went with it. Water had life-giving properties, especially when used with the craft. "Let's get to work."

27

BACK FROM THE BRINK

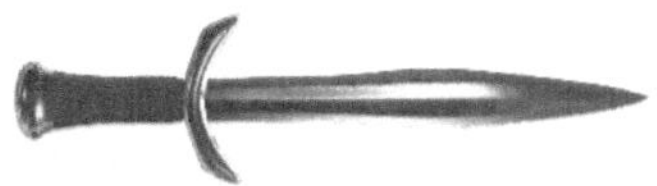

IT WAS LATE, yet Nessa still sat at Hugh's side.

Blinking, as a veil of sleep attempted to settle over her, she jerked awake.

Hugh lay there, unmoving. However, his breathing was a trifle deeper and the pallor upon his cheeks had lessened.

The Grim Reaper no longer stood above him, scythe at the ready. Nonetheless, he wasn't out of the woods.

Nessa straightened up, wincing as she rubbed her aching back. It had taken every last shred of skill she possessed to bring Hugh back from the brink. The moment she'd placed her hands on him, she'd felt death's shadow.

She'd fought it, pushed it back with softly whispered words.

Thomas had watched her all the while, his gaze wide and frightened.

No doubt, observing her at work, the lad had realized she was employing witching to heal the knight. A witch-wind had gusted through the tent as she drew from the craft—the scent of pine-resin, crushed herbs, and earth—making the banks of candles gutter and the coals in the brazier pulse to life.

At a certain point, Thomas Charlton had murmured a prayer and crossed himself.

Yet to his credit, the lad hadn't fled, hadn't run off to fetch guards.

He'd been afraid of the strange practice he'd witnessed, but he'd known that she was trying to save Hugh, and so he'd stayed.

His fortitude had impressed Nessa.

Eventually though, fatigue had claimed the lad. The squire now slept, curled up in his blankets near the brazier, leaving Nessa and Hugh alone.

Wringing out a cloth, she leaned forward, wiping his clammy brow. "Fight, Hugh," she whispered. "*Fight.*"

A draft fluttered across the tent then, and Nessa straightened up to see two regal figures enter.

Despite that Nessa had spent days with the English army, she'd yet to set eyes on King Edward of England and his queen consort, Margaret of France. She'd almost forgotten their large pavilion sat just a few yards distant from Hugh's.

Still dressed in a heavy hauberk, his golden crown gleaming in the candlelight, Edward strode to the bed, his crimson surcoat fluttering. He towered over his queen, a small dark-haired woman wearing a fur-lined mantle. The king stepped around Thomas's sleeping body; the lad slumbered so deeply, he didn't even stir.

Nessa's heart started to pound wildly at the sight of the royal couple. She hadn't expected to see either of them here, especially not at this late hour.

Swallowing hard, Nessa watched them approach. Then, remembering her manners, she dipped her chin.

Of course, now was her chance. The Hammer, nemesis of the Scots, stood before her. She should lunge for Hugh's dagger, which sat sheathed on the table next to the bed, and slit Edward Longshanks's throat.

However, Nessa didn't. Exhaustion pressed down upon her tonight, and her worry for Hugh obliterated everything else.

"Where's my physician?" Edward Longshanks's voice was low yet powerful. He'd spoken to Nessa in French, for he likely didn't realize that she spoke the English tongue.

"You just missed him," Nessa replied in French. "He was sure Hugh would die … and can't believe he's still with us."

The English king's greying brows raised. "How *is* Hugh?"

"It's still too early to tell," she replied. "But … if he is with us at dawn, there may be some hope."

The Hammer nodded, stepping close to the bed. His gaze, ice-blue, rested upon Hugh's face.

"I lost one of my guard today," he murmured. "I don't wish to lose another."

At Nessa's look of confusion, the queen spoke up. "Robert le Breton died defending the king … he was a close friend of Hugh's."

Nessa nodded, remembering the two knights who'd been with Hugh the day they'd met at the gates. Was Robert le Breton one of them? Le Breton had apparently been one of a number of English knights and men-at-arms who'd died during the skirmish.

Thomas had told her what had happened, of the Highlanders that had attacked, and how the king's men had pushed them back before the Scots had fled, leaving them vulnerable to missiles from the wall.

And as Thomas had recounted the tale, she'd known who was responsible.

The Guardians of Alba.

Her sisters had been successful in rousing support from the Highlands. The attack, and the ruse that followed, had been a success for the rebels. The English had suffered a stinging defeat today, one that the defenders of Stirling Castle would use to their advantage.

Once again, conflicting feelings churned through Nessa.

She wanted her countrymen to win, for the English to be driven from these lands. But the last thing she wished for was for Hugh de Burgh to die.

"Hugh has been with me many years," the king continued, his gaze still upon the knight's face. "His loyalty has been unquestioning. He fought at my side in the Holy Lands … a young soldier then. Over the years, he's always been my right-hand ... campaign after campaign."

"He fell defending you, my love," Margaret murmured, placing a hand upon her husband's arm. "As did Robert ... his loyalty never wavered."

Edward of England nodded, although his face tightened. He glanced up then, those cool blue eyes spearing Nessa.

"I've never seen Hugh de Burgh waver once ... not until he met a Scotswoman at Dunfermline ... one who had the nerve to follow him on campaign."

Nessa stared back at him. The challenge in the king's voice made her hackles rise.

When she didn't reply, the king's mouth curved. "And here you remain ... at his side."

Nessa drew in a deep breath before replying. "I'm a healer ... and I've done my best to aid him."

Beside the king, his wife smiled. She was pretty with luminous brown eyes. Nessa spied a tell-tale bulge under her gown; she hadn't realized the queen was with bairn. However, there was a knowing look in the queen's eyes that made Nessa tense. "You are in love with him, I think," Margaret murmured.

Nessa's breathing hitched, heat flushing through her before icy cold followed in its wake. Her lips parted to deny the queen's comment. She was wrong, a Guardian of Alba couldn't love one of the enemy. And yet, the words wouldn't come.

The queen continued to hold Nessa's gaze, giving her the uncanny sensation that Margaret knew who she really was.

Nervousness fluttered in Nessa's belly. She hoped that wasn't the case.

"I'm glad for you both," Longshanks said then, breaking the weighty silence. "A soldier's life can be a lonely one."

Nessa's eyes widened. This was the infamous Edward Longshanks of England, the warrior king, the 'Hammer of the Scots'. The man's blistering temper and thirst for conquering and glory were legendary. He'd killed countless Scots, and most likely would kill many more.

And yet he'd just revealed an unexpectedly soft side. One that left her speechless.

The shock must have shown on her face, for the king issued a soft laugh as he linked his arm through his wife's and stepped back from the bed. "Aye, I've lived my life by the sword," he said, still smiling ruefully. "But over the years, I've discovered that it is love that truly makes life worth living."

And with those parting words, the king and queen turned and left the pavilion.

Nessa stared after the couple, unsure what to make of either of them. Life of late had shown her that when one scratched beneath the surface, nothing was as she'd believed it to be.

In truth, she was still reeling from Queen Margaret's comment.

She wasn't in love with Hugh de Burgh. Her attention shifted to the knight's pale, sleeping face. Was she?

Nessa's shoulders slumped then, exhaustion settling over her as if a heavy pair of hands pressed down upon her. She glanced over at Thomas. Still huddled within his nest of blankets, the lad slept on, oblivious to the fact the king and queen had just visited them.

Placing a hand upon Hugh's chest, she felt the slow yet steady thud of his heart and the reassuring warmth of his skin. There was no sign of fever as he wasn't hot to touch.

Nessa's throat thickened then, and she bowed her head, closing her eyes. "How I wish we were different people, Hugh," she whispered, "and that we'd met in peaceful times." She paused there, sudden tears scalding the back of her eyelids. "How happy we might have been together." Her chest now ached. "But even though we aren't to be … promise me ye shall fight … that ye shall live." Her voice hitched then. "May yer future be filled with happiness, mo ghràdh … and may The Three watch over ye for the rest of yer years."

Nessa trailed off there; she literally couldn't continue.

Queen Margaret's words had hit her like a mallet to the chest. And at that moment, she realized that, somehow, she'd had fallen for Hugh de Burgh. Like a thief, it had crept up on her.

The ache in her chest was so strong now that she reached up with her free hand and rubbed at her breastbone. For the first time, she felt the true weight of what she could never have, and the loss of it was a yawning abyss within her. But she'd weather it if the goddesses spared him.

Blinking rapidly as her eyelids burned with unshed tears, Nessa was about to move back from the bed, and to find her own upon the sheepskins in the corner of the tent, when a warm, strong hand covered hers.

Hugh was awake and looking up at her. His expression was tired, yet his hazel eyes were soft.

Nessa's breathing hitched, mortification flooding through her. Crone's tears, had he heard her? His fingers closed tighter over hers, and she knew then that, indeed, he'd heard every word she'd spoken. He'd heard, and he understood.

"Sir Hugh lives!" Lady Philippa burst into the tent where the queen and Lamia had just settled down at their looms. "I've just heard it from his squire."

Queen Margaret picked up the basket of wool she was about to weave and smiled at Philippa. "I can't say I'm surprised."

Seated opposite, Lamia cut her mistress a startled look. "Whatever do you mean, Margaret?" she asked. "Last night the physician told me Sir Hugh wouldn't survive the night."

"Well, he has!" Lady Philippa moved over to one of the large stuffed cushions decorating the tent where the queen and her ladies spent rainy afternoons and sank into it. "It appears that Hugh's Scottish lover is a healer. She saved his life."

Lamia fought the urge to scowl at the lady-in-waiting. Lady Philippa was one of the most goose-witted young women she'd ever met; she couldn't understand why Margaret suffered her.

However, the queen merely bestowed the court lady with another knowing smile. "I must discuss something in private with Lady Lamia," she said after a pause. "Please leave us for a spell."

Lady Philippa's pretty face tightened just a fraction, her gaze snapping to Lamia. Like the other ladies-in-waiting who'd accompanied them on campaign, she resented Lamia her close relationship with the queen. Margaret often preferred to spend time alone with Lamia instead of gossiping with the others. Nonetheless, Philippa wasn't foolish enough to argue with the Margaret about it. She rose gracefully to her feet and left the pavilion.

When she'd departed, Lamia turned her attention to Margaret, quirking an eyebrow. "You know something I do not, I'd wager?"

Margaret gave a soft laugh before she wound wool around her shuttle and started to loop it through her loom. "Hardly ... but Edward and I visited Sir Hugh late last night. We were sure to find him breathing his last ... but, instead, we discovered color in his cheeks and his lover at his side." The queen paused there. "She must be a skilled healer indeed to have saved him."

Lamia stiffened. *Lover.* She didn't need to be reminded of her own failure to entice Hugh into her bed. The rejection still stung.

She was still nursing the bitter bite, when Margaret glanced over at her, a groove appearing between her eyebrows. "Why is she here?"

Lamia paused at this question. Sensing her disquiet, Fantôme moved against her arm. "I told you ... the woman is clearly besotted with Sir Hugh."

Margaret fixed her with a level look then, one that made Lamia shift uncomfortably upon her stool. "I think there's more to it than that."

Lamia frowned. "You do?" She knew her tone verged on patronizing, yet she couldn't help it. Margaret didn't possess the slightest amount of witching ability.

"Perhaps all these years in your company has made me sensitive to such things ... but I 'smelt' witch-craft in that tent and felt the same power I sometimes sense in you." Margaret paused, her gaze fusing with Lamia's. Her eyes glinted then. "You can be prone to overconfidence, my dearest Lamia," she said softly. "If Nessa can bring a man back from the brink of death ... she may be more powerful than you believe."

28

I KNOW WHAT YOU ARE

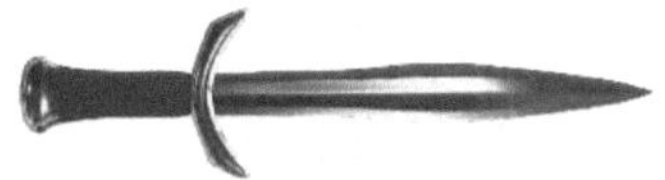

LAMIA HURRIED ACROSS the inner perimeter toward her tent, clutching her cloak tight against the wind that gusted across the hillside. The boom and rumble of war rolled over the camp, and when she glanced up, she spied *le Berefry*, the great wooden siege tower, trundling up the hill on runners toward the walls of Stirling Castle. The men had just finished erecting it, and today the siege tower would be put to use. *Le Berefry* also possessed a heavy timber battering ram that they would be using to weaken the castle defenses.

Lamia's attention shifted up, to where smoke curled from the fortress's thick curtain walls. The attack had resumed with the dawn, with even more ferocity than before. Edward was understandably furious at their trouncing and wanted to hit back.

But Lamia's thoughts weren't on the siege. Yesterday had merely been a setback, one they would swiftly recover from. Instead, her thoughts were on the witch who sat at Hugh de Burgh's bedside.

She may be more powerful than you believe.

Those words stung. The queen's gentle manner sometimes made Lamia forget that she was sharper than most folk gave her credit for. She hadn't missed the rebuke and challenge in Margaret's eyes.

And yet, sometimes Lamia felt as if Margaret didn't know her at all. They'd been best friends since childhood, but Lamia had always hidden her most secret desires from Margaret. Her friend had made the kind of marriage most noblewomen could only dream of—and Lamia wanted the same for herself. She wouldn't wed a king, yet she wanted lands, a title, wealth and luxury, and a powerful husband.

Lamia had grown up an orphan amongst strangers and had learned early on that, to survive, she had to be cleverer and quicker than others. Her mother had died birthing her, and she barely remembered her feckless father—yet she wouldn't live and die in obscurity as her parents had.

She would make something of herself. And to do so, she had to be one step ahead of everyone else. She didn't like that Margaret had picked up on something *she* had missed.

Ducking into her pavilion, Lamia went straight for her scrying bowl. Fashioned out of obsidian, its surface shone like a black looking-glass.

She set the bowl down on the table at one end of the tent and carefully poured water into it. Fantôme slid forth from her hiding place up Lamia's sleeve, curling onto the table. Her ivory head peeped up as she observed the witch at work.

"I've been a goose, Fantôme," Lamia muttered. "And I fear that I may have overlooked something important."

Lamia had always been confident in her witching, and in her ability to assess any potential threats. But had her own hubris gotten the better of her? Had it blinded her?

She'd been standing before her tent when they'd brought Sir Hugh in the day before; she'd seen the way he was bleeding. Although she'd been sore about the fact he hadn't yet come to her pavilion for bed-sport, the sight of his grave injuries had chilled her blood. As such, she'd tracked the physician down and demanded to know if Sir Hugh would live. The man had given her a blunt answer.

For the first time, Lamia had wished her skills extended to healing. However, she'd always preferred the darker, more exciting arts, and knew little of healing besides a few simple charms.

No, Hugh shouldn't have survived—and yet he had.

Was his survival down to witching? Lamia hoped the bowl could allay her worries.

"Come here, Fantôme." She reached out a hand toward the grass snake. "I need your assistance."

Dutifully, Fantôme slithered across the table toward her before wrapping around Lamia's wrist. Scrying required the deepest of concentration, and her familiar helped her achieve it. The moment the snake's scaled body tightened around her wrist, she relaxed.

Breathing deeply, Lamia waited for the water to settle so that it formed a clear skin. And then she bent over it, whispering to the water. Lamia had never had any formal training in the craft, only a hoard of forbidden books she'd discovered in the castle outside Paris where she'd grown up. Those books had opened up an exciting new world, and she still carried some of them with her.

She'd developed some skill at scrying, although it had taken her a while to find the right vessel for it.

As her words died away, Lamia gazed upon the mirrored surface within the bowl, looking for patterns in the shapes and shadows that played across it.

And as she watched, her breathing grew slow and still.

The images were unclear at first, merely formless shapes. But then, as time drew out, and her breathing slowed further still, Lamia began to make sense of them.

Blue-robed figures—women, all of them.

Lamia's gaze narrowed, and she peered closer still.

A waterfall appeared, spilling over the edge of a lake down a craggy rock face.

Lamia's frown deepened, and then another image came into focus.

A small woman with a crow perched upon her shoulder. A deep, earthy power emanated from the woman, making the fine hair on the back of Lamia's neck prickle.

Drawing back from the scrying bowl, she muttered an oath.

Fantôme tightened her grip around her wrist, urging her to reveal what she'd seen.

"Witches," she whispered. "And they were all dressed in blue ... just like Nessa."

Lamia rose to her feet, her pulse, which had beat so slowly during the scrying, now raced. She'd initially thought Hugh's lover nothing more than a harmless hedge-witch, yet in reality, the woman was part of a coven. Margaret, curse her, was right. There was far more to Nessa than met the eye.

Spitting out another oath, Lamia turned on her heel and hurried from the tent.

Nessa moved through the inner perimeter, bending her head against the gusting wind. Pushing the hair out of her eyes, she shifted her attention to the castle perched high above her and spied the massive wooden siege tower that now battered the curtain wall.

"Thrice-cursed bastards," she whispered aloud. "How did they build that so fast?"

Indeed, she hadn't been out of Hugh's pavilion in days, except to use the privy, and had little idea of how things were progressing for either side. Still reeling from the revelations of the night before, Nessa had been momentarily distracted from the reason she was here— the reason she hadn't tried to escape. However, the sight of that monstrous siege weapon brought her sharply into focus.

Surely, Stirling couldn't withstand it?

Breathing in deeply, Nessa fought to calm her rising panic. The gates still held, and while they did, there was still hope.

Peering up at the siege tower, her gaze narrowed. It was made of wood—surely the defenders could somehow set fire to it?

Pulling her cloak tightly about her, Nessa continued her walk.

It was late morning, and Hugh had fallen asleep. Thomas had gone off to run some errands for the knight, and so Nessa had seized the opportunity to slip outdoors for a spell. Of course, she wasn't supposed to venture outside without Thomas escorting her, but since she'd saved Hugh de Burgh's life, the man couldn't be too harsh with her. Well, not yet, anyway.

Deep in thought, Nessa circuited the space once more. They were well into spring now, and although today was cold and windy, it had rained nearly every day since their arrival in Stirling, and the camp had turned into a swamp. Nessa's boots squelched through sticky mud.

She circuited the clearing at the heart of the camp, but instead of returning to Hugh's pavilion, she took the path behind the tents. It felt so good to stretch her cramped muscles that she didn't want to go back just yet. She walked along the narrow passage between the backs of the pavilions and the wall of supply wagons that made up the inner perimeter.

Nessa was halfway around the loop walk when a dark shape fluttered in from above.

With a flap of wings, a large black crow flew down, settling upon one of the wagon wheels.

Nessa halted, a wide smile creasing her face. "Eclipse!"

The crow cocked its head, glassy, dark eyes fixing upon her.

"I was hoping ye'd pay me a visit."

Glancing around, to ensure she was alone, Nessa shifted closer to the High Bandruì's familiar. She had to give her news quickly before anyone saw her.

"Things didn't go quite as planned," she told Eclipse, her voice breathless with urgency. "Sir Hugh resisted my attempts to charm him and took me prisoner … however" —Nessa held up her unshackled hands to show that she was free for the moment— "I have learned two things of importance … the first is that The Hammer has a witch traveling with him. Her name is Lamia Delamare, and she's one of the queen's ladies-in-waiting.

She's strong ... for she has a familiar. She may be a threat to our cause."

Nessa paused then, leaning closer. "They have also erected a massive wooden siege tower, with a battering ram ... someone needs to deal to it." She straightened up, favoring Eclipse with a rueful smile. "That's it ... I wish I had more to reveal, but—"

The crow erupted skyward with a violent flap of wings. Nessa reeled back, and, whirling around, she saw a cloaked figure standing a few yards back. Lamia Delamare had just stepped onto the path. Pale hair, braided and coiled, glinted despite the dull day.

The scent of hot iron and musk enveloped Nessa then.

Pulse quickening, she turned to face the witch squarely.

Lamia was frowning. However, her focus was skyward at where Eclipse was now flying away.

A moment later, the witch lowered her gaze and met Nessa's eye.

Nessa favored her with a tight smile. "You are too late," she said in French.

Lamia's mouth pursed. "So I see." She took a step forward. "I know what you are, Nessa. It seems you aren't a lone healer as I'd thought ... but part of a powerful coven."

Nessa arched an eyebrow, even as her pulse started to hammer against her ribs. How had Lamia discovered that?

Warning prickled across her skin. It was best she didn't linger here to find out.

She was just about to duck into the gap between two pavilions when Lamia's voice forestalled her. "You're no infatuated lover ... what's your real purpose here?" Nessa felt the woman's witch-will emanate from her, like mist wreathing out from the Wailing Widow Falls. She was trying to coax an answer from her. "Are you planning to kill Edward?"

Nessa frowned. "Why, are you planning on running to him?"

Lamia's jaw tensed, and Nessa watched her with interest. It was then she knew that Edward of England had no idea he had a witch in his midst. She'd suspected as much before, yet Lamia's reaction now confirmed it.

"Are you a spy then?" Lamia ground out, her pale eyes glittering.

Nessa lifted her chin. She longed to fling her mission in the witch's face—to tell her she was here for Scotland. The English would never take this land as their own, not while the Guardians of Alba existed. But caution checked the instinct.

Instead, she stared her adversary down. "The reason I'm here matters not," she replied, her voice turning flinty. "But remember this, Lamia Delamare … I know who *you* are … and I'll wager the king does not."

With that, Nessa left the path, moving between two tents toward the clearing beyond.

When she re-entered Hugh's pavilion moments later, Nessa's pulse hammered in her ears. She'd presented a fierce face to Lamia, yet in truth, the encounter had rattled her. Her palms were now damp, her legs shaky.

A few feet away, Hugh still slept deeply, the whisper of his breathing filling the tent. Thomas still hadn't returned from his errands.

Hands trembling, Nessa dug into one of the pouches at her waist, grabbed a handful of salt, and sprinkled it across the threshold to ward herself against the witch. She then whispered a protection charm.

She wasn't taking any chances with Lamia Delamare.

Nessa had seen the fear in the woman's eyes as she'd left her. Her threat would hopefully prevent Lamia from going to the king. However, somehow, the witch had discovered the existence of the Guardians. That knowledge made her dangerous—both to the order and to Scotland.

29

YOU'VE EARNED IT

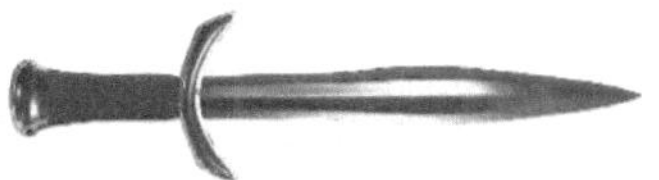

HUGH EYED THE cup that Nessa passed him, his gaze wary. "What's in that?"

Nessa's mouth quirked. "I once told a man in a similar situation to ye that it's best not to ask such questions." She held the cup to him, waiting until he took it. "Best ye don't know. Just drink up."

Hugh frowned yet relented, lifting the cup to his lips and taking a tentative sip. "Christ's bones," he muttered. "It tastes awful."

"And it'll do ye good. Go on … drink."

Watching Hugh do as bid, Nessa considered that the knight was definitely feeling better. Men only tended to make a fuss about such things when they were no longer rubbing shoulders with death. Five days had passed since the skirmish, and with each passing morning, he appeared stronger.

Hugh emptied the cup before muttering another oath under his breath. "I don't want to sound ungrateful, Nessa … but I swear these drafts you make me taste like horse shit."

Nessa laughed. "And ye are familiar with that taste, are ye?"

He grumbled something, yet his eyes twinkled.

Warmth spread through Nessa at the sight of mirth on his face. Hugh had been so forbidding of late, she'd forgotten his dry sense of humor and the banter they'd once shared.

Smiling, she took Hugh's now empty cup from him. "Now, are ye going to let me check yer wounds without complaining?"

He pulled a face. "Yes, I'll behave myself ... go ahead."

"Good lad," Nessa quipped. She helped him into a sitting position and then started to unwrap the bandages. "Ye'll heal a lot faster if ye do as ye are told."

Hugh snorted a laugh before wincing. Although his injuries were healing well, they still pained him.

Removing the bandage, Nessa inspected the wound to his back—out of the two of them, this was the one that had threatened his life. But it was healing well, a scab now forming. He'd been lucky, for the crossbow bolt had narrowly missed piercing a lung.

Rubbing ointment carefully onto the injury, she then wound a fresh bandage around Hugh's naked torso. Then Nessa moved down to his leg. Her brow furrowed as she examined the wound.

The bolt had ripped a hole in the muscle of his thigh, and although the injury appeared healthy enough, thanks to her ministrations, she worried it would leave lasting damage.

"Any reason for the frown?" Hugh asked.

Nessa glanced up, cursing herself for letting her concern show so clearly. "Ye are going to walk with a limp from now on," she murmured.

Hugh's eyes shadowed. "How bad will it be?"

Nessa held his gaze. She didn't have an answer for that.

"Will I be able to ride?"

She nodded.

"And fight?"

"Perhaps," she said cautiously.

Silence stretched out between them. Hugh's light mood had vanished. His handsome face had turned to stone, and his gaze was shadowed.

Watching him, Nessa understood. Fighting was his life, and as commander of the English army, he couldn't show the slightest weakness.

"It's still early days," Nessa said eventually, seeking to reassure him. "Every man heals differently."

He met her gaze then, the harsh look on his face softening. "I haven't forgotten," he said, his tone gentle now. "That I'm only alive to grumble about my lot because of you, Nessa. You've saved my life, not once, but twice."

Their gazes held.

He'd heard her whispers that night, the words straight from her heart. But neither of them had spoken of it in the aftermath. Perhaps because they both knew it was hopeless to fight the truth and pointless discussing it.

They were from vastly different worlds, and soon—if Hugh allowed it—she would return to hers. Neither of them had fanciful characters; they were both realists. Nonetheless, it didn't ease the ache deep in Nessa's chest whenever she dwelled on the fact that she'd have to leave him.

Ever since Hugh had awoken from his life-threatening injuries, he'd softened toward her. Nessa hadn't worn shackles on her wrists since then.

"Ready for supper?" Thomas entered the pavilion then, carrying a heavily laden tray. As he neared the table, Nessa caught the whiff of mutton stew.

"Aye," Hugh replied gruffly, tearing his attention from Nessa. "And if you both help me, maybe I can even sit up at the table this eve."

Thomas and Nessa did as bid, helping to lift him under each arm, and a short while later, Hugh sat gingerly eating his supper. Nessa had taken her place opposite, watching him closely. His healing was still in the early stages; she wouldn't be able to rest properly until he was able to stand without assistance and walk again.

Her mood shadowed then as she reached for some bread.

She hadn't wanted to be so brutally honest with Hugh, yet that wound on his thigh was serious enough to lame him permanently.

They both knew the truth of it, even though neither voiced it aloud.

Hugh de Burgh's military career was drawing to an end.

A week later, Hugh stood before the king, trying to ignore the dull ache in his upper back and thigh.

Nearly two weeks had passed since the day of that fateful attack—since Robert le Breton and many others had died under the hail of Scottish crossbow bolts. Hugh could walk, yet as Nessa had warned, he had a terrible limp and needed the assistance of a cane at present. However, he'd deliberately left his stick back in his pavilion.

He had to appear strong and fit before the king.

"You've served me well over the years, Hugh," Edward said, pouring them both goblets of wine. The two men were alone in the reception area of the king's pavilion. Outdoors the sun was setting in a blaze of red and gold over the smoky, dirty camp.

Over the past days, Hugh had noted a change in mood amongst his countrymen. Whenever he'd ventured outdoors, leaning on his cane for support, he'd seen the grim expressions on the soldiers. Even Nicholas Harrington looked uncharacteristically serious these days. With Robert dead and Hugh recovering from his injuries, the responsibility for the siege had passed to him.

He'd visited Hugh the evening before and given him a report over tankards of ale. Things weren't progressing well for them. Stirling still held. More stone from a nearby quarry had been hauled in for missiles. Every day, Greek Fire, stone, and lead flew at the walls of the fortress, yet although the great curtain walls of the castle were now blackened, they showed no sign of crumbling.

Nicholas's report had left Hugh on edge. He was anxious to recover, so he could help bring Stirling under English control once more.

And yet, as he stood there, his gaze taking in the king's unusually solemn face, he knew this was not to be a conversation about siege tactics or replenishing their rapidly dwindling food and weaponry supplies.

The king's first words had warned Hugh that this exchange was to be far more personal.

"No man has ever shown me such loyalty," Edward continued, handing Hugh a goblet.

"You are my king," Hugh replied. "I would lay down my life for you."

Edward quirked a greying brow. "And you almost did." He inclined his head. "If it hadn't been for that comely Scottish healer you keep, you'd be lying six feet deep in Scottish soil." His gaze shadowed. "Like Robert."

They fell silent then. It was hard to believe that Robert le Breton was gone. Hugh kept expecting the knight to stride into his tent, a flagon of wine in one hand and a bag of knucklebones in the other, the small crucifix he wore about his neck glinting. *Time for a game ... I've thrashed Nicholas this eve, and now it's your turn.*

"We've lost many good men over the years," Hugh murmured. Suddenly, the weight of all those losses pressed down upon his shoulders. Most of the time, he pushed the memories of all the friends that had fallen aside, yet today he felt every one of them.

The king nodded, and then his gaze raked down over Hugh. "You're as strong as a mountain, Hugh." He then gave a rueful shake of his head. "I can't believe you're actually standing here before me after the blood you lost." Edward's expression became solemn once more. "But you aren't infallible ... and it's time for you to step down."

Hugh's breathing hitched. The way the conversation was going, he'd sensed something of this nature was coming.

"The siege goes ill," he said, stubbornness rising within him. "You need me."

The king shook his head. "You know as well as I that an injured man is more of a hindrance than a help."

"I'll heal," Hugh muttered.

Edward huffed a laugh. "Aye, you will. But you'll do it back at Grosmont Castle. Go home, Hugh ... get to know your son, wed that comely Scottish healer of yours, have a family, and look after my borders." Their gazes fused then. "You've earned it."

Hugh was still reeling when he stepped from the king's pavilion.

The last of the sun's rays stained the western skies, the crenelated walls and towers of Stirling Castle silhouetted against it.

But the sunset was fading now, just like Hugh's career.

Heaving in a deep breath, he walked forward a few paces and halted, letting his gaze sweep around him. A pall of wood smoke—from the hundreds of hearths that dotted the camp—hung over the tents. As always at this hour, the camp was a hive of activity. In addition to the knights and men-at-arms that made up the fighting force, the army had a large number of craftsmen, including carpenters, masons, and laborers. Clanging and banging drifted through the warm dusk air, for the craftsmen were erecting two more trebuchets after the siege weapons had taken a hammering from the defenders.

Four days before, the Scots had tried to set *Le Berefry* on fire. Nicholas had assured Hugh that the damage was only minor—yet it was another frustrating sign of their lack of progress. And then, just two days earlier, the Scots had conducted another night raid on the camp. There had been a few since the siege began. However, this one had caused more damage than the others. The attackers had killed a number of sentries and set fire to the perimeter fences, before slashing their way through the first rings of tents. They hadn't gotten any further, yet the night raid had put the camp on edge.

Hugh's attention went then to the large wooden viewing platform, erected just behind the inner perimeter. Edward wanted a safe vantage point for the queen and her ladies to have an uninterrupted view of the siege. However, the platform was empty at this time of day.

Swiveling, Hugh then gazed upon Stirling Castle itself. Smoke trailed from the walls, and the air still held the familiar throat-searing reek of Greek Fire.

All of this was as familiar to him as the beating of his own heart. But he was being forced to give it all up. What would he do with himself if he wasn't campaigning for the glory of England?

The fine hair on the back of Hugh's neck prickled then. He was being watched. He shifted his gaze from the castle to where a flaxen-haired woman stood on the other side of the perimeter.

Lamia Delamare. Hugh hadn't seen her in a while, since before he'd fallen in battle. After she'd invited him to her pavilion, he'd done his best to avoid her.

The lady-in-waiting held his gaze for a few instants longer. She then favored him with an enigmatic smile before turning and disappearing into the shadows.

Hugh watched her go before shaking his head. She was an odd woman, Lamia Delamare—almost as strange as Nessa.

Nessa.

She'd nursed him back to health and had hardly left his side over the past fortnight. He'd long ceased shackling her wrists, which meant she could have likely escaped, had she truly wanted.

And yet she'd stayed. He wasn't foolish enough to believe she'd forgotten her old life or the cause that had brought her into his life. All the same, her whispered words that night after she'd saved his life had broken down the barriers between them. They'd fallen into an easy rapport over the past days, but there had been no talk of the future, and Thomas's presence prevented them from broaching more sensitive topics.

And yet the weight of all those unsaid words hung between them, creating tension that grew with each passing day.

Hugh's chest constricted. The king had told him to go home, to Grosmont and his family. And although the shock of being dismissed from service still made it hurt to breathe, a latent excitement now kindled in the pit of his belly.

Home.

He imagined riding over the forested hills toward the Grosmont, the stone keep rising against the sky. Thomas would return with him, of course. The lad was sworn in his service for a while yet. But there was someone else he wanted at his side.

Someone he now couldn't imagine his future without.

30

A WOMAN WITH SECRETS

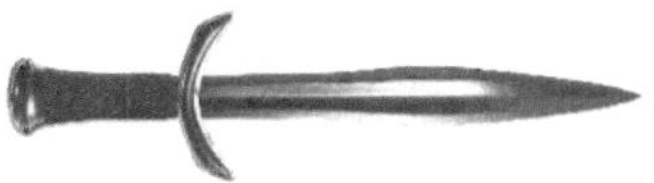

NESSA SPRINKLED SALT over the threshold before digging her fingers into the leather pouch she held. Empty. Her mouth thinned, tension coiling within her. Salt was essential; she'd have to ask Thomas to fetch her some more.

After her run-in with Lamia, she'd taken to warding the pavilion every morning.

She hadn't seen Lamia since that night, although she'd been cautious whenever she left the tent, making sure that either Thomas or Hugh stayed with her, and that she never strayed out of view of others.

Even so, she could feel Lamia's presence nearby, a faint hum in the air—like an angry hive readying itself to attack.

Nessa frowned then. It vexed her that the witch might think she feared her. Aye, Lamia's witch-will was stronger than her own, but Nessa could defend herself, and inflict serious harm, if necessary.

However, her goal now was to stay out of trouble.

Restlessness churned within her. Of course, she wasn't much good to Scotland or Robert Bruce stuck in this tent. Her usefulness as a spy here had ended. It was time for her to return to the Wailing Widow Falls and accept her next mission.

Heaviness settled upon Nessa at the thought, yet she shrugged the sensation off. Enough. She had to focus on what really mattered: Scottish freedom.

Nessa glanced over then, at where her saddlebags sat in the corner of the pavilion—packed and ready to go.

Hugh hadn't actually said he'd release her—and the siege of Stirling Castle continued—yet she sensed he would let her go if she asked.

A sigh escaped her. She should have been relieved about the eventuality, but she also felt conflicted. These past days would remain with her forever. She and Hugh were no longer lovers, yet the time she'd spent with him, nursing him back to health, had felt the closest to a 'normal' life that she'd ever had. They were a family of sorts—she, Hugh, and Thomas—in the midst of a busy camp while the boom and rumble of the siege surrounded them day after day.

But just like those nights in Dunfermline, this too was a stolen moment in time. One that was drawing to an end.

Hugh would let her go, and she'd never see him again.

Goose. Nessa's mouth thinned. *Harden yer heart! The cause is more important than yer pining for this man.*

And it was. Robert Bruce had to be protected.

The reminder made Nessa strengthen her resolve— just as Hugh entered the tent.

He was limping heavily, his face taut with discomfort.

"Ye left yer stick behind," she greeted him, motioning to the cane one of the carpenters had made him.

"I wasn't going before the king looking like a cripple," he grumbled, his brow furrowing. Hugh halted before her, his gaze meeting Nessa's. "Not that it made any difference ... he's discharged me from duty."

Nessa stiffened. "So soon?"

Hugh made a face. "You knew how this meeting would go then?"

"Aye," she admitted softly. "Ye are healing well, Hugh ... but those injuries will stay with ye forever. Ye can't go into battle with them."

Tension rippled across his face, as silence fell between them.

"Nessa, you are free to go," he murmured. "You have been for a while, but I think you know that anyway."

Nessa swallowed. "Aye, thank ye, Hugh."

Another moment of awkward silence stretched between them before, unexpectedly, he stepped close to Nessa, reached out, and took her hands. "I'll admit it felt like a kick in the teeth," he said gruffly, "to be sent away after so many years at my king's side." He paused then, his hazel eyes gleaming in the dimly lit interior of the tent. "But when I left him and really thought about what I was giving up ... and the future that lies before me ... something became clear."

Nessa's breathing hitched. It was as if a curtain had just been lifted from his face. He suddenly looked years younger—and hopeful.

Hugh's fingers tightened around hers. "You don't have to return to your outlaws, Nessa. Come back to Grosmont with me instead. I wish to make you my wife, to have a family with you ... grow old with you." He released one of her hands, lifting his own to her cheek and caressing it gently. "You might have drugged my wine back in Dunfermline, and I wish I could remember telling you how I felt ... yet even though I didn't realize it then, I do now ... I *am* in love with you." He broke off then as his voice turned husky. He stared down at her, his eyes dark and expectant.

"Hugh," she whispered. Her chest started to ache. "I lied to ye about that ... ye never told me that ye loved me back in Dunfermline."

His gaze shadowed. "I didn't?"

She shook her head, guilt crushing her chest.

"And the things you said that night ... after you'd healed me." His features tightened. "Were they also lies?"

"No," she gasped. "I meant every word."

His expression softened, and he cupped her chin. "Then come back to Grosmont with me ... start again." He paused then. "I'm not asking you to change who you are. You can continue your healing ... your craft ... I will have a space made for you in the castle."

Nessa's heart fluttered against her ribs. Mother's milk, how she was tempted. She'd never wanted anything more than to ride off into the sunset with Hugh de Burgh. He gave her something—a feeling of completeness she hadn't even realized was missing in her life. Aye, she'd been lonely at times over the years, yet she hadn't realized that it was love her heart had been yearning for.

But she couldn't leave the order, couldn't turn her back on her people. It would be the ultimate betrayal to Colina, Fyfa, Breanna, and the others. They'd all sacrificed their lives for the Guardians. What right did she have to abandon them all, especially now when Scotland needed them so much? The order was her life—she knew no other one.

But deep down, there was another reason she resisted him. Fear. Nessa was terrified of stepping away from the role that had always defined her. Who was she, if she wasn't a Guardian of Alba?

And yet the temptation to agree rose like a springtide within her. It would be so easy to say 'aye', to melt into his embrace.

Dragging in a deep breath, she stepped back from him, releasing his hand. "We Scots have a saying," she whispered. "If wishes were horses, beggars would ride."

He frowned. "And it means?"

"My life is here, Hugh. I cannot go to England with ye … I cannot be yer wife."

Hugh's eyes guttered.

It was an awful thing, to see hope die, and a sickly sensation washed over her. Nessa swallowed, trying to dislodge the lump that had now risen in her throat. "Some things are just not meant to be, Hugh," she whispered.

"I don't understand." A nerve flickered in his cheek as he continued. "Is it that I'm English?" When she didn't answer, his brow furrowed. "The Scottish cause will go on without you, Nessa … just as this siege will continue without me at the helm. Maybe it's time to step away from your old life. Things won't fall apart without us."

Ye are wrong, Hugh ... they might ... I might ...

How she wished she could tell him who she really was—of the oaths she'd sworn to her sisters and the High Bandruì when she'd entered womanhood. Perhaps then, he'd understand.

But she couldn't reveal the truth to him, for that would break the greatest oath of all—one of secrecy.

"It's not just that we are on different sides," she admitted then. "I made promises ... and I must keep them."

Their gazes remained fused, silence stretching out between them. The disappointment on Hugh's face pained her, yet she sought to wall herself off from it. This had to be done.

"You are a woman with so many secrets," he said finally, bitterness lacing his voice. "I don't really know you at all, do I, Nessa?"

Her pulse quickened. "Aye, ye do," she whispered. She drew in another deep, shuddering breath. "In amongst all the lies I told ye ... there were also many truths."

Hugh stared at her before shaking his head. Long moments passed, and then his gaze veiled. His shields were going back up.

"I was a fool," he said, his voice roughening, "to fall for a woman who shrouds herself in mystery like you do ... but it can't be undone. The offer still stands though. If you wish it, you will always have a place by my side."

Hugh stepped back, widening the gulf between them, and raked a hand through his short hair. The gesture left it in spiky disarray. Nessa ached with the need to reach out and smooth it.

But she couldn't, she wouldn't. Not now.

"Well ... since our fates have been decided, there's no point in prolonging this," he muttered. "I'm leaving at dawn tomorrow ... and I suggest you do the same." He paused then, his gaze shadowing. "Go back to your outlaws, Nessa, and continue your cause ... I'll pretend I know nothing about it."

It was a strange, silent evening.

Thomas reacted badly to the news that the king had released Hugh from service, but after a few stern words from the knight, the lad slunk off to make sure the horses would be ready for the morning's departure.

Supper was tough, boiled mutton with coarse bread. Food supplies were running low in the camp; the king had called for provisions from across the border, yet they would need to make their dwindling reserves last until then. *A good time to leave*, Nessa thought dryly.

Thomas returned from ensuring that all the tack was ready. His usually cheerful face was drawn, and his blue eyes red-rimmed. Nessa realized the lad had been weeping.

The knight himself said little. Hugh's expression was inscrutable over supper, and he ate in silence, preferring to keep his own counsel rather than talk to Nessa or Thomas.

Nessa wasn't offended; he was trying to prepare himself for the morning in the only way he knew how. Even so, she felt wretched and was barely able to force down more than two mouthfuls. A boulder now sat on her chest.

After the meal, they readied their bags for departure. Thomas tried to insist that Hugh let him do all the packing, yet the knight barked at him to stop fussing like a mother hen.

Nessa understood. He wanted to keep busy this evening. They all did.

They retired to their beds early, a tense silence settling over the interior of the pavilion. Unable to sleep, Nessa lay upon her sheepskin, staring at the poles that held up the roof of the canopied tent.

Her churning mind drove sleep away.

Hugh lay just a few feet distant, and she could tell by the shallowness of his breathing that he too couldn't rest. Only Thomas—who could sleep through anything—slumbered, his gentle snores filling the tent and shattering the ponderous quiet.

Finally, Nessa could bear it no longer.

This was her last evening in the presence of the man she loved. Aye, even though she hadn't actually said the words, she did love him. She couldn't undo her decision, and she couldn't change who she was. But she also couldn't lie there, letting them both pass the night alone.

And so, she cast off her blankets and padded over to Hugh's bed.

Hearing her approach, he turned, his handsome face caressed by the ruddy glow of the brazier a few feet away.

Their gazes met, understanding passing between them. And then he shifted sideways, lifting the covers so that she could slide into the bed next to him. Nessa climbed in, relaxing as the warmth of his body enveloped her.

Wordlessly, Hugh put his arm around Nessa, allowing her to snuggle against the hollow of his left shoulder. His healing wounds were to the right thigh and back, so she didn't risk hurting him if they lay together like this.

Nessa wrapped her arm around his chest, squeezing her eyes shut. Tears burned against her eyelids, and she tensed her jaw as she fought them.

Of course, holding him like this made their upcoming separation even harder to bear. She could feel the strong and steady beat of his heart, and every time she inhaled, the masculine spice of his skin filled her lungs. His arm around her could have fooled her into believing that everything would be all right.

But it wouldn't.

Unspeaking, they lay together, held fast in each other arms.

31

OUR PATH LIES TO THE NORTH

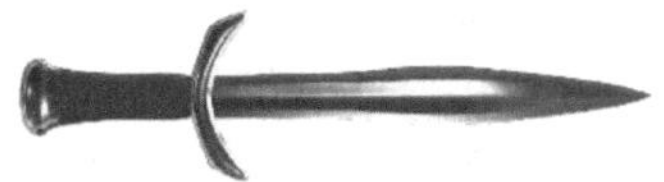

HUGH AWOKE IN the early hours of the morning.

Lying there, listening to the light rain that pattered against the roof of the pavilion, he soaked in the feeling of Nessa's soft, warm body curled against his.

If he could imprint one memory of her on his mind forever, it would be this.

He didn't want the night to end, for the treacherous sun to rise. For when it did, time would march on, and Nessa would leave him.

Even now, his belly still ached from the disappointment of her rejection. He knew he could be arrogant at times, yet even he hadn't assumed she'd swoon at his feet at his proposal. Nessa was too fiercely independent, too resolutely *Scot* to do that.

But he hadn't expected her to refuse him so adamantly.

It had stung.

Nessa had hidden many things from him—and still held her secrets close to her chest—yet he no longer cared. He only wanted her. He didn't care about anything else.

Nessa sighed in her sleep then, murmuring something unintelligible before snuggling closer to him. Hugh lowered his face to her hair, breathing in the scent of rosemary—a scent that he would forever associate with this woman. Her hair tickled his nose, yet he remained like that a while, inhaling the perfume of her.

He still wasn't in a fit state to swive a woman, and Thomas lay snoring on the floor just a few feet away, otherwise, he'd have been unable to resist the temptation of her lush body.

But tonight wasn't about giving in to lust, about slaking the need that burned like a fever in his veins. The past weeks had been sweet torture. Once his anger at her had dimmed, desire had taken its place. He'd tried his utmost to quash it, but every time he'd looked Nessa's way over the past weeks, he'd drunk her in, the memories of what they'd shared in Dunfermline tormenting him. And then, that day when she'd massaged his shoulder, he'd been unable to bear it any longer. He'd hauled her onto his lap and kissed her—and would have done much more if his squire hadn't interrupted them.

Hugh's throat thickened then, and he squeezed his eyes shut. Nessa's breathing feathered across his chest; he could feel it through the thin material of his tunic.

But after tonight, he'd never do so again.

Life's a cruel bitch. The day before, it had kicked him in the cods twice—as if it wished to teach him humility. Despite his loveless marriage, fortune had largely shone on Hugh de Burgh. He'd survived countless battles and never known the agony of wanting someone he could never have. Until now.

"That's the last of the bags, Sir Hugh," Thomas announced, his voice listless this morning.

"Good," Hugh replied, his tone clipped. "It's time we were off then."

Nessa's belly cramped at these words. The night had flown, and now the moment she'd been dreading was upon them.

The three of them stood with their horses in the enclosure behind the inner perimeter.

Hugh had just returned from saying farewell to the king and queen. His expression was stern when he entered the enclosure to find Thomas strapping on the last of their bags. Likewise, Nessa had saddled Honey and secured her two leather bags behind the saddle.

The time to say goodbye had arrived.

Dawn was breaking, lavender and gold painting the eastern sky. Around them, the English camp was readying itself to begin the siege anew. Men moved about, their voices rumbling over the sea of tents. Nessa could also see helmeted and armored figures moving around on the castle ramparts.

Stirling's defenses still held.

For an instant, Nessa forgot her sadness at leaving Hugh. Thomas had admitted to her earlier that the siege was proving much more onerous than the English had expected. Now, supplies were getting low—and unless The Hammer received more provisions and reinforcements from across the border, he wouldn't be taking Stirling.

Her gaze lingered upon the castle walls, determination gathering within her. *Keep fighting, Fyfa. More of our allies will rally to yer side.*

Feeling Hugh's gaze upon her, Nessa glanced away from the fortress.

Dressed in his heavy hauberk and armor and blood-red surcoat, a dark plum cloak rippling from his broad shoulders, he was a formidable sight.

"Ready?" he asked, his gaze searching her face.

Nessa nodded.

Their gazes held then, and she let herself remember what it had felt like the night before, to lie in his arms, to listen to the thunder of his heart. She wanted to keep hold of those memories, yet they would fade—and one day, she'd forget the details of his face, the exact shade of his eyes, and the velvet timbre of his voice.

It felt hard to breathe when she thought of it. This was too raw, so much harder than she'd ever thought leaving would be.

The moment drew out, and nearby, Thomas shifted uncomfortably. Nessa could feel his gaze upon them, flicking between their faces. No doubt he was wondering at the delay.

A crowd had also started to gather, as soldiers readied themselves to say farewell to the man who'd commanded them for the past years.

But Hugh and Nessa continued to stare at each other.

"Come here, Nessa," he said, his tone roughening.

Nessa did as bid, moving from Honey and crossing to him. However, as she drew near, her step faltered and she halted.

Hugh bridged the distance between them, reaching out and hauling her into his arms.

Crushed against his chest, bent over the iron strength of his arm, Nessa raised her face to his. Hugh's mouth covered hers, his tongue delving between her parted lips for a deep, passionate kiss that had the men nearby whistling and cat-calling.

The knight paid none of them any mind. Instead, he continued to kiss Nessa as if they were alone. Reaching up, Nessa wrapped her arms around his neck, returning the embrace with equal fervor.

The taste of his mouth, the slide of his tongue against hers, the rasp of his shaven chin—she imprinted all of it onto her soul.

It was a kiss that spanned the gulf between them, between two different worlds. The Scottish witch and the English knight were never meant to be, yet that wouldn't stop either of them from kissing as if their lives depended upon it.

They were both out of breath when they broke apart.

Hugh's eyes gleamed. "I'll never forget you, lass," he said huskily. "And if you ever change your mind, Grosmont Castle awaits."

Blinking back tears, Nessa managed a nod. She couldn't speak; if she did, she'd start weeping. She was aware then that they'd amassed quite an audience now.

Dignity was the only thing she had left.

They mounted their horses: Hugh upon Ajax, Nessa upon Honey, and Thomas upon a shaggy cob weighed down with saddlebags. In single file, Hugh leading, followed by Thomas, with Nessa bringing up the rear, they rode out of the enclosure and down the path that led out of the camp.

Hugh's comrades were there to see them off.

One of them, a big, heavily-muscled knight with a bald head, raised a hand as Hugh passed.

"Stay well, Nicholas," Hugh said, raising a hand in farewell. "And try not to catch the pox."

The knight barked a laugh. "And a safe journey home to you," he replied. His gaze then shifted to Nessa, his dark eyes curious. "To *all* of you."

They rode down the avenue of men. The knights and men-at-arms all formed a column, and many of them raised a hand to Hugh as he passed, while others slapped a fisted hand over their heart.

On the way toward the gates, Nessa spied another figure in the crowd—one she'd done her best to avoid over the past fortnight.

A woman wearing a fine silver-blue cotehardie that matched her eyes stood behind the ranks of soldiers, silently looking on. Lamia Delamare watched her intently.

Nessa stared back—a silent challenge passing between them. Foreboding prickled her skin. She had the uncanny feeling that the Guardians of Alba hadn't seen the last of Lamia.

Something else caught her eye then. Gold glinted in the first rays of the morning sun—and it was then that Nessa spied a couple standing back from the crowd.

The Hammer had come to see his commander off. He stood with an arm draped around the shoulders of his queen, his expression veiled. Hugh had already said his farewell to the king and queen, yet they'd ventured out to see him leave nonetheless.

Hugh looked to the king then and raised a hand to him.

The men's gazes fused, and then The Hammer smiled.

Nessa glanced away, her belly tightening. She now saw Edward of England as a man, and not merely as a symbol of oppression. However, that didn't mean she liked him any better for it.

The trio rode on, passing through the gates and taking the road that would bring them to the River Forth and the great stone bridge that spanned it. The English and the Scots had fought here, a few years earlier—a battle that had ended in a resounding English defeat. William Wallace had been the hero of that victory, yet so much had happened since that it seemed a lifetime ago now.

Hooves clattering on stone, the three horses crossed the bridge and reached the other side. Here, the road forked: one path leading south, and the other north.

Hugh reined in Ajax. The destrier snorted, tossing his head. The stallion was impatient to be off, as was Thomas's cob. The squire's horse jogged on the spot.

Nessa's attention settled upon the squire. "All the best, Thomas," she said, noting the brittle edge to her voice. "I'm sure you shall make a fine knight one day."

The lad's cheeks reddened. "It was a pleasure to know you, Nessa," he mumbled through his embarrassment.

Nessa smiled back. She then shifted her attention to Hugh.

"A safe journey to you," Hugh spoke up, his lips lifting at the corners. However, his eyes were solemn. He then spoke in Gaelic. "May life treat you well, Nessa."

"And ye, Hugh de Burgh," she whispered back in the same tongue. Her heart suddenly felt as if it were lodged in her throat.

She watched, as the knight and his squire turned their horses south and urged them into a canter, away from Stirling.

Honey issued a shrill whinny after them, pulling at the bit to follow. Nessa held her back before reaching down and stroking the mare's neck, soothing her. "No, lass," she murmured. "Our path lies to the north."

32

GOING HOME

Grosmont Castle
The Welsh Borders

Two weeks later ...

THE SIGHT OF his home on the southern horizon made a smile curve Hugh's lips—the first real smile in a while.

They'd been riding through woodland when the trees drew back. And there, perched atop a velvet-green hill, with the shadowy mountains behind, Grosmont called to him. The scent of wood smoke and crushed grass reached them, carried on a warm afternoon breeze.

"It's been too long," he murmured, voicing his thoughts aloud. "I should have come home earlier."

Next to him, Thomas cast the knight a surprised look. No doubt the squire had heard the longing in Hugh's voice, the regret.

"But I thought you liked campaigning?" Thomas asked.

Hugh huffed a laugh. "Aye ... too much." His gaze returned to the stone walls that seemed gold-hued in the afternoon sun. "But I neglected things ... I forgot where I'm from."

With that, he urged Ajax on, taking the road through the village below the castle, and up the rounded hill—indeed, the castle's name meant 'big hill' in French—to where the drawbridge had been lowered over a deep moat.

The sight of Grosmont's towers made Hugh's skin prickle. The fortress was one of the 'Three Castles of Gwent' that had been built by the Normans three centuries earlier to control the Welsh border. It was formidable.

The gatehouse loomed over the two riders as they clattered across the drawbridge and into the bailey beyond. Geese scattered, honking when Hugh and Thomas pulled their horses up.

They'd dismounted, and were about to lead their mounts into the stables, when a tall, broad-shouldered figure emerged from the keep.

Kit de Burgh strode toward them, his light-brown hair ruffling in the breeze.

"Christ's teeth!" His younger's brother's face was alight with joy. "Hugh! Is that you?"

Hugh grinned. "Aye, little brother ... I'm certainly not a wraith returned to haunt you."

He stepped forward then and hugged Kit. The pair had been born four years apart and spent most of their adult lives living separately, yet when Hugh drew back, he saw Kit's hazel eyes shone with tears.

Kit had always been the more emotional of the two of them.

Even so, Hugh's throat thickened, and he cleared it. "I've missed you, Kit." He slapped him on the shoulder then. "I received your last letter during the winter ... you are wed?"

Kit grinned. "Aye." He glanced back then, at where a small woman descended the steps from the keep. "Emily has finally tamed me."

Hugh raised his eyebrows, taking in his sister-by-marriage as she approached. Emily's brown hair was braided, coiled about her crown, and covered with a fine net, as was the custom of wedded women south of the Scottish border. Noticing the style, Hugh's belly tensed. He recalled then Nessa's wild red-gold hair that tumbled over her shoulders.

Shoving aside the treacherous memory, Hugh marked then that the dove-grey cotehardie Emily wore revealed a swollen belly.

Smiling, he turned back to Kit. "I see other congratulations are in order."

His brother's grin now split his face. "Aye." He reached out then, drawing Emily into the circle of his arm. The young woman beamed up at her husband. She then glanced at Hugh before dropping her gaze demurely.

"Aren't you going to introduce me to our visitor, Kit?" she asked.

"Of course," Kit replied, winking at her. "Dearest, I'd like you to meet my brother, Hugh ... Lord of Grosmont."

Warmth suffused Hugh as he smiled at his brother's wife. Despite his own bruised heart, it pleased him to see Kit so happy.

At that moment, two more figures emerged from the keep and made their way down the stairs to the bailey. In the yard itself, other inhabitants of the castle—guards, servants, and retainers—had gathered, as word of Hugh's return drew them from their chores. But Hugh's gaze wasn't on them, but on the small boy who gripped his grandmother's hand.

Hugh's throat thickened. "Richard," he breathed.

He'd last set eyes on the child shortly after his birth. He'd raced home upon hearing that his wife wasn't faring well in the latter stages of her pregnancy. Anne had died by the time he'd reached her bedside, yet the small, squalling babe had survived. Hugh had departed once more from Grosmont just a few days later.

The child before him was a stranger, and yet he saw Anne in his face: her neat nose and flaxen hair. The lad's stubborn jaw and hazel eyes though belonged to Hugh.

"Aye," Kit murmured. "He's growing into a fine lad, although he's almost as bull-headed as you."

Hugh swallowed, his throat aching. Richard was approaching four now and was already tall for his age. Hugh had missed so much of his growth—precious years that could never be taken back.

Leaving Kit and Emily's side, Hugh went to his mother and son.

And when he met his mother's eye, Hugh's chest constricted. She looked older, tired. Aye, he'd been away from Grosmont for far too long. "Greetings, mother," he said, his voice roughening.

Isabeau de Burgh stepped forward, before reaching out, taking one of her son's hands, and squeezing gently. "It's good to have you home, Hugh," she said, her voice catching. She then released her grandson's hand and smiled down at him. "Greet your father, Richard."

The lad's gaze widened while he gazed up at Hugh. "Are you really a brave knight?" he asked.

Something deep within Hugh twisted, and the back of his eyes burned. Struggling to remain composed, he hunkered down so that his gaze was level with his son's. "Aye," he replied, his voice catching. "And I've finally returned to you, lad."

Wailing Widow Falls
Assynt, Scotland

Nessa was lying on her cot, staring at the wall, when Breanna entered her alcove.

Her sister halted in the doorway, letting the hanging fall shut behind her before she issued a huff of irritation. "Are ye planning on rising from yer bed today?"

"Aye," Nessa muttered, pulling the blankets up around her chin. "Just not yet."

Breanna snorted. "The sun is high in the sky." She then pulled up a stool and settled down on it. "Ye aren't usually so lazy."

Nessa snorted, tearing her attention from the pitted stone to her sister. She adored Breanna, yet sometimes her blunt tongue was vexing. Nessa had been back with the Guardians nearly a week now, and a strange lethargy had come upon her. She'd been finding it increasingly hard to rise from her pallet in the mornings.

Breanna had clearly grown tired of her sluggishness.

Arms crossed over her breasts, her strong-featured face set, Breanna's dark eyes bored into her. "When are ye going to talk to me?" she asked, her brows drawing together. "The others are starting to think ye are ill."

Nessa rolled over on her back. "I'm perfectly well, thank ye … I just need a little time to myself."

Ignoring her assertion, Breanna moved forward and placed a hand on Nessa's brow. "Ye aren't fevered." She settled back on her stool and made an impatient noise in the back of her throat. "It's *him*, isn't it … that *Englishman*?"

Nessa's jaw tightened. It was clear from Breanna's frown and the inflection in her voice what opinion she held on Hugh de Burgh. She'd never met the man, yet the fact he was English was enough for her to mutter a curse whenever he was mentioned.

Fortunately, Nessa had said very little about him.

Upon her arrival at the Falls, she'd settled down before one of the hearths, while Colina and her sisters gathered around, and told them of the events that had occurred after she'd last left them. She'd kept her story emotionless, factual, and yet the rasp to her voice, when she'd spoken of Hugh, had likely given her away.

She'd seen the way Colina's face changed, her features tightening, her usually distant gaze sharpening. Nessa had also seen the surprise, the disgust, on some of the faces of her sisters—including Breanna's.

They didn't understand—and she didn't blame them. No doubt, Breanna was readying herself to give Nessa a tongue-lashing about her taste in men.

Nessa's jaw tightened further. She wasn't herself at the moment, yet she would bite back if Breanna started hectoring her. "Leave it, Bree," she said, injecting a warning note into her voice. "I don't want to speak of him."

Breanna scowled. "So, it's as I thought. Ye have gone and fallen in love with one of the enemy."

Nessa sat up, pushing the blankets aside. "Have ye got porridge in yer ears? I said I didn't—"

"Ye can't lie here moping forever," Breanna shot back, cutting her off. "The news ye brought means that we need to be more vigilant than ever. That witch, Lamia, knows of the Guardians ... and that means she could jeopardize our cause."

"I'm aware of that," Nessa replied through gritted teeth. "Why else do ye think I rode back here as if The Hammer himself were after me?"

And she had. However, she'd also traveled back to Assynt in a daze, hardly noticing the glens, valleys, and forests she'd ridden through. She'd left her heart behind her, and with each furlong she journeyed north, the emptier she felt.

A hole had been carved out of her chest, and even when she'd returned to her home under the waterfalls, a place she'd always felt safe and sheltered, the yawning sense of loss didn't ease.

Nessa couldn't go on this way. The night before, she'd lain awake, staring up into the darkness, mulling over her situation. Something had to be done. She just wasn't sure exactly what.

"Then why aren't ye up and about ... and helping to do something about it?" Breanna demanded.

Nessa spat a curse before rising to her feet and reaching for her kirtle.

"Where are ye going?" Breanna asked, her dark brows drawing together.

"Anywhere ... as long as I don't have to suffer yer bladelike tongue a moment longer."

Nessa pulled on her kirtle, and was lacing her bodice, when she felt Breanna's gaze boring into her. Glancing up, she saw her sister's proud features had softened.

"Believe it or not, I didn't come in here to berate ye." Breanna's peat-brown eyes shadowed. "I've missed ye of late ... and Fyfa too ... I just want things to go back to how they were."

Nessa held her gaze. "We were inseparable once, weren't we?" she murmured. "Three fierce young bandruì ready to take on the world." She paused then. "Well, ye and Fyfa were always fierce … I was perhaps less so."

Breanna favored her with a wry smile. "Ye are a healer … ye have to be softer than us." She rose to her feet then, dusting off her blue skirts. "Come on … there's some fresh bannock on the griddle if ye want some."

Nessa sighed. Her appetite had been off ever since her return. Food had lost its taste of late. And it would remain so until she faced things. "Aye, in a wee bit," she replied. "But first, I must speak with our mother."

33

YER HEART CALLS YE

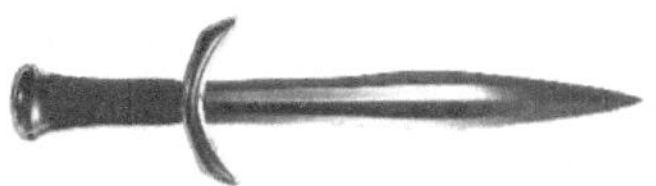

NESSA FOUND THE High Bandruì upon a ledge, halfway up the rock-face.

She'd climbed a rope ladder inside the cavern and then crawled out onto the damp ledge to find Colina already seated, her back up against the mossy rock, her farsighted gaze unfocused. For once, her familiar wasn't with her. The Wailing Widow, a frothing column of water, fell just a few feet away, sending a misty cloud of water over the ledge. Droplets settled over Nessa's face as she crawled over to Colina and settled down next to her.

This ledge was the High Bandruì's special place—one of the few spots that allowed her quiet, meditative time away from the rest of the order.

Few others joined her up here, but this morning Nessa had intruded upon her peace.

Seated there, Nessa breathed in the fresh, rich air that the waterfall created. The ledge afforded them a lofty view across the stony, wooded gorge. Looking on at the unchanging scene, it was hard to believe that, to the south, the English were still laying siege to Stirling Castle.

At the Wailing Widow Falls, the world seemed to stand still.

"Ye aren't yerself these days, Nessa," Colina greeted her with disarming bluntness. Her voice was gentle, as always, yet there was a strained edge to it.

Nessa's throat tightened. Was the High Bandruì disappointed in her?

"Aye, I'm sorry about that," Nessa replied, cursing the sudden huskiness in her voice. "It just that things ... have caught up with me." She broke off then, wishing she had the courage to speak her mind—to voice the conflict within her. However, she held her tongue. Once again, fear had her in a stranglehold. Letting go of this life seemed impossible.

Likewise, Colina lapsed into silence. Watching the older woman's face, and the lines of care upon it, Nessa wondered what the High Bandruì was thinking. She was wise and kind, and yet in many ways an enigma—even after all these years.

"Things do catch up with us," Colina murmured. "Eventually."

Nessa didn't reply, wondering at the comment, and the brittle edge to her leader's voice.

Colina looked at her then, her gaze suddenly sharper than it had been in years. When Nessa had been a bairn, the druidess who had mothered her had managed well despite her poor vision. But with the passing of the years, her shortsightedness had worsened.

Yet this morning, as their gazes met, it was as if Colina could once again see as clearly as she had in her younger years.

"Sometimes I think I failed ye, Nessa," the High Bandruì said, reaching out and taking her hands in hers, squeezing gently.

Nessa's eyes prickled, tears threatening. "No," she whispered back. "Never."

Colina's throat bobbed before she shook her head. "I've only ever been proud of ye," she whispered. "When I found ye all those years ago, chilled to the marrow in the woods, wrapped up in nothing but a sheepskin, ye gazed up at me with such trust in yer eyes that I swore then and there that I'd protect ye as if ye were my own." The High Bandruì's gaze glistened. "Ye were such a happy bairn ... so full of curiosity and gentleness ... I knew early on that ye would be one to follow the healing arts." Colina broke off there, her fingers squeezing tighter. "The three of ye all came to me in the space of one cold spring ... and I knew that ye'd all have a role to play in the fight that was coming ... a fight I'd seen in my visions."

Nessa listened silently. She knew of Colina's premonitions; she recalled the High Bandruì speaking of them when she was a bairn.

The English would come.

The Scots would rally against them.

A freedom fighter who'd lost his woman to the enemy would raise an army against them.

And Colina had been right. The English had indeed crossed Hadrian's Wall and marched upon Scottish soil—and William Wallace, whose love, Marion Bradfute, died at English hands, had led an uprising.

Colina was indeed skilled at divination.

"Ye see ... I knew that ye would lose yer heart to an Englishman, if I sent ye to Dunfermline," the High Bandruì continued.

Nessa's breathing caught, her gaze widening. "Ye *knew* that would happen?"

Colina nodded.

Nessa's belly contracted. "Couldn't ye have sent someone else?"

"No one else could have done the job as well as ye, Nessa ... perhaps Fyfa, but she has a vital role at Stirling Castle." Colina paused there. "Breanna is too quick-tempered, and none of the others have yer patience, yer skills with potions and earth and moon workings—and yer independence."

Nessa's pulse now beat in her ears. "So ye sent me anyway."

A nerve fluttered in one of the High Bandruì's eyelids. "Aye ... the cause came first."

Nessa held her gaze. She didn't know how to respond. She was angry with the High Bandruì, and yet she also took responsibility for her own decisions. Colina might have caught a glimpse at the future, yet Nessa had agreed to the mission, and no one had forced her to let Hugh de Burgh into her heart.

"I think," Colina said finally, shattering the silence between them, "that the time has come for ye to leave us."

Nessa's lips parted, a gasp rushing out of her. Although she'd been wrestling with that very decision, her mother's words shocked her all the same. "What?"

Colina's grip tightened, to the point where it was almost bruising. "I don't say this lightly, lass ... I say it because I know in my gut that to keep ye with us would only bring ye sorrow."

"But—"

"Ye have given yer life to this order, but it's time now to pass the torch to another." Colina released one of her hands, raising her own as Nessa once again attempted to interrupt her. "Some of the young ones are developing strong healing skills. They will take yer place in that role."

Nessa swallowed hard. Once again, conflict twisted within her. In her heart, she wished to go, yet the part of her that clung to the safe and familiar rebelled. She felt like a baby bird, about to be shoved from the nest. "Am I that easily replaced?"

Colina shook her head, her eyes glittering. "No ... ye are the daughter I always wanted, Nessa. *No one* can ever replace ye."

Nessa stared back at the High Bandruì. Her candid words robbed her of any response. She knew Colina was fond of her, yet she'd never realized just how deep her feelings ran. Nessa's eyelids now burned, and a tear slid free, rolling down her cheek.

"I only ever saw ye as my mother," she whispered. "I have only ever wanted to do ye proud."

Tears now wet Colina's cheeks too. "And ye have," she said, her voice husky. "Thanks to ye, we had advance warning of the siege upon Stirling. We were able to furnish them with extra supplies, and a number of our allies have ridden south to help defend the castle ... they continue to harry the English as we speak. And now we know a witch resides within the English camp. These details are vital to us ... if ye did nothing more for the rest of yer life, these deeds would be enough. We still don't know where the threat to Robert Bruce will originate from ... but at least we are forewarned."

A beat of silence passed between them before Nessa replied. "Hugh de Burgh has my heart, mother."

The High Bandruì's mouth quirked. "Aye, lass ... I release ye from the oaths ye swore to this order. I give ye the freedom to leave us ... to ride south and wed the man ye love."

Nessa stared back at her. "I'm afraid," she whispered. "What if I don't fit in anywhere but here?"

Colina shook her head, her smile widening. "Ye are a survivor, my daughter ... ye would fit in *anywhere*. Yer heart is calling ye ... and ye would be wise to answer it."

Grosmont Castle
The Welsh Borders

"Something is amiss with you, brother," Kit observed as he eyed Hugh over the rim of his goblet. "Yet I can't put my finger on exactly what it is."

Hugh snorted, even if tension rippled through him at Kit's words.

His brother was far too perceptive.

"Nothing's wrong," he replied, frowning. "I'm just getting used to my old life ... that's all."

Kit nodded, although his gaze didn't change. "I imagine it must be a change from leading the king's army," he admitted. "And I'd expect you to feel a bit restless here ... but it's not that. You've always been a surly bastard, yet you hardly speak these days. Just now, I caught you staring off into the distance like you were hundreds of leagues away." Kit paused then, letting his observations sink in. "What happened in Scotland?"

Hugh muttered an oath under his breath, before reaching for the ewer of wine, and topping up his pewter goblet. The brothers sat in the solar, upon the first floor of the keep. Just over a week had passed since his return to Grosmont, and after supper, the brothers had settled before the hearth to share a goblet of wine and talk over the running of Hugh's lands.

So many years had passed since Hugh had managed them himself, he needed his brother to update him.

However, Kit wasn't interested in telling him about their last harvest, their tenants, or the taxes they collected for the king. Instead, he wanted to know about things that Hugh didn't wish to discuss.

"Nothing happened."

"Aye, it did. Why are ye so tight-lipped about it?" Kit held his eye, his own expression stubborn. Moments passed as their stare drew out, and then Kit's eyes widened, understanding dawning. "It's a woman, isn't it?"

Hugh couldn't help it, he flinched—and victory flared in Kit's eyes. "I knew it!"

"Shut your beak," Hugh growled, taking a gulp of wine. "I don't want to discuss it."

Kit reclined in the high-backed chair, nursing his goblet of wine as he viewed his brother with a hooded gaze. "A Scotswoman too, I'd wager."

Hugh heaved in a deep breath, fighting his rising temper. Kit was never one to leave a subject alone. However, short of shoving his brother's teeth down his throat, he wasn't going to shut him up this evening.

"All right," he muttered. "There was a woman ... but it's over."

Kit watched him, taking this in. "And was she a Scot?"

Hugh nodded, fighting the images of Nessa that crept in, tormenting him. Her smile, both knowing and innocent, her sharp green eyes, and the soft lilt of her voice. He missed her with an ache under his ribcage that only seemed to grow with each passing day.

Kit gave a rueful shake of his head. "Well, that was an unfortunate choice, wasn't it?"

Hugh snorted before taking another deep draft of wine. It was—and yet despite that Nessa could never be his, he didn't regret knowing her. Before Nessa, he'd cared about little save the glory of England. His loyalty to Edward had narrowed his world to the point where he sometimes forgot who he really was, and what he'd left behind. His empty marriage had been his own doing, and Nessa had made him realize that he didn't want to die alone on a battlefield.

Glory was a cold mistress.

Aye, he missed Nessa with every waking breath, yet he was thankful to her too. She'd taught him what was truly important.

34

THE RIGHT CHOICE

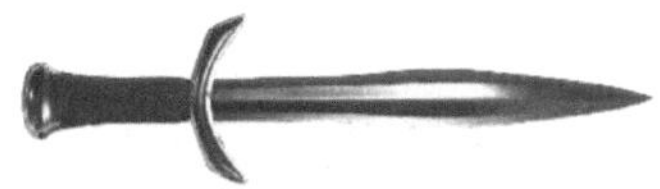

NESSA LEFT THE Wailing Widow Falls on a bright late-spring morning.

She urged Honey through the gap she'd forged in the wall of water, the garron's hooves crunching over wet stones.

She didn't look back, even as she felt the weight of her sisters' gazes upon her.

Breanna was among them.

They'd hugged, and when Breanna had pulled back, her cheeks were wet with tears. Few words were spoken, for the night before, the pair of them had argued. Breanna had eventually broken down, her outrage merely a shield for her grief at losing Nessa.

They'd talked then, and Nessa had fully explained her decision. She wasn't sure if her sister truly understood, yet Breanna had ceased railing at her. Instead, she'd turned her anger upon the High Bandruì for colluding with her.

"How could she send ye away?" Breanna had demanded, her eyes red-rimmed, her cheeks flushed. "We are kin!"

"She isn't. This is my choice."

"But ye wouldn't be going if she didn't allow it."

"Our mother understands us, Bree," Nessa had replied, taking her sister's hands and squeezing them gently. "Better than we do ourselves."

Colina stood among the others this morning too. She'd enfolded Nessa in one last hug, and the grief that had welled up within Nessa had almost made her want to stay.

These women were her kin.

But it was time to leave her family now, to embrace a future outside the order. She could hardly imagine such a life, for the Guardians had been her world.

Yet Colina's words had freed her. She had to follow her heart.

Honey jumped up onto the mossy bank of the burn, and Nessa reined her around, watching as the waterfall closed behind her, sealing the others inside. She was now alone, with the dawn chorus and the gentle rumble of the cascade.

"Goodbye," Nessa whispered, her voice catching. "I will never forget ye all."

It hurt to leave those she loved, yet it would have hurt her more to stay.

Swallowing to ease the tightness in her throat, even as her belly fluttered with excitement and trepidation at what lay ahead, Nessa turned away from the Wailing Widow Falls.

She then gathered the reins and urged her garron south, toward her destiny.

A month later, Nessa rode through the woodland that lay just north of Grosmont Castle.

Jittery with nerves, she strained her gaze into the distance, hoping to make out the castle walls. However, she wasn't yet close enough. It was hard to believe that, after weeks of travel, her destination—and the man she loved—were just out of sight.

It hardly seems real.

An overcast day pressed down upon her, and she breathed in air that was heavy with the promise of rain. Nessa was sweating under her new chemise and cotehardie. She'd bought the garments, along with knee-high hose, which felt strange against her skin, in the town of York on the way south.

As she'd walked amongst the narrow, cobbled streets, she'd been keenly aware that Englishwomen dressed differently to their Scottish counterparts. Obviously, there were no plaid shawls, but many women wore bell-sleeved robes over their kirtles. They also dressed their hair differently. Nessa was used to letting her long red-gold hair flow loose down her back, yet she soon noted that in England only unwed maidens seemed to wear their hair thus.

At thirty, Nessa could no longer call herself a maiden, and she'd noticed the stares she attracted in her travel-stained blue kirtle and unruly hair.

As such, she now wore her hair in a neat bun at the base of her neck. She'd then covered the bun with a delicate veil, as she'd seen Englishwomen do. She'd also shed her beloved blue robes for a moss-green cotehardie over a slightly darker green kirtle. Around her hips, she'd cinched a heavy belt.

Despite the warm day, she wore a light woolen traveling cloak, with the hood pulled up. Resisting the urge to shove the hood back, Nessa slowed Honey to a trot, her gaze scanning the roadside. She'd attracted a lot of unwelcome attention over the last month, something that had turned her wary.

A woman traveling alone was always at risk, even in Scotland. However, the farther south she'd ridden, the more trouble seemed to cross her path. She'd had to threaten a drunk with her dirk in an inn just north of Hadrian's Wall, and had been forced to use witching when a group of outlaws chased her two days later. In York, she'd narrowly missed being robbed by a cutpurse. Colina had gifted her a small purse of silver pennies, and the lad had nearly run off with it.

Unfortunately for him, she'd cast a jinx on him as he fled, and the urchin had sprawled on the cobbles.

Nessa had managed to get this far unscathed, yet, even so, the incidents had put her on edge.

The night before, she'd stayed in the village of Pontrilas, her last stop before Grosmont. The innkeeper had kindly provided her with a steaming iron tub of water, and she'd been able to bathe properly for the first time since leaving the Highlands.

She didn't want to arrive at Grosmont coated in grime and sweat.

What if Hugh has changed his mind about me?

Nessa clenched her jaw. The thought had surfaced periodically during the journey south, although as her destination approached, it now niggled at her.

Goose, she chided herself. *The man offered ye his heart and a place at his side. He won't spurn ye.*

But even so, the nervousness lingered, fluttering in her belly like a cluster of moths.

She'd taken great care with her appearance that morning and set off from Pontrilas shortly after dawn, crossing Afon Mynwg, the river that locals said formed the border between England and Wales.

Pushing aside her worries, Nessa peered ahead. The trees seemed to be drawing back. Indeed, moments later the woodland—oak, ash, and beech—fell away, and a great fortress with dun-colored walls rose before her, perched upon a green hill.

Nessa's breathing caught, and she slowed her pony to a walk. "Look at that, Honey," she breathed. "It's even grander than I'd imagined."

Indeed, Grosmont was quite a sight. It commanded over the lands below it, two crenelated towers outlined against the dull sky.

Suddenly, despite the care she'd taken with her appearance, and the new garments she'd bought for her arrival, Nessa felt shabby and out-of-place. What if Hugh had returned home and deliberately cast her from his mind? What if he'd eventually concluded she wasn't the right woman for him?

"Stop it," Nessa muttered to herself. "Ye'll find out soon enough."

She'd come this far, braved letches, bandits, and thieves to reach Grosmont—she'd not let her own fears hold her back. Not any longer.

Drawing in a resolute breath, she rode on, through the village of squat stone cottages with thatched roofs. Locals stopped work in the fields to watch her pass. Honey plodded dutifully on, her furry ears flicking back and forth at the sound of a donkey braying nearby. The garron snorted; she wasn't fond of donkeys.

On they rode, up the hill and to the lowered drawbridge. A wide, deep moat, full of still, dark water surrounded the castle. It was a reminder that this fortress sat on lands that had once belonged to the Welsh—it sat on the frontier and would always have to weather assaults.

Honey clip-clopped across the drawbridge, and they passed under the portcullis and the gatehouse, under the watchful eye of guards above. Two more men in hauberks and helms stepped out to bar her way into the inner ward.

Nessa drew up her pony, pushing back her stifling hood.

Finally, she'd arrived.

"Sir Hugh … you've got a visitor."

Hugh glanced up from where he'd been checking the steward's ledger against the stocks in the granary. Frowning, his gaze alighted upon the guard who now stood framed in the doorway.

"Aye, who?" Hugh wasn't in the best of moods this afternoon. His right thigh, although it had healed well, was aching—the result of him being on his feet all day. This task, which he'd thought would be brief, had turned out to be a laborious one. The steward, his aging uncle, had miscounted most items.

"A woman," the guard replied, his gaze gleaming with unabashed curiosity. "A Scot."

A jolt arrowed through Hugh. Wordlessly, he passed the ledger to the servant who'd been helping him with the inventory. He then left the granary, stepping out into the grey afternoon.

Kit was still there, helping to shoe horses, as he'd been earlier when Hugh had entered the granary. However, his brother and the farrier had ceased their work.

Instead, their gazes were trained on the woman upon a shaggy dun pony, who waited, flanked by his men just inside the gates.

Hugh's breathing stopped. For a moment, he merely stood there, unable to believe his eyes.

The woman, tall and curvaceous, sat proudly upon the saddle. He barely recognized her, dressed in a fine cotehardie, her lustrous hair netted and tied back in a prim bun. Green suited her, yet he'd only ever seen her in blue.

Hugh stepped forward. "Nessa?"

She favored him with a smile then, a knowing expression with a slightly mischievous edge, and Hugh's heart bucked against his ribs.

Christ's bones ... it's really her.

Nessa swung down from the saddle, allowing one of the guards to take the reins of her faithful garron. Then she moved toward Hugh.

"Hugh," Kit called from behind him, amusement lacing his voice. "Aren't you going to introduce us to your visitor?"

Hugh ignored his brother. He ignored everything except Nessa.

"You came," he said, a trifle stupidly. "I never thought you would."

Nessa's full mouth quirked once more, although her eyes were limpid, soulful. "Some things are too precious to cast aside," she said, her voice growing husky. "If ye will have me, Hugh de Burgh, I am yers."

A beat of silence passed while their gazes fused. Hugh was aware of Kit asking him something else, yet he didn't even recognize the words.

His pulse now thundered in his ears.

The shadow that had fallen over him since Stirling shifted then, gliding away and leaving hope in its place. Above Grosmont, the dull sky cleared: the cloak of grey parted, and the friendly face of the sun shone down upon them once more.

Slowly, Hugh smiled. "Aye," he murmured.

He moved forward then and scooped Nessa up in his arms.

She squealed in fright, clutching at him. "Hugh! What are ye doing? I'm not willow reed ... ye'll do yer back in."

"Silence, woman," he replied, turning his attention to the grinning guard who held Nessa's pony. "Look to my bride-to-be's mount." He then spun around, taking care to do so on his good leg, and cast his brother a wide grin.

Kit was staring at him as if he'd just taken leave of his wits, as was the bemused farrier.

"Send word to the village church, and bring Father Gregor to our chapel," Hugh told his brother. "There will be a wedding at dusk."

Kit nodded dumbly.

Not waiting for any further response, Hugh strode from the inner ward. His limp was still pronounced, and his right thigh protested at the extra weight, yet today he barely noticed.

Today nothing mattered except the woman in his arms—the woman he would soon make his wife.

35

MY WILD SCOTTISH LASS

"WHERE ARE WE going?" Nessa asked, clinging to Hugh as he entered the great hall, made his way past a group of stunned-looking servants, an older woman who bore an uncanny resemblance to Hugh, and a small brown-haired woman with a pregnant belly, and started up the stairs to the first floor of the rectangular keep.

"To my solar," he replied. "Away from prying eyes."

Excitement arched through Nessa, the sensation so strong that her breathing caught.

Hugh didn't need to say anything else. She knew what he intended.

Moments later, they were inside the solar. Richly woven mats covered the stone floor, and tapestries of hunting scenes hung from the pitted walls. A large hearth burned at one end of the generous space. At the other hung a heavy curtain, beyond which was, presumably, the lord of Grosmont's bed-chamber.

They didn't get that far.

Hugh let Nessa down, allowing her body to slide over his as he did so. And then he spun her around, pressing Nessa against the door as his mouth captured hers.

She drank him in, devouring his lips and his tongue with her own. The kiss was savage, hungry—a song of how much they'd both missed each other. Reaching up, Nessa wrapped her arms around his neck, as she'd done during their last kiss back at Stirling.

But then, they'd had an audience—and then the embrace had been tinged with sadness.

This time, she pulled him against her, reveling in the feel of his large, muscular body. His time away from the fighting, and the injuries he'd recovered from, hadn't weakened Hugh de Burgh at all.

She thrilled at his strength, his masculinity, at the possessive way his hands removed her cloak, tossed it aside, and then ran down the length of her back. Gripping her backside, he pulled her hips to his, grinding his arousal into her.

Wild need caught fire in the cradle of Nessa's belly.

How she craved him.

Back in Dunfermline, back when they'd hardly known each other at all, Hugh had been a leisurely lover, taking his time with her. But neither of them wanted that today.

This was a claiming, one that couldn't be delayed a moment longer.

Their clothing came off, the garments rippling to the floor, the rasp and pant of their breathing filling the solar.

And then when he'd stripped Nessa's clothing away, save for her hose, Hugh took a step back, his gaze raking over her. Likewise, Nessa drank him in, taking in the breadth of his chest, the whorls of crisp hair that covered it—angling down to his belly—and the erection that thrust toward her.

"Hades," Hugh ground out. "I've missed you."

Nessa flung herself at him, her mouth bruising his, her fingers splaying across his strong chest. Lust drove all coherent thought from her mind. She couldn't speak; she could only reach for him.

Hugh kissed her back, his hands reaching up to remove the veil from her hair and loose the bun.

Drawing back a moment to view her hair as it rippled down over her shoulders, his mouth curved. "That's better," he rasped. "That's how I remember my wild Scottish lass."

Nessa huffed a shaky laugh, her blood roaring in her ears. "I wanted to do ye proud, Hugh ... to appear before ye looking a little like a lady."

He snorted. "I don't need you to change, my love. I want you exactly as you are."

And with that, his mouth claimed hers once more.

Still kissing her, Hugh picked Nessa up, carrying her to the large oaken table that dominated the solar. There, he sat her down as he gently peeled off her hose, caressing the curve of her calves as he did so. Nessa watched him, aching for him.

Hugh then spread her thighs wide and drew back, his gaze devouring her. "Lovely," he whispered hoarsely. "Are you really mine?"

"Aye," she whispered. "Claim me, Hugh."

Needing no further encouragement, he reached for her. His big hands stroked her breasts, lifting them to his hungry mouth as he suckled her. Nessa writhed under him before wrapping her legs around his hips, drawing him to her.

She couldn't wait. She had to have him buried deep inside her.

Reaching down, her fingers wrapped around the thick girth of his shaft. His rod pulsed eagerly as she gripped him, guiding him. And when he slid into her, Nessa let out a deep groan, her head falling back.

Maiden's blood, how she'd yearned for this. How she'd yearned for *him*.

Hugh buried himself to the hilt, yet Nessa tightened her grip around his hips, drawing him in deeper still. She then circled her hips, whimpering at the pleasure that now pulsed through her loins. She cried out his name, and he groaned hers.

Gripping hold of her thighs, Hugh unwrapped her legs from around his hips, parting her wider still while he withdrew almost entirely from her. He took her then in slow, deep thrusts. Propping herself up, hands splayed across the scrubbed surface of the oaken table, Nessa arched her hips up to meet him.

They fitted together perfectly, and the feel of him, iron-hard, sliding into her softness, her heat, unraveled the last of her restraint. She sobbed out his name once more, her body trembling while wetness erupted deep within her.

Nessa reached up then, clinging to his shoulders. But Hugh didn't let up. Sweat glistened upon his body as he took her, continuing in slow, deliberate strokes, his gaze fused with hers.

The intimacy of it caused another sob to rise within her. The love, the tenderness in his hazel eyes, undid her entirely.

"You are mine, Nessa," he ground out, a nerve flickering upon his cheek. She could feel tension vibrating through his big body as he fought his release. "Say it."

"I'm yers," she whispered, her voice catching. "I'm yers, Hugh … for always."

He let himself go then, as she wrapped her legs about him once more, arching up so that he could drive deeper still. It was as if he wished to lose himself within her.

And he did.

Hugh's eyes fluttered shut, the expression upon his face almost pained as he gave himself up to her, to the passion that stole both their breaths. She urged him on, never taking her gaze from him, clinging to her lover when his body went rigid.

An instant later, Hugh flung back his head and—for the first time in all the occasions they'd coupled—roared his pleasure.

Lying upon the bed naked, sweat-slicked limbs tangled, Nessa and Hugh recovered from the storm of passion that had just broken over them. After their coupling, Hugh had carried Nessa into his bed-chamber.

They lay in silence for a bit, while they both recovered their wits. Then, murmuring an oath, Hugh rolled onto his back, flinging an arm over his eyes. Nessa propped herself up onto one elbow, viewing him under hooded lids. The man was a delight to look upon.

Hugh's chest still rose and fell sharply in the aftermath of their passion.

"I swear my heart will give out if we do too much of that," he eventually murmured.

Nessa laughed before she traced a line with her fingertips from the hollow beneath his neck, down his chest and belly, to where his shaft had started to stir once more. "Really? The rest of yer body disagrees, I believe."

Hugh removed his arm from over his eyes, viewing her with a lopsided smile. "I'm not a lusty lad of eighteen, Nessa ... I can't go all night."

She snorted, stroking her fingertips over his stiffening rod. "We shall see about that, Sir Hugh."

He grasped her wrist then, pulling her up so that she lay on top of him. Grinning down at him, while at the same time acutely aware of his arousal pressed against her belly, Nessa's gaze met Hugh's.

He stared up at her, his mouth curving. Yet his gaze was limpid, tender. "You're a wicked woman," he murmured. "What am I to do with you?"

She lowered her eyelashes. "I can think of plenty of things."

Laughter rumbled in his chest, although he caught her hand and brought it to his lips, kissing the back. "I thought I'd lost you forever," he said huskily. "I'd resigned myself to having nothing more than memories."

"So had I," she whispered. "But I set myself free." She paused then, noting the confusion in his eyes. "If we are to be wed this eve, Hugh, then there can be no more secrets between us. I must tell ye of my past ... the real story."

Hugh nodded, his gaze never leaving hers as he waited for her to continue.

Nessa inhaled deeply. "As I told ye, I was a foundling ... abandoned by my parents to the woods. However, it wasn't a hermit who found me, but a druidess ... a woman who heads an ancient order. She raised me, and many others, as her daughter ... and taught me her craft." Nessa paused then, relieved to see that Hugh's expression hadn't altered. He wasn't angry at her—not yet anyway. "We are the Guardians of Alba," she said softly, "and now that I have been released from the oaths I swore, I can speak to ye of the order. Over the centuries, the Guardians have protected Scotland from invaders. That is why our paths crossed … why I tricked ye as I did … and why I was bid to return to ye en route to Stirling."

Hugh swallowed. "And that's why I'm alive." He cast her a rueful look. "The physician told me I should have bled out from those injuries, yet I lived to see the dawn … because of your craft."

Nessa nodded. "So, ye aren't angry?"

"Why would I be?"

"I'm a witch, Hugh. Do ye wish to wed such a woman?" Fear fluttered up within Nessa as she spoke. Yet she had to say it; she had to know.

"That's only part of who you are, my love," Hugh replied softly, reaching up and brushing away a lock of hair that had fallen across her forehead. "Just as being a knight is only a part of me. Perhaps we both let those roles define us … for too long. But those chapters of our lives are done with. Edward released me from service, and you have left your order." He halted then, his throat bobbing. "Maybe that is what makes us right for each other … we're both loyal, Nessa. But now it's time we looked to ourselves … our own happiness."

She favored him with a soft smile. "Aye … ye English will continue to harry my countrymen, with or without ye leading them." Her smile faded as she imagined Fyfa at Stirling and Breanna helping to ready the order for what was to come. "And my sisters will continue the fight for Scottish freedom."

"We both gave our lives to the things we believe in," he replied, his hand cupping her face, the pad of his thumb caressing her lower lip. "And now it's time to let others continue in our stead. I no longer wish to devote myself to the glory of England. I wish to give my loyalty to you."

She stared down at him, tenderness and love swelling in her breast so keenly that it made her chest ache. "And I will gladly accept it," she whispered.

Hugh favored her with a soft smile, his eyes crinkling at the corners. The moment drew out, and then he reached down, smacking her lightly across the bottom.

"Well, then, we'd better get ourselves up and dressed." His smile widened at Nessa's affronted look. "The priest awaits ... and I'm eager to be wedded."

Epilogue

I MAKE YOU A PROMISE

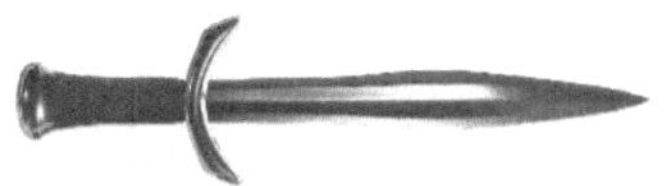

Grosmont Castle
The Welsh Borders

Two months later ...

"YOU NEED TO keep the bandage dry," Nessa
instructed, as she finished binding the lad's lower leg.
"Or the wound risks souring."

"Fret not, Lady de Burgh," the lad's mother replied.
"I'll make sure Will looks after it."

Nessa met the woman's eye and smiled. She was a
farmer's wife, a careworn woman from Grosmont
village—this six-year-old boy was one of her huge brood
of bairns. Will had tripped while out in the fields with his
father, catching his leg on the blade of the plow.

Lady de Burgh.

Even now, two moons since she'd become Hugh's
wife, the title sounded strange.

Who would have thought she—Nessa the healer,
Nessa the bandruì—a woman with not even a clan name
to cling to, would become the wife of Hugh de Burgh,
lord of Grosmont Castle.

Not only that, but the folk of this place—Hugh's kin
and servants alike—had welcomed this strange
Scotswoman into their midst.

Hugh had given her this space, a chamber in the
northern block next to the chapel, as her infirmary. It
wasn't a big room, yet Nessa had made it her own.

Bunches of drying herbs hung from the rafters, and the shelving Hugh had made for her groaned under the weight of bottles and vials she'd already accumulated. True to form, she was having trouble keeping the space tidy.

Neatness wasn't really part of Nessa's nature.

"I'm glad to hear it, Alice," she replied. "Here ... I've made up some extra salve. Be sure to rub it on the cut every morning before applying a clean bandage."

Alice nodded, tucking away the small clay pot Nessa had just handed her into her apron. "Thank you, Lady de Burgh."

Watching the pair leave her infirmary, Nessa leaned back against the edge of the small table—which was laden with linen bandages, her pestle and mortar, and baskets of dried herbs—and wiped her hands upon a clean cloth.

A smile curved her lips.

Hugh had promised her a space of her own, and he'd kept his word.

She'd used witching rarely since establishing herself as Grosmont's healer—only occasionally employing it when absolutely necessary. She wouldn't forget her craft, or the witch-will that hummed around her during a full moon, yet it didn't guide her life as it once had.

Nessa's smile widened, contentment settling deep into her bones.

She'd never known happiness like this. Sometimes she felt she could burst from it.

And then, as if the greatest source of her joy had been drawn to her by her thoughts, a tall figure entered the infirmary, ducking under the low doorway to prevent cracking his skull on the lintel.

Hugh de Burgh straightened to his full height, casting a look around the space.

"God's teeth," he murmured. "This place could do with a tidy-up."

Nessa snorted. "Everything is in its place, dear husband. I know exactly where to find what I need."

Hugh quirked a brow, approaching her. "Glad to hear it." He stopped before Nessa then, his expression sobering. "I didn't wish to interrupt you in here ... but I've just received a missive from the north ... from Scotland." He paused, watching her face. "Stirling has fallen."

Tension coiled under Nessa's ribcage. She'd whispered to The Three nightly, asking for their assistance so that Stirling might resist their besiegers. The defenders had done an admirable job—for it was now nearing the end of July—yet they had not outlasted the English as she'd hoped.

"Do ye know the details?" she asked, frowning.

"Edward used a new weapon," Hugh replied. He moved close and took her hands. "A massive trebuchet ... bigger than any built before ... it tore a hole in Stirling Castle's walls."

"And what of those defending it?" Nessa was afraid to ask, her heart now racing. Yet she had to know of Fyfa's fate.

"I don't know," Hugh replied, his gaze meeting hers. "The missive didn't say ... I'm sorry, Ness."

Nessa drew in a deep, steadying breath. She was glad she was leaning against the table, for her legs suddenly felt weak.

Hugh's gaze shadowed. "I know you have a friend at Stirling ... hopefully, she was spared."

Nessa swallowed. "I hope that too."

They looked at each other, the moment drawing out. Over the past weeks, Nessa had told Hugh more about the life she'd led before meeting him—and about her bond with her sisters, Fyfa and Breanna. The two women might not have shared the same blood as her, but she would always look upon them as kin. And despite her happiness with Hugh, the joy that waking up every day next to him brought, she missed them both.

"One day," Hugh said, squeezing her fingers tightly, "when the fighting is over, and things quieten down, you will be reunited with them."

Nessa lowered her gaze. "Will I?"

Hugh released her hands before hooking a finger under Nessa's chin and lifting her face so that she met his eye once more. "I make you a promise, my love, that one day I will take you back to Scotland to see your sisters again."

Nessa stared back at him, her gaze misting with tears. The resolute tone of his voice, the determination in his eyes, was impossible to argue with. Hugh wasn't a man who made oaths lightly. He was a knight; his word was his bond. Her heart lightened in the knowledge that he would do his utmost to keep it.

She raised a hand, her fingers entwining with his. "Fortune was indeed smiling upon me, Hugh de Burgh, the day it ensured our paths would cross."

The corners of his mouth lifted. "Fortune ... or that wily woman who leads your order."

Nessa laughed, the sound carrying through the infirmary. She told Hugh many tales of Colina, and he'd been fascinated by every one of them. "She's a seer after all ... I think she knew that ye and I were meant for each other," Nessa mused, lifting his hand to her mouth and kissing each of his fingers.

Hugh smiled back, and was about to answer, when a small figure burst into the infirmary.

Richard de Burgh had joined them.

Warmth filtered through Nessa as she took in the lad's animated face, easing her worry for Fyfa. He looked so much like his father. "Da ... look at what Kit made me." The lad waved about the wooden sword. "A proper longsword, like yours!"

Hugh grinned, ruffling his son's hair. "And a fine sword it is ... shall we go out into the inner ward and have a duel?"

"Aye, Thomas says he's too busy to fight me."

"Well, I will accept the challenge."

Nessa snorted. "Hugh ... don't encourage him."

Hugh cast her a look of mock innocence. "What? A lad needs to know how to defend himself." Reaching out, he took her by one hand and Richard by the other. The lad was beaming now, overjoyed to have his father with him.

Watching them together warmed Nessa's heart. Who knew if she and Hugh would ever have bairns of their own—even though she'd stopped taking that herbal draft, her womb hadn't yet quickened—but she was already deeply fond of Hugh's son.

She had a new family now. It was a different one to the Guardians, an order of women bonded together for a single purpose. She missed them—her mother and sisters—and she worried for Fyfa. She hoped her sister had evaded The Hammer's wrath.

Nessa swallowed in an attempt to ease the sudden tightness in her throat. Like her, Fyfa was a survivor. Not only that, but the other guardians would be watching and waiting, ready to aid her.

Nessa's tension eased at this thought. Aye, she had to remember that.

Hugh had spoken true when he described life as a series of chapters. Indeed, the first chapter of her life—one that she had embraced—had ended, and now another had begun. She intended to dedicate herself to it with the same fierceness she once had to her order.

"Come on." Hugh led them both to the doorway and outside to where the morning sun basked the inner-ward. Then, releasing his wife's hand, he headed with his son toward the armory to collect his practice sword. "Let the battle begin!"

Nessa watched them go, smiling.

Aye, this was where she was meant to be.

The End

FROM THE AUTHOR

NESSA'S SEDUCTION was so much fun! I loved Nessa and Hugh—both practical and driven individuals who finally find peace in each other's arms. This was my first Scottish/English different worlds romance, and I have to say, I'm now a bit 'obsessed' about English knights.

Maybe I need to find a way to incorporate a knight or two in my future books?

I introduced readers to Nessa in DRACO (Book 3: The Immortal Highland Centurions). I was immediately intrigued by her sassiness and just knew I had to write a story about her. Likewise, Hugh appears in that novel. As I finished DRACO, they both tapped me on the shoulder and said "write our romance next!" ... and so I did!

I hope you loved their enemies to lovers/different worlds romance ... now get ready for deception and second chance love with Book 2 in the series, FYFA'S SACRIFICE.

Jayne x

HISTORICAL NOTES

I did A LOT of research for this series!

Of course, this story-world blends a touch of fantasy with real historical fact (as *The Immortal Highland Centurions* did), however, I took care to base my witches of the Guardians of Alba order on ancient Celtic druidic and Wiccan practices, to give the order a feeling of authenticity.

My references to The Three goddesses (The Maiden, The Mother, and the Crone) come from Celtic mythology, as do my references to their power being related to the moon. Each moon of the year had a different name and significance, and each phase of the moon held a specific power. From the Wiccan religion, I brought in the use of the elements, candle magic, and crystals—and the use of the words 'craft', 'witching', and 'workings' to describe magic and spell casting. Both Celtic and Wiccan practices had a strong 'feminine' influence, which I really enjoyed exploring with my bandruì. I wanted their practice to be largely positive and life-affirming.

I really enjoyed researching the historical backdrop to their novel (and indeed the whole series). If you read *The Immortal Highland Centurions,* then you will have already met King Edward I of England (also known as 'Longshanks' or 'The Hammer of the Scots'). That series also featured William Wallace as a side character. However, this one is focused on the rise of Robert Bruce to power (with the 'behind-the-scenes' help of our witches!). We'll be meeting the Bruce in the next book! In 1304, when this novel is set, Robert Bruce had yet to start causing problems for the English.

In 1304, Edward of England lay siege to Stirling Castle. The siege lasted from the beginning of April and ended on 24 July. Sir William Oliphant defended the castle with a garrison, while Edward attacked with a number of siege engines (including *Le Berefry*) and the infamous Warwolf (which you'll also meet in the next book in this series!).

Edward attacked the castle for four months, using lead balls (stripped from nearby church roofs), stone missiles (from a nearby quarry), and Greek fire. When Oliphant initially refused to surrender, Edward was quoted as replying: "If he thinks it will be better for him to defend the castle than yield it, he will see." I used a slightly altered version of this statement in this novel!

During the siege, Edward of England nearly lost his life twice. Once when a crossbow bolt struck his saddle, and then when a boulder (launched by a catapult on the walls) fell just a foot or two from him. I incorporated both those incidents in the battle scene where Hugh is injured.

Eventually, Oliphant surrendered to the English ... but I'll provide more historical details about that in the back of the next installment in the series, FYFA'S SACRIFICE.

As with my previous series, I've tried to remain largely faithful to the historical representations of Edward I England. He was indeed an aging warrior king, and his son Prince Edward did accompany him on his campaigns to Scotland, helping him to conquer the Scots. His second wife, Margaret, also traveled with him. As I show in this novel, Edward was famously 'lucky in love'. He adored his first wife, Eleanor (who bore him 16 children!), and although his second wife, Margaret, was indeed forty years his junior, the couple were reputed to be very happily wed. She bore him three children, and when Edward died in 1307 (of dysentery), she said: "When Edward died, all men died for me."

All the settings in this novel are based on real locations:

Dunfermline: this town, which is overlooked by a commanding abbey, was where the English army did winter in 1303/4.

Stirling: this fortress (which I also feature in my *Immortals* series) was indeed 'the brooch that holds Scotland together'. The Siege of Stirling was a landmark victory for the English during the Wars of Independence. However, it was not an easy one.

The Wailing Widow Falls: I came across a picture of these waterfalls a few years ago ... and just knew that, one day, I'd write about them. Located in the northwest of the Highlands in Assynt (Caithness/Sutherland and Ross-shire), these massive falls run out of Loch na Gianmhich, crashing into a narrow gorge at the bottom. There are many tales associated with their evocative name, although the one I used is a variation of a story of a deer hunter who fell from the top while hunting in a thunderstorm. The next morning his mother, filled with grief, hurled herself to her death from the same spot. In my version, it's his *wife* who does so ... after all, it is calling the Wailing *Widow* Falls. Of course (to my knowledge) there isn't a cavern hidden behind the waterfalls!

Grosmont Castle: the fortress (today an impressive ruin), which indeed means 'big hill' in French, is located in Monmouthshire on the Welsh Border. Grosmont (as well as Skenfrith and White Castle) was one of the 'Three Castles of Gwent' built by the Normans to control this key section against Welsh uprisings. The De Burghs did rule the castle for a spell—one Hubert de Burgh was once lord of Grosmont. However, my hero, Hugh, is an entirely fictional character.

I also used an old Scottish proverb in this novel: *If wishes were horses, beggars would ride*. It actually wasn't first recorded in written form until the 1600s, but I decided to alter the timeframe a little!

I hope you enjoyed this window into the research, settings, and background to the novel. All these details help to make the story all the richer!

ABOUT THE AUTHOR

Award-winning author Jayne Castel writes epic Historical and Fantasy Romance. Her vibrant characters, richly researched historical settings, and action-packed adventure romance transport readers to forgotten times and imaginary worlds.

Jayne has published a number of bestselling series. In love with all things Scottish, Jayne also writes romances set in Dark Ages Scotland ... sexy Pict warriors anyone?

When she's not writing, Jayne is reading (and re-reading) her favorite authors, cooking Italian feasts, and going for long walks with her husband. She lives in New Zealand's beautiful South Island.

Connect with Jayne online:
www.jaynecastel.com
www.facebook.com/JayneCastelRomance
https://www.instagram.com/jaynecastelauthor/
Email: contact@jaynecastel.com